WHISPERS FROM THE
SILENCE

TIM CAGLE

Tim Cagle

Excerpt from Whispers from the Silence

"I need to tell you the real reason why country music gets to me. After my dad was killed when I was ten, music and I became estranged. Sad songs reminded me of him and made me break down. I felt ashamed because crying was not the way a man should act. About a year later, my mother got sick and we were forced to move to Texas to live with my grandmother. One day, Mom called me in and said before my father died, he told her I had more musical talent than anyone he had ever seen. She made me promise to honor his memory by becoming a songwriter."

I stopped and swallowed hard. "A week later, she died. I refused to show any emotion, telling myself that my broken heart should stay hidden. As I sat in church, an image appeared of Dad and Mom. One sad song after another started torturing me. After the funeral, I broke down in the car and almost bit through my bottom lip trying to stay strong, but hot bitter tears kept flowing like raindrops trickling down a windowpane."

I looked off into the distance.

"When the car stopped, I jumped out and vowed no one would ever see me lose control again because it was a sign of weakness. Then, music appeared and I grew angry. I went on the attack and shouted that country songs were harsh and cruel. When I finished, the silence whispered in my ear for the very first time."

"What did it say?" Trapp asked, as her voice trembled.

"It told me to write my own lyrics so I could cry inside."

"So no one can see you?" she asked. I nodded.

"Every time I write a song, it lets me shed a huge lump of sorrow, and no one will ever have to know."

DEDICATION

To Linda,

Always the dance

ISBN-13:978-1548103057

ISBN-10:1548103055

:

CHAPTER ONE

As Orville Wright once asked his brother, Wilbur, "How do I start this son-of-a-bitch?"

The first time I heard that line, I was a seventeen-year-old kid making my college quarterback debut. It came from my roommate, Billy Joe Crowder, a maniacal middle linebacker. I nicknamed him "Hooker," because he used to wrap his arms around a ball carrier's chest like grappling hooks. He once hit a back so hard the runner's sternum cracked. That was eighteen years ago.

Since then, that line has helped me launch songwriting marathons, pyrotechnic love affairs and amnesia-tinged hangovers. Tonight, it popped up as I walked onstage, picked up my guitar and did a sound check. The bass was a little tinny, so I adjusted my amplifier and took a deep breath.

Like always, an image appeared in my mind of the thirteen-year-old boy I once was, performing for the first time in front of the student body. My voice cracked and the shrill sound sent ripples of snickers racing like a tsunami across the auditorium. Ashamed, I saw myself fleeing toward the wings. Thank God my coach was waiting. "Son, you can brand yourself a coward for a lifetime or go back out there and kick fear in the ass like a soccer star on amphetamines," he said, turning humiliation into triumph.

The crowd kept filing in as I hit a G9th. As the sweet tone resonated throughout the room, I smiled down at my Martin guitar, a Model D-28, I referred to as my "Stradivarius in drag." The citadel of sound was always full-bodied and lush, like vintage wine aged in rosewood casks.

The touch of the hand-lacquered finish reassured me when I had to perform for belligerent whack jobs or obnoxious drunks. The Martin and I have acted like conjoined twins for years. It was my reward for getting a signing bonus when I got drafted by the Pittsburgh Steelers. The first time I held it, the sensation was like scooping up a ballroom dancing partner. The quilted maple wood was precision balanced while the frets were elegantly spaced, leading to action with more fluidity than a Gothic novel.

When I got traded to the Patriots, I even bought it a seat next to me so I wouldn't have to risk shipping it. Playing the Martin also made my confidence soar when I found one special woman in the audience and sang my first song just to her.

My eyes swept the room, but candidates for inspiration were scarce. I wound up focusing on the pony-tailed guy in front of me in the stained tee shirt, Fu Manchu moustache, nose rings and tattoos. He was sitting next to the chartreuse-tipped pig-tailed woman in the soiled white shorts, skimpy halter top, neon blue mascara and mother-of-pearl studs triangulated on the top of her tongue like an arrowhead.

On his right forearm, there were smoking, crossed Colt 45 pistols with the words: "I Wish I Was Deep Instead of Macho." He sneered at me like he just came down with hepatitis C, and I got pissed at myself because I'm still stuck playing in this dump, at least for tonight.

My lifelong dream is to be a songwriter in Nashville. I wanted to go after high school, but gave it up to play football in college. Then, I went to the NFL and played for six more years. After I got hurt and retired, my wife, Carol, refused to leave Boston. Last year she threw me out, and now I'm forced to stay, because she drained our joint account and left me so broke I can't afford to pay attention.

I'm convinced this will be my last chance to leave. It's time to follow the love of my life, music, instead of spending the rest of my days pretending I'm someone else.

Three beautiful blondes with pulled back hairdos, short skirts and snowflake white smiles pranced into the lounge like lingerie models on a runway. I took a deep, euphoric breath, and moved that the inspiration nominations cease.

"I'd like to start off with a medley of my favorite Gregorian chants," I said softly, trotting out my favorite icebreaker as the stage illumination came on.

My spirits soared as the blondes raised their glasses toward me in a toast. I smiled like I just won Powerball, hit an E7 chord and spoke to the crowd.

"Good evening, ladies and gentlemen. I'm J. W. Steele, former Texan, coming to you on this hot Monday night from the Temptation Lounge in Boston. As Toby Keith once said, 'I Should Have Been A Cowboy' so, sit back and relax because the more you drink, the less you'll have to testify about when a grand jury gets convened later."

I led off with the old Eagles' hit, 'Take It Easy'. When I got to the part about having all those women on my mind, the trio cheered. Midway through my first set, the blondes stood up, blew me a kiss and left. At the entrance, they passed a striking brunette in a designer-looking suit.

I made eye contact and went through my final sets of country, rock and pop tunes. It seemed like she was following my every move like a sniper. At eight o'clock, I said good night and was packing up when someone touched my arm, and I turned to see the brunette.

"J. W., I'm Amanda Parsons. I'm an agent from Nashville," she said, as my entire body quivered. Up close, she was a dead ringer for Ann, my high school love and the first woman who ever broke my heart.

"Nice to meet you," I replied, grasping her hand like it was a royalty check.

"I got your name off the marquee and Googled you. Your football days are over, right?"

"I'd love to play but my knee needs a note from my orthopedic surgeon." I smiled.

"Are you here every night?"

"Just weekends. The regular act had an emergency tonight so I got called in," I said.

"What about future plans?" she asked.

I felt my face light up like a meteor shower, as I told her about moving to Nashville in January.

"Why wait until then?" she asked.

I explained about Hooker with the new coaching job and us planning to reunite once football season was over. I skipped the part about needing my next gig just to survive.

"Do you have a manager?" she asked.

I grinned and jerked my thumbs toward my chest. I felt my heart pound as possibilities raced through my mind while I surveyed her long chestnut hair and lightly-tanned face. Watching Amanda made me picture Ann as we used to sit by the lake, awestruck as a falling star turned the Texas sky into the color of burnished steel.

"Let me get to the point because I'm catching a flight. I have a friend in Nashville who's a producer. I think he could turn you into a star."

I felt the back of my legs semi-buckle. My chest rose and fell as her words were like injections.

"I counted at least three songs that were originals," Amanda said. "From what I heard, you have a real gift for songwriting."

"Tell me about the producer," I said, visualizing Ann and the first time I made love.

"His name is Sam Presley. He's worked with a lot of big names, like Waylon and Dolly," she said, looking me over like an item she found on final sale.

"Let me give you my contact info," I said. We exchanged numbers, while a limo driver came in to notify Amanda it was time to leave.

"I'm talking big money and a real chance at stardom, J. W.," she said, scoping out the hotel lobby. "No offense, but it's not like what you have here. Sam will lead you to the big time."

* * *

My mind was racing all the way home. Writing songs is the one thing I've dreamed of since I was a ten-year-old kid. When my music made people's eyes light up, it meant I've unlocked a door in their soul. It almost seemed like a spiritual release, one filled with the purity of a love sonnet. The high reminded me of a drug, one that triggered a response like when true love blossomed and a partner turned into a soul mate.

I arrived at nine o'clock and made sure the door to the other half of the duplex was secure. That side was occupied by my landlady, Julie Gretsky, and her twin daughters, Emily and Alexa. Once inside, Dr. Coors became my anesthesiologist on call. I plopped on the ancient glen plaid sofa, thankful that the apartment came furnished. Everything was worn and dated, but Julie made sure the place was sparkling before I moved in.

I activated the sound on my phone, and heard so many pings from emails that I looked to see if my cell phone had mutated into a harpsichord. A huge grin appeared as I saw the last one from Hooker.

He addressed me as "Wilbur" and said he was in non-stop meetings all week. He's headed to Oklahoma on Thursday to escort their top recruit to training camp. Tonight, he had a date with the third different woman he has fallen in love with this week. He said we could catch up on Sunday unless he was still entangled with a mattress mambo marathon.

My phone rang. The caller ID made me suck in a deep breath before I heard a deep voice. Its sound made me picture an antebellum mansion, a frosted pitcher of mint juleps and the caller petting a huge, floppy-jowled bloodhound named 'Stonewall.'

"Mr. Steele, Mah name is Sam Presley. I'm a colleague of Amanda Parsons and a record producer in Nashville," the voice said, with a deep Southern drawl.

"Good evening, sir," I said, my throat drier than a John Kerry speech.

"Befoah you ask, Ah'm no relation to the King, heh, heh," he said. "Ah would like to invite you to meet me in Nashville."

"I'm starting a new gig next week but I can come down this Wednesday. Is that OK" I blurted.

"That would be mighty fine," he said, as a lump formed in my throat while we exchanged backgrounds for a few more minutes.

"Amanda talked about an original song you did called 'All Ah Am is Free.' Ah'd admire it if you could send it before we meet," he said.

I told him it would go right out. After we finalized our meeting details and hung up, my heart was pounding so hard it felt like a bass drum was in my chest.

I texted Hooker and Julie, the only friends I felt close enough to share the news with. Hooker said he would pick me up at the airport. Julie said she would stop by after work. I found a flight on Wednesday morning with a return Thursday. The tickets cost me five hundred dollars and I panicked because there was barely six hundred left in checking. Thank God I still had some credit.

Sadness came over me as I remembered my life in football and how things had gone downhill since then. After my knee injury, I took a job as a salesman for the company owned by my father-in-law, Allister "Boomer" Lyle. I sold shortening, frying fat and cake mixes to all the bakeries, restaurants, hotels and food service institutions in Boston. On my first day, I discovered that going to work was as exciting as watching C-SPAN reruns of Pakistani parliamentary debates without subtitles.

At least, I had a job until Boomer fired me after Carol kicked me out. He even fought my claim for unemployment benefits. I won that fight but my checks will run out in two weeks. I've been able to live by picking up extra cash playing at clubs even though I make barely enough to get by.

My new gig starts in a few days. It will net me fifteen hundred a week until January. I'll have enough money to move and cash in on Hooker's recent relocation to Nashville.

I got out my guitar, recorded my song and sent it to Sam. A few beers later, it was almost midnight, when I heard a soft knock at the door. It was Julie.

She had a wine bottle in her right hand and a takeout bag from a Chinese restaurant in her left. Her hair was fixed in a ponytail, she stood a regal five foot eight, and wore a navy top, white shorts, flip-flops and a frenzied smile. The top's color was a sharp, distinguishing compliment to her light auburn hair and robin's egg blue eyes. She came over and took me in her arms.

"You're on your way to the red carpet, big guy," she said.

"Well, let's not write my Hall of Fame induction speech yet. It's just a start."

I got her a wine glass and sat next to her on the couch. Her eyes danced like a wheat field waving in the wind. I thought about all the nights she stopped by after work and the times she talked me down, especially when I was pissed. One night, I let my guard down and a few angry tears fell. It was the first time I had ever cried in front of a friend.

With no romance between us, our friendship took off after I started to fill the void in her daughters' lives. She dated sporadically, and told me she refused to get involved with a man because it would interfere with her relationship with the twins. At times, she even inspired my lyrics. Above all, she became my closest friend. My biggest regret was that she never let me fall in love with her.

"You seem worried. I thought you'd be bouncing off the wall with joy," she said.

"I'm scared. Playing at the hotel is one thing. Auditioning in front of a big-time producer is a higher level of fear."

"Maybe making it in Nashville will soften your layer of scar tissue," she said.

I flashed back to the night she told me my inner self was surrounded by a dark shroud of sorrow. That let me start a song called, 'Clouded Soul'. So far, I only had the title.

"Why am I getting your Freud impersonation?" I asked.

She paused and looked me up and down.

"When you're not trying to out-clever yourself with quips, I hear agony when you sing. I don't know the real you because you're always onstage," she said, as I started to pace.

"I've wanted this my whole life. What if I find out I'm not good enough?"

"What does your heart tell you?"

"That I'd better suck it up."

"Like in front of the whole high school?" she asked.

My face tingled as I stared at her, but she wasn't finished.

"You might be like that old Leonard Cohen lyric you gave me about being as free as some poor old drunk in a midnight choir. Maybe you're searching for the freedom to fail," she said.

I let out a short, smooth whistle at her talent for cross-examining me with the skill of a seasoned prosecutor. She touched my left hand and I felt like a guest who stayed just a little too long.

"At least I'm not some kind of manic depressive. Besides, now I can teach the twins all those heartbreaking songs. How long will they be at the beach?"

"My sister's bringing them back Friday night. I said they could spend a few dollars from their puppy fund," she said.

I grinned at the memory of how they asked me to convince Julie to let them have a dog. I said they should offer to pay for it, then reached into my wallet and gave them a ten to start the ball rolling. They had over ninety-four dollars in the fund, from doing chores around the house and babysitting gigs, now that they had completed their child care class.

"They took the Yamaha with them and wrote a poem so you can turn it into a song," she said.

A vision of our first music lesson appeared. The girls showed up with a battered acoustic guitar they bought for five dollars at a garage sale. It was worn, the neck was too wide and the strings were set too far above the frets. They grew frustrated as they struggled to depress the strings. I knew the answer was a new guitar, but I was tapped out.

The next day was my unemployment hearing. Boomer testified I was discharged for cause as a result of misconduct, but the hearing official saw right through all of the bluster and bullshit and awarded me benefits. To celebrate, I went to a music store and found a beautifully preserved, secondhand Yamaha.

It had a thin neck and low frets and was perfect for twelve-year-old feminine fingers. Julie insisted on paying me but I said no, just like I refused to take money for teaching. Being with the twins was far too much fun to get paid, so she started sending desserts or casseroles instead.

"Did you tell them about meeting this producer in Nashville?" she asked.

"I wanted to talk to you first," I said, after shaking my head.

"They're going to be crushed when you move there," she said. "You're the only dad they've ever known."

My eyes glistened as I remembered how she told me their father deserted the twins a decade ago. A vision formed in my mind of me taking them to their first father-daughter dance last June.

"If you're trying to make me feel guilty, it's working," I whispered.

"Remember how you said you grew up Catholic and I said I'm a Jew?" she asked. I nodded. "Same guilt, different holidays," she said, flashing a grin.

We talked for several more minutes as Julie urged me to check Sam out. A moment later, she leaned back and closed her eyes. I re-corked her wine bottle and we walked arm in arm to her door.

As she turned, I couldn't stop reflecting on how uncanny her insight was. Her best reveal was when she said I entered the twins' lives at the exact same age I was when my mother died.

I kissed her on the cheek. An image formed in my mind of me acting as Julie's date for hospital functions. At times, that made me feel strange and filled me with a longing I could not explain. I even composed a lyric about the two of us, '*Like a flame that's banked too long.*' Too bad it has stayed sequestered in the unopened pages of a work in progress.

I headed back to my music, while I questioned life's mysteries. Julie had turned into a platonic wife who never asked me to justify my actions or questioned my loyalty. I was especially mystified as to how the two of us ever became so close without activating episodes of heavy breathing and five-fingered, frenzied groping.

Maybe I should be happy Julie was not my lover. That would make it almost impossible to leave her. The pain of parting would make me question my decision. The heartache would leave a deeper scar and be saturated with guilt.

At present, I was seeing only one woman, Erica. Our sex life was hot and heavy, but light on involvement. Neither of us wanted anything permanent or complicated. That made perfect sense to me. It even had my stamp of approval based on an old Kristofferson lyric about how the lovin' would always be easy, unlike the livin' which was nothing but hard.

* * *

It was late Wednesday morning when I landed in Nashville and marched off to meet Hooker. We've stayed in touch by phone, especially after Carol left me.

Hooker is the only guy who can sense exactly what I need—a rousing pep talk, a few beers or a swift kick in the ass.

We've been making plans to reunite since he moved to Nashville two weeks ago. He's now an assistant football coach at Tennessee Baptist College. He's also a marriage dodging bachelor, a semi-transvestite and more fun than Lady Gaga picking out a new chicken parmesan evening gown.

We're probably as close as two men have ever been without exchanging diamond pendants. In Texas, he said and did things that formed the basis for a song. The best one was the time he told me, "Love is just a gamble based on the promise of a lie."

Once, I was leaving a bar and asked if he was ready. He said in the middle of an intoxicated hiccup, "S'loon." That led to a tune called, 'It's Too Saloon To Tell.' He once said that the best way to tell if someone was a true friend was whether it felt right when you cried in front of them.

He's a big bastard, six foot four and close to two hundred fifty pounds, an inch taller and twenty-five pounds heavier than me. I turned thirty-four years old two weeks ago. He beat me by four months. I have a full head of light brown hair, but he's showing a little skin yarmulke that he tries to deny.

I rounded the corner and saw him holding a huge handwritten sign that said, "Welcome to the only guy who reminds me of St. Paul—a small, boring town in Minnesota."

"Let's drop your bag off at the apartment. I've got time for a quick lunch before afternoon meetings," he said.

"Tell me again why you're coaching at a Baptist college," I said.

"It's the fastest route to a division one coaching gig. So, I put up with the God jocks in exchange for career development," he said.

"You're safe as long as you never show up for an inspection in your underwear," I said.

"Thong you," he answered, as we both chuckled.

I grinned as I thought about Hooker being a semi-transvestite. It's not like he's a real heavy-duty drag queen, sporting around town in Carolina Herrera ball gowns or Jimmy Choo stilettos. But, he's really into women's panties. He says it's a lot easier being a guy than a woman, so women get to wear the best underwear. His official reason for cross-dressing is because the texture of silk or chiffon does more for romance than Fruit-of-the-Looms, but I don't buy that.

One night, when we were drunk, he told me his mother didn't want another boy and dressed him in girl's clothes until he was three years old. Maybe he associates women's clothing, and especially panties, with the love of a mother he always chased but never caught.

A smile formed as I realized I was about to reclaim RuPaul Light for a cellmate. I gave thanks it wasn't Rand Paul, as I heard Aerosmith singing 'Dude Looks Like A Lady', in my mind.

It was a short trip, until we reached the last building in a row of apartments and entered the first unit on the third floor. I was shocked to see that it was sparsely furnished, an upgrade from our last pad in Beaumont, when we used an aluminum storm door stacked on bricks for a dining room table. It was a typical single guy's apartment, with its drab, semi-disgusting clutter suggesting that it had been decorated by someone who thought an Oriental rug was a Chinese toupee.

Fifteen minutes later, we found a space in front of a bar and grill. When the server arrived, we both ordered burgers, fries and iced tea.

"I can't do beer, man. Too much to go over later," Hooker said, folding his arms.

"I need a clear head myself."

"Son, talk to me about Carol. You gave me footnotes on the phone, but now I want the whole term paper," he began, like he was ready to update his will.

As I began, he interlocked his fingers and reminded me of a coach telling me to start going to class or lose my scholarship.

"Things started to go downhill after I blew out my knee and had to retire from football. I was out of the spotlight and so was she," I said.

"You caught her with your boss?" he asked.

I nodded. "Yeah. My flight got canceled and when I got home, Russ Hartley's car was there."

"Then you found the note about her diamond ring, right?" he asked.

An image flashed through my mind of me reaching for my laptop next to Carol's attaché case the next morning, when my hand accidentally knocked the case to the floor. As I picked everything up, I saw a handwritten note from Russ that he was in love with Carol.

"That was only the beginning. I went to the bank and discovered that our joint account had less than five dollars. I found a bank officer who told me Carol transferred the money," I said.

Briefly, I remembered how everyone said there wasn't one goddamned thing I could do about it, because the money was held jointly. My sources were impeccable, two husbands who went through the same thing. One said a good lawyer might help if I could afford one by hacking into the Pentagon's budget. The other told me finding an honest, competent lawyer was as easy as finding a used Yugo sub-compact that ran.

"That still wasn't the worst part," I said. "After the bank, two cops came to my door with Carol and Boomer. The first cop handed me an emergency restraining order and said I couldn't have any contact with her."

"That's when Boomer fired you, right?"

I nodded as my anger flashed.

"Why did you go to work for him when you couldn't stand him?"

"I never finished my degree and recruiters weren't exactly breaking down my door when I retired. So, Boomer became my only alternative."

"Carol refused to move here after your football career ended, right?" he asked. I nodded. He looked at me and I knew an impression was coming. His greatest gift was spot-on mimicry and politicians and celebrities comprised his alter-ego. At times, he'd throw in a foreign accent and I'd start roaring like we were drinking with Sam Kinison. "I can hear her now. 'Why thayah? Ah Mississippi and Ah-kann-soo-wah closed foah the summah?" he said, capturing her native Massachusetts accent, where the letter "r" is pronounced "ah," and infusing the phony British dialect she added because it convinced her she sounded just like a Kennedy.

"She'll never leave Boston. Not with her monthly quest to see how much she can increase profits for St. John, Gucci and Giorgio Armani," I said, picturing Carol's four walk-in closets, one just for shoes.

"Ever since I met Carol at your wedding, I wondered how you two ever got together."

"I had never met a woman like her. Bright, beautiful and a blueblood. Maybe she picked me because I was a pro athlete and her friends were off the wall jealous."

"Didn't she want to be a charter member of the upper crust more than anything?"

I nodded, as an image of me moving to Boston appeared, with a picture of my teammates warning me about the city's aristocratic class, known as "Brahmins." Descriptions ranged from "cotillion assholes," to "they think they piss champagne."

"Carol's crowd convinced me that Brahmins are terrified about mingling with social inferiors, so they weed out those with low-tier college degrees and proletariat kinfolk. Every time Carol introduced me to someone, I got their educational pathways. As in, 'This is Quinton Wingtip, of the Beacon Hill Wingtips. Phillips Andover and of course, Harvard.' I started getting the jump on people by saying, 'I'm J. W. Steele, of the Stainless Steeles. Trap Play Prep and of course, Screen Pass University.' Go long, y'awl." I pictured that exasperated look Carol got when I wouldn't swoon if she told me somebody was a descendant of King George the Third. The only Georges I swooned over were Jones and Strait.

"You're still playing at the hotel, right?" Hooker asked.

"Yeah. Cocktail hour on weekends. Friday is my last night. I start my big one next week."

"Why don't you come down here now? You could live with me."

I shook my head and sipped my iced tea. "I need to save a few bucks first."

"I could cover you, man. You can pay me back when you start shipping platinum," he said.

"No, I'll pay my own way. Tonight might be my big break."

"Did you check this producer out?"

"I tried but there wasn't much. He gave me a reference but I couldn't reach him."

"Tell me about your new landlady-slash-therapist," he said.

"I met her through her brother-in-law, Greg, an assistant trainer from the Patriots. Her name is Julie, but Greg said she likes to be called 'Jewels.'"

"I sense a friends with benefits moment. You could also get an alternative way to pay the rent."

"Just friends, no benefits."

"You're shitting me. Did your joy stick get repossessed?"

"She told me romance is not in the cards."

"She must be homely enough to use barbed wire for dental floss," he said.

"No way. She's smoking hot."

"Friendship with a beautiful woman with no hope for a fuckathon? Impossible," he declared.

I told him how the twins met me before I became a tenant. The girls were shy and a little standoffish, but I must have passed the test. Julie told me they both thought I was a "hoot" and couldn't wait to ask me about playing the guitar. She said if their attention bothered me, I was under no obligation to show them anything.

When I told Julie about splitting up with Carol, she replied that she didn't expect me to be a cloistered monk, but hoped I would show some dating discretion as the girls noticed everything. Then, she looked me right in the eye and said there was one rule that was a deal breaker. She said to me, 'I'm divorced and you're separated. I'm sure we could steam up the windows while the twins are in school, but I'm determined that won't happen. I can't let myself get distracted by romance with you so close by. So, you won't be spending time here reading the screenplay from *Fifty Shades of Grey* with the girl next door'."

"Tell me about the twins," he said.

I could feel my face grow a grin the size of a sinkhole in Florida.

"They saw me carrying my Martin. Emily asked if they could hear me play and Lexi said Taylor Swift was their favorite. I told them her music was perfect for young girls, but not so much for an old bastard like me."

"Where's their dad?"

"He left after their first birthday. Jewels said he never wanted children, so the selfish prick just bailed out on them."

"I never thought of you as the fatherly type. What's it like to be with kids?"

"Unvarnished honesty. I was terrified at first, because I never had much of a childhood. But, I didn't want them to grow up fatherless like I did."

"How often are you with them?"

"Almost every day. Julie works as a private duty psych nurse on the three o'clock to eleven o'clock shift.

The twins come over after school and we play some music. Then, they do their homework and we make dinner, usually with enough left over for Jewels when she gets home around midnight."

"How old are they?"

"Twelve."

"What happens when you have to work?"

"I'm there except for weekends and Jewels has those nights off. She was worried when she took the shift and told me if I wouldn't have come along, she might have passed it up. The pay differential is a real shot in the arm and she's relieved to know I'm next door."

He gave me a look like he was calculating the budget deficit.

"So, you get to babysit the twins, teach them the guitar, be their surrogate dad, make dinner for Mom and the only sex you get is on pay-per-view. Remind me to never let you negotiate my next contract or I'll have to pay the school."

He looked at his watch and told me he had to get to the stadium. I said I would keep him updated as to when he should start building a wing to hold my future Grammys.

* * *

Hooker dropped me off downtown just before one o'clock so I decided to explore before meeting Sam. There were a dozen street musicians with instrument cases open for contributions.

I saw an old man with a beat-up guitar and shrouds of stark white hair protruding from his cowboy hat. Behind him was a woman wearing a soiled bandana and accompanying him on violin. I thought the scarf was strange because of the August heat, until it slipped down to reveal the edges of a jagged, bumpy scar. Someone had deliberately disfigured her, probably with a shattered beer bottle.

It was obvious neither had found the luxury of a bath for some time. I stuck a ten dollar bill in his battered guitar case. He tipped his hat, smiled and told me Jesus was coming soon.

As I passed a historic-looking, red brick building, my mind told me something was familiar. I pulled up the address from Sam Presley's email, went inside and felt the blood rush as I checked the directory. When I couldn't find Sam's name or Syntron Productions, apprehension spread. Finally, I convinced myself there had to be a logical explanation.

A few minutes later, I entered the Country Music Hall of Fame. Many exhibits went back to long before I was born. I felt goosebumps when I came to the display of Alan Jackson's handwritten lyrics to 'Where Were You When The World Stopped Turning?' written soon after the attacks on September eleventh. It was eerily moving, sad and enraging, all rolled into one. Those words spelled out in longhand made me feel a songwriter's kinship like I never have before.

Before leaving, I went to the souvenir shop and found tee shirts for Julie and the twins. The shirts for the girls were covered with images of guitars. My joy escalated because they came in different colors, a must because the twins told me that dressing alike would make people think they were a couple of real "dorkers".

* * *

It was just before five o'clock when I arrived at the hotel. My breath came out in spurts, as I spotted an older gentleman and young woman occupying two easy chairs by an off-white sofa.

Sam was in his late fifties and dressed in a dark suit, cowboy boots and a string tie. He had wavy white hair and reminded me of the actor, William Devane. The woman's name was Darla and her curve-clinging, silver-sequined mini-dress was up to her thighs. Her hair was long, frizzy and blonde, and her eyes were a deep blue.

I felt my mouth grow dry as we all shook hands. The last time I was this nervous was when two three hundred pound linemen were chasing me, before they made the inside of my knee feel like shredded broccoli hugging overcooked fettuccine.

Darla sat next to me on the sofa and Sam flanked me in the chair on my right. I clenched my teeth to keep my lower jaw from dropping and making me look like a panting King Charles Spaniel staring out the window of a Ford pickup. My pulse felt like a ticking time bomb.

"Thank you for comin'," Sam said, as Darla smiled like Vanna White about to turn over a vowel. As she slid closer, I caught a whiff of perfume, a blend of jasmine and roses.

We spent the next thirty minutes getting acquainted. Sam said he and Darla had to leave early and asked how long I would be in town. When I said until tomorrow, he made me promise to meet them for dinner next time I came back, hopefully in a week or two.

I told them about my athletic career and how I grew up in Texas. Sam eyed my right hand and I saw him focus on the black and gold ring with the five diamonds at the top.

"Is that a Super Bowl ring?" he asked, with a hushed, reverent voice.

I grew a look of caution before nodding. People sometimes had weird reactions when they found out I used to play professional football. Some were mesmerized, some attentive, while others were jealous. I never felt like a celebrity, just a guy who worked hard to develop my skills and loved playing a kid's game after I became an adult. That's why I always downplayed the ring.

"It is. I was with the Pittsburgh Steelers then," I answered.

"You mus' be the only man evah to combine pro football and songwriting," Sam said dryly.

"What about Mike Reid? Cincinnati Bengals defensive tackle, classical pianist, Grammy winner and Songwriter's Hall of Fame. He wrote for Ronnie Milsap," I said.

Sam shot me a look of confusion before he quickly recovered.

"Oh, oh, yeah, Mike Reid. He was a legend, all right," he said.

I could swear he had no idea who I was talking about and suddenly, felt on edge. At once, I told myself it was nothing more than a small mental miscue anyone could make. Besides, Mike hadn't been current since the '90s. I felt edgy, but wanted this meeting so much I convinced myself everything could easily be explained.

"What position did you play?" Darla asked.

"I was a gunner on kicking teams and the third string quarterback," I said.

"What's a gunner?"

"One of the point guys flying down the field and hitting everyone in sight," I said.

"How many songs have you written?" Sam asked.

"Over four hundred," I said. Then, I took a deep breath and told Sam he wasn't listed at his office address. He said he was expanding his base of operations to Memphis, and had just secured a new satellite office here. His lease expired so his name was removed from the directory and he hadn't updated his contact info.

I was ready to ask about the reference I couldn't find, when Sam reached into his briefcase, removed an envelope and slid it toward me. It showed my name on a check underneath the cellophane window. My pulse pounded as I realized it was time to make a deal. I no longer cared about references or jocks becoming songwriters.

"J. W., ah want to buy your song. We think you're a superstar songwriter," he said.

My hands shook as I opened the envelope. Inside, there was a check made out to me in the amount of five thousand dollars. I resisted the urge to jump up and shout as Sam slid another document in front of me.

"We gotta keep the books straight for ol' Uncle Sam. That there's a form W-9 we have to file with the IRS, so I can send you a 1099 for your tax returns," he said.

My hands shook as I competed the form. A broad grin popped up as I thought about the lyrics to the old Clint Black song, 'When My Ship Comes In.'

"We'll want you to come back in a week or two to do some recordin'," Sam said.

I tried to respond but my voice quavered. Finally, the words appeared.

"I hope Amanda can meet us next time. I have a lot to thank her for," I gushed.

"You can count on it," Sam said, as we all shook hands and left.

* * *

I called Hooker like I just won the Heisman Trophy and told him we had a lot to celebrate. I said everything was my treat because I was now five grand richer. He got to the hotel thirty minutes later and we drove to a bar and grill called Panhandle's, a dive located on the west side of town, to see the local talent.

Everything was the same color: dirt. The last time the floor was swept, it was by General Sherman's boys, who stopped to tidy up before making full-time work for the Atlanta Fire Department. Bacteria moved out years ago, after their demands for cleaner, brighter working conditions were ignored.

Hooker confiscated the last run-down booth opposite what passed for a bandstand. As I slid in over the seat, trying not to catch my Levi's in the mosaic of cigarette burns that formed quills on the red plastic, he waved toward the bar. Our server arrived and we both ordered ribs.

We turned toward the bandstand and I saw a tall man in a huge black Stetson approaching a small stage. Hooker told me he was the owner.

"All right, Earl," he said to the bartender, sounding like Michael Moore introducing Harry Reid to a remedial reading class. "Unplug the juke box, and git that shit off. Folks, we're gonna start tonight off with our first act, Rib-Eye and the Gravy Stains, so give 'em a big welcome."

Four men in faded, ripped Levis, stained tee shirts and mud-crusted boots walked up to the stage. The tallest band member, whom I assumed was Rib Eye himself, went to the microphone. He was about six foot two, and skinny with straggly hair. He wore a look that said he was exhausted from plowing since dawn, or that an OxyContin dealer had filled his back-order.

I licked my lips as our server arrived with what seemed like two truckloads of ribs, a steamer trunk packed with rings and fries, and a forklift filled with coleslaw. We greeted her like we just escaped after a month in Bangladesh. Hooker said to hit us again on the beers and began gnawing on a meaty rib.

Right then, as another alleged band took the stage, two women in cutoffs and halter tops approached our table. Each was twenty-something, shapely and had light brown hair.

The smiling one spoke first. "Howdy, Billy. How's the football team doin'?"

"Well, hidy there, Bobbie," Hooker said. "They're great. Come and join us."

"This is J. W. Steele," he continued. "Ex-quarterback for the New England Patriots and Nashville's newest songwriter."

"Hi, kids," I said, extending my hand.

Bobbie reached her hand across the table. "Hiya, J. W. This is my friend, Susannah."

I stuck out my hand, but Susannah kept looking around and shaking her head from side to side.

"I'm heading for the library before this place gets quarantined," she said, and left.

"So Bobbie, how's life treating you?" Hooker asked, motioning for her to join us.

"Well, I'm almost over the broken heart you gave me," she replied.

He reached over and kissed her hand as the owner returned to the mic.

"Now we come to our last act, a first time performer who comes from the great state of Texas. Put your hands together for Ms. Jillian Loving, singing her own creation, 'All Over Her'."

A woman in her late-twenties, wearing tight jeans and a tee-shirt, took the stage and adjusted the microphone. Her skin was tanned to a gorgeous bronze, like coffee with real cream. Her eyes were a beautiful shade of amber, and sparkled when she looked up. Perfectly straight teeth the color of white porcelain, gave her a smile that, when contrasted with her skin, was startling. I pictured a marshmallow inside a Godiva chocolate.

Her auburn hair with sunburst golden streaks was long and straight, and tied in a ponytail. She was barely five foot three, and looked as healthy as an aerobics instructor. I watched her every move like a freshman nerd who discovered a cheerleader smiling back at him, then told myself the true test would be when we talked. A grin formed as I prayed she didn't have a fake British accent.

She walked to the stage, placed her purse on top of the amplifier and opened her guitar case. I could see her instrument was also a Martin. The bar maintained a high-level of noise as Jillian plugged into the amplifier and sat on the barstool in front of the microphone.

The noise grew louder. Jillian waited for the sound to die down, but it only intensified. With no lull in sight, she finally strummed a chord, grinned at the crowd and said: "I like to start off with Billboard's l-l-list of top ten Paderewski mazurkas."

I laughed my ass off as she began to sing in a smooth, silky voice.

* * *

> *When you stared at me,*
> *Said you'd swear to me*
> *That none other*
> *Would ever come between;*
> *Candlelight and wine,*
> *Then came lovin' time*
> *But you took my hand*
> *And called me by her name*
> *Chorus*
> *You won't get all over me*
> *Till you get all over her*
> *You won't find me*
> *Standing in your line;*
> *Although you say you love me,*
> *One thing you can be sure*
> *Our love's called off,*
> *While she's still on your mind.*

All of a sudden, four guys, who looked like they were waiting for a decision from the parole board, began raising hell off to my left. The main event was about to start when one of them yelled to Earl, "Hey, we've heard enough of this pansy shit. Turn on the jukebox."

I was hoping his conviction was for income tax evasion, as opposed to serious bodily injury, when I stood up. Immediately, one of his sidekicks walked over and plugged in the jukebox. It came on with a loud roar.

When I got to the guy, Jillian confronted him. He

was about six foot five and towered over her. Out of the corner of my eye, I saw the owner take out his cell phone. I hoped he was calling 9-1-1 instead of his bookie to get down a last-minute bet on the other guys.

"What gives you the r-r-right to do that?" Jillian stuttered.

"Two hundred and fifty pounds and a couple of wrecked eardrums from listening to that shit you're warbling."

"Hey asshole, whaddya think you're doing?" I asked, in my best Steven Seagal voice.

Jillian turned and gave me a look of disgust.

"I'm not a d-damsel in distress, you m-m-m-macho shithead," she said.

"I'm sorry, ma'am, but I was..." I began, as she turned and faced the bully.

"Wanna come home with me, honey? You can bring these with you." He sneered, reached out and grabbed her breasts.

I was ready to clock him when Jillian quickly stepped forward, bringing her right boot down hard on the bully's left instep, then repeating with her left boot on his right instep. The stupid bastard went down screaming in pain, as she slammed her fist into his groin and straddled him.

His three friends approached. One of them gave Jillian's amplifier a vicious kick, denting the speakers and sending her purse and guitar case flying.

"Hey, you bitch, what do you think you're doin'?" he asked.

Hooker and the bouncer joined me. The bouncer looked about five foot ten and thirteen thousand pounds. He had a neck so huge, his head looked like a bowling ball sitting on top of a short refrigerator. I wondered if he was big enough to have his own Google coordinates as I looked behind him to check if he had a balcony.

I was about to step forward, when the bouncer smacked the bully in the jaw with his raised forearm. I could almost hear his cheekbone splinter as he grunted, then slumped to the floor, plunging downward faster than shares of heart valve stock after a product recall.

Two deputy sheriffs walked in. The bouncer pointed toward the gang of four and signaled they started everything. I walked over to Jillian, who was trying to recover the contents of her purse and guitar case. She seemed angry and embarrassed as she refused to look up.

"Are you okay?" I asked, but there was no answer.

She continued gathering items from her purse. I searched for a way to get noticed. She refused, trying to make an exit as soon as possible. Finally, I invited her to have a drink.

"I'll pass," she said.

"Hey come on. I grow on people," I said.

"So does t-t-toxic mold."

"Come on over and let's get acquainted," I pleaded, taking her arm.

She tore her arm away faster than a lobbyist leaves a concession speech.

"Take this in the spirit it's meant. You'd do me a s-s-solid favor if you'd fuck off," she said, turning to leave as 'Trouble' by Travis Tritt, began to play.

Hooker grew a contented look and said we handled those guys like Jean-Claude van Damme and Jackie Chan. I said my contribution was closer to Niles or Frasier. Of course, depending on his choice in lingerie, an argument could be made that we performed like Bonnie and Clyde.

Suddenly, I spied a dark object lying under the bass drum. Walking onto the bandstand, I saw that it was a woman's black leather wallet wedged in by the drum. Inside, I found a driver's license, credit cards, assorted cash and a membership card to a songwriters' association. I ran toward the door but it was too late. At once, I realized tomorrow might be a perfect way to meet her when I returned it on my way to the airport. My pulse quickened as I could almost hear the sound of her voice blended with mine. Then, I laughed out loud when I realized I had just met the first woman in years who would think of a lock and not a legacy if I shouted, "Yale!"

* * *

Thirty minutes later, Hooker and Bobbie were holed up in his bedroom while my mind was filled with thoughts of Jillian and how to pursue her. I ran my fingers over Sam's check and had a vision of introducing her to my music. I felt myself blush as another picture formed of us in bed together, and my whole body stirred.

At that moment, Brooks and Dunn began singing 'Only In America,' in my subconscious.

Bartender, set everyone up with some spacious skies and an amber wave of grain and put it on my tab, was my last conscious thought as I drifted off to sleep.

CHAPTER TWO

The sounds of Hooker and Bobbie moaning in the next room, while they tested the mattress's rebound quotient, brought me to life in the morning. I headed for the kitchen and found the coffee pot when Hooker popped out of his bedroom.

"Sorry, I'm not used to having anyone in the stands when I'm at the fifty and driving for the goal line. Bobbie's one of those steamy little goddesses who makes John Henry stand at attention," he said.

John Henry is the name of his joy stick. The reason escapes me, but I promise to post it on Facebook the instant the FBI needs the answer to complete my background check. Besides, my dearest friend and traveling companion has a significantly more inspiring name. It's Deene. That's French for 'hope.'

"Do all the women you date need a fake ID?" I asked.

"I'm just trying to be a father figure for twenty-something fillies," he said.

I told him about my plan for reuniting later this morning with the woman of my dreams.

"Can I borrow the Jeep? I'd like to look Jillian up on my way to the airport."

"Sure. My flight's not until six o'clock, so just text me where you park," he said.

Bobbie walked out of the bedroom wearing only a long tee shirt that hit her at mid-thigh. She shuffled over to the refrigerator and her face grew into a scowl as she saw the barren shelves.

"I'll stop for a muffin somewhere on my way home. I'm late for work," she said, before heading off toward the bathroom.

"What does she do?" I asked.

He took a sip of his coffee, then ran his hand over his hair.

"Dental hygienist."

"So she was grabbing your balls all night, and now she'll be grabbing people's teeth all day," I replied, absent-mindedly running my tongue over my third molars and praying that, during a dental cleaning, I had never performed a homosexual act on anyone, by proxy.

"Son, as Barack Obama once said to Mike Pence, 'It gives her something to cling to besides her guns and religion'," he said.

Bobbie came back, looking ready to dig around the gum lines of some rotting bicuspids.

"Bye, J. W. I'd love to hear your songs sometime. Bye, Billy. You better call me, you hear?"

After Bobbie left, I told Hooker about what I found in the wallet.

"The driver's license says Angela Trappani, not Jillian Loving."

"Jillian is probably her stage name. Why do you think she changed it?" he asked

"Maybe she wanted to sound like a singer, not Carmella Soprano's stunt double," I said.

"Why don't you call and make sure she's there?"

"She has an unlisted number."

"What if she's involved with somebody?"

"I'll probably just slink away."

He asked if I knew where Franklin was. My GPS app was on the fritz so I told him to pretend he was Rand talking to McNally.

"Head south on I-65. Only about twenty minutes."

* * *

We left at eight-fifteen. After dropping Hooker off, I headed south. Traffic was stalled and I didn't reach the exit ramp until almost nine o'clock. The road led east for almost three miles, and took a sharp series of turns. I searched the numbers on mailboxes until I found the one that matched her driver's license. Shaking slightly, I walked to the door of the first three-story, red-brick townhouse, rang the bell and heard a voice inside. My breath started coming out like water spitting from a pulsating shower head.

"Who is it?"

I almost lost my nerve until a picture of blood, fistfights and broken bones from six NFL training camps appeared. I shook my head from side to side and realized this was much worse. I never wanted to romance any of my teammates.

"Excuse me, ma'am. I'm from Panhandle's. I found your wallet."

Instantly, she opened the door. Jillian-slash-Angela had only a towel wrapped around her. Her hair was dripping wet. She had a trace of shampoo at her temple.

"W-W-Where's my wallet?" she asked, as her face grew a look of fear.

"Right here," I said, extending my right hand. "I found you from the information on the license."

"I was getting ready to c-c-cancel all my credit cards," she said. "I'm s-s-shocked you're from Panhandle's. When I called to ask if anyone turned it in, the man on the phone sounded like I was crazy." Suddenly she appeared uneasy. "Wait a minute. Aren't you the same g-g-g-guy who tried to pick me up last night?"

"Not guilty by reason of diminished musical capacity. I'm hoping you'll let me plead it down to misdemeanor leering with a sentencing recommendation of probation. I'm J. W. Steele," I said, extending my hand.

After hesitating, she shook her head.

"I'm involved with someone. So, thanks for the wallet but I'm not l-l-looking for romance."

"I'm a songwriter. I have one that's perfect for you," I pleaded.

"I don't know you. You could be anyone, from J-J-J-Jack the Ripper to some drugged-out whacko with a sign that says 'Will Work For Food.'"

I tried to get in my rebuttal, but she closed the door and the deadbolt engaged. As I walked to the car, I saw a Black Audi convertible in her carport. I filed that information away for later use and vowed to return as soon as I came back to town, even if I had to bring the cast of *Glee* with me to serenade my way into her life.

I smiled as I remembered Sam offering to record me. Selling my song meant I had plenty of money to fly back and forth until January. Gushing, I ran my fingers over his check in my pocket and fantasized about how my life was about to change.

When I called Julie to update her, she said she knew I was on my way to the top because I had three huge fans who thought I was a "savage" songwriter. I grinned and remembered the first time I played for the twins and they told me I was a savage musician. Lexi said it was a really cool compliment because she was a savage in math and Emily was a savage in science, so it was up to me to turn them into savages on the guitar.

After our flight took off, a mechanical problem developed and we were forced to land in Philadelphia. The delay and air traffic congestion made it so I did not get home until after midnight. Julie texted me and said she was working an extra shift and she and the twins would see me tomorrow night after I finished performing.

* * *

On Friday, I went to the bank when it opened and felt a thrill as I deposited my check. After treating myself to a first-class, leisurely breakfast, I got to the hotel early in the afternoon and went to the room number I received by text. Erica Spaulding opened the door and let me in. She gave me a short kiss, then drew back. She was smartly dressed, in Ferragamo high heels, navy suit and white silk blouse. A single strand of pearls covered her neck down to the first button of her amply-filled blouse. She wore only a gold chain-link bracelet on her left hand and a small filigree ring on her right ring finger. Chic, silver-framed glasses covered her eyes. Every phase of her appearance added sex appeal. Like a Monet painting, maybe a dab of extra paint here or there, but still a time-honored masterpiece. She had shoulder-length, light brown, butterscotch-highlighted hair, reminding me of the vivid colors of sunset.

She took off her suit jacket and slipped it over the back of a chair. I felt myself harden because my trip had me in the mood for romance. As our eyes met, I saw a look that told me something was coming down so I saved my Nashville story for later.

"J. W., I have to talk to you," she said tentatively.

"Uh-oh," I said. "Whatever I did, I'm really sorry."

She stared at me for a long moment and an empty feeling appeared.

"When we first went into this fling, we agreed that either of us could call it off at any time, right? Well, I can't see you anymore," she said flatly.

"What did I do?" I asked.

"Nothing. I met someone and I think it could go somewhere."

"But I thought we had a great thing together. No ties, no commitment."

She stood there and looked pensive, like I had just hacked into her bank accounts.

"We did, but now I want more than that. I can't sleep with you both at the same time."

I sat on the side of the bed. Suddenly, I felt a pang of loneliness.

"Why dump me now?" I asked.

She looked deeply into my eyes as her lips curled into a wry smile.

"You were never mine to begin with so I can't dump you."

She rose and began to pace, then came and took me into her arms. As she held me close, I felt her body rub against my front, I was astonished to find myself start to grow hard. I pulled back and stared into her eyes as images flashed of the two of us in bed.

"I'll miss you," I said finally.

"No, you won't," she said, shaking her head from side to side.

I tried to respond but she grabbed my upper arms and looked me right in the eye.

"What's my favorite TV show of all time?" she asked.

I looked up and shook my head.

"Where does my son go to college? Where's my perfect vacation spot? What movie scene always brings me to tears?" she asked.

I tried to turn away but she pulled me back and gave me a slight shake.

"You can't answer any of those things, can you?"

I tried another mental calculation.

"I know you think the best band of all time is the Eagles. Kenny Chesney and Patty Loveless are your all-time country singers and Kris Kristofferson and Jim Webb are your top songwriters. You just taught Emily 'Rip Tide' and Lexi 'Girl Crush'. I know you are not sleeping with their mother because you respect her too much, whatever that means," she said.

I felt trapped, like a burglar surprised by a homeowner with a baseball bat. She was standing there in a provocative pose and my joy stick was dangerously close to getting hard again.

"Look at you," she said, extending her hands in my direction. "I'm giving you a free therapy session and you're thinking we would have time for one more round if I would just shut up with this silly girl rant."

I looked down and tried to hide my face because she was dead-on accurate. Suddenly, I felt panic-stricken.

"When we started this fling several months ago, I was worried that I could fall in love with you. I knew from the beginning I couldn't let myself get involved. I don't think you can let yourself fall in love. Plus, no woman will ever be as important as your music."

That's exactly what Jewels told me, I thought.

"I've racked my brain to figure out how this could be the best sex I've ever had, but every time I leave here I feel empty," she said.

I began to shift like a schoolboy standing in front of the principal.

"Why do you think I know all those things about you and you know nothing about me?" she asked. I shrugged. "Because, when we're not making love, I listen to you. But, you make me feel like we're a couple of robots. I don't want to move in with you, but I would like just a teaspoon of humanity stirred in when we're together."

"I'm sorry. I didn't mean to be selfish," I said.

She shook her head. "At first, it didn't bother me. I was coming off a twenty-two year marriage and the last thing I wanted was a relationship. Now, I don't understand how you can kiss me like we're star-crossed lovers, but I'm not sure you'd give me CPR if I went into cardiac arrest," she said. She folded her arms again. "Okay, tell me one thing I said that's not true," she said.

I stared at the floor and was ready to swear I would give her CPR, but knew that was the wrong answer.

"I guess the silence says it all," she said. "I would certainly recommend you to any of my friends who could use an hour or two of a rockets-red-glare, bombs-bursting-in-air hump festival, but you have the emotional intelligence of a statue."

I looked away as she continued.

"You once told me there's a song that explains every situation. Sometimes, I wonder if you ever really listen to any of those lyrics," she said.

"I'm not sure what you mean," I said.

Erica picked up her suit jacket and slung it over her right shoulder.

"I think the last line to the old Eagles' hit, 'Desperado', that you always sing in the lounge, fits this moment to a T," she said.

My mind heard the soulful, raspy sound of the voice of Don Henley as he told me that it was time to let somebody love me. Then, he paused before delivering the hook: ...'before I found out it was too late.'

My mind was reeling after she left. I really did care about her, but kept my feelings in check after we decided from the start this affair wasn't going anywhere. Besides, I learned long ago that I had to hold something back in my relationships with women.

Erica was assistant manager of the hotel by the airport and could get us a room anytime we wanted. For the past few months, we've had standing dates on Mondays and Fridays. She was married to a cop and their divorce was becoming really nasty. He was insanely jealous and had not come to terms with the fact that their marriage was over. Erica had just reached her forty-sixth birthday, a nice age differential that I figured would let us go on indefinitely.

An intense feeling of sadness spread over me like a velcro storm cloud. I knew the answer to every question she asked and wanted to scream 'I love you,', but the words stuck in my throat.

I got to the bandstand just before six o'clock. and a teenage boy wearing a kitchen uniform approached.

"Excuse me, Mr. Steele. Ms. Spaulding asked me to give you this envelope," he said.

"Who's it from?"

"I don't know. She said someone left it at the front desk and asked me to deliver it. She also said it would be okay if I asked you a question," he said.

"Sure it is, as long as you call me J. W." I smiled.

"Great. Can you show me how to play a G thirteenth?" he asked.

I nodded, picked up the Martin, formed the chord and strummed. As the sound filled the room, his eyes lit up like an eight-year-old ogling a Blizzard at Dairy Queen.

"Wow, you really get a major amen for that one," he intoned.

"Tell me your name," I said.

"Timmy Cahill," he answered, in an awestruck voice.

"Okay, Timmy, here's the best part. If you move your pinkie like this, the chord becomes a G ninth."

Timmy's lower jaw dropped and his semi-open mouth convinced me I'd just made a friend.

"I have to go on stage now. If you have any more questions, you can call me," I said, quickly giving him my number.

"Thanks, J. W. My dad is taking me camping, but I'll be back Monday," he said.

He stuck out his fist for a bump and left me feeling somewhat old, but deeply satisfied that I still had something valuable to share.

I tore open the envelope and read a handwritten letter on a piece of hotel stationery. It was from two brothers, Nick and Matt Bentley, who said they were members of a group called Power Sweep, and were awed by my performance last Monday night. They had to leave before they could talk to me. The band was based in Atlanta, and getting ready to start a Caribbean tour. They wanted me to contact their manager about writing songs and possibly performing together.

Overjoyed, I slipped the letter into the string compartment of my guitar case. I was on a streak of good luck with no end in sight.

My session went flawlessly and two hours later, I headed out to the parking lot. After placing my equipment in the back, I heard the sound of someone walking swiftly. When I turned, I was slammed into my car and my hands were jerked behind my back. The sensation of something being slipped over my wrists took over. An angry voice appeared next to my left ear.

"You're busted, asshole. Possession of a firearm, assault and battery on a police officer and resisting arrest. An unlicensed gun in this state means a year in the can, pal, and no pussy judge can let you off without jail time," the voice snarled.

"What the hell are you talking about? You've got the wrong guy. I play music in the hotel lounge," I said, my voice filled with fear.

"Yeah, you think you're some big time, football playing singer. But that ain't all you do, you prick," the voice continued. "You specialize in fucking other guy's wives."

Out of my peripheral vision, I saw the man draw back with a stick. Instantly, I felt a huge blow behind my knees and collapsed onto the pavement. He stood there and snarled.

A blow to the side of my head stunned me, and I felt myself being loaded into the back of a police cruiser. As we sped away, I slipped into semi-consciousness and realized I had just met Erica's husband.

* * *

We arrived at the police station where I was photographed, fingerprinted and put in a holding cell. I claimed my own little corner, while my attitude sent signals that I was not ready to friend any of my cellmates.

An hour later, I was taken to a separate room. A middle-aged, serious looking woman, peered at me over her reading glasses.

"Mr. Steele, I'm Magistrate Callahan. Because it's Friday night and you will not be arraigned until Monday, I'm here to see what bail should be set in your case," she said coldly.

"Ma'am, I swear I'm innocent. This must be mistaken identity," I said. I refused to say anything about the cop, because the last thing I wanted to do was involve Erica, especially since it happened where she works.

"You can bring that up to the judge. This hearing is only about bail and you as a potential flight risk," she said, while reaching for a folder as I stayed silent. "The charges against you are serious—especially possession of the firearm with no license. You have no priors, so I'm setting your bail at five thousand dollars cash, or fifty thousand surety."

I swallowed hard. It might as well be five million.

"Can I call someone?" I asked.

"You can," she said, after directing the officers to let me use a telephone.

Soon, an officer returned with my cell phone and told me to make it quick. My hands were shaking as I dialed Julie. I gave her Hooker's number so she could ask him for bail money because Sam's check had not cleared yet. She told me to sit tight and she would get back to me.

* * *

At quarter of nine on Saturday morning, an officer shouted, "Steele, you made bail!" I walked quickly out of the cell door as the desk sergeant handed me an envelope with my belongings. I signed a release and was told to report to Middlesex District Court at eight o'clock on Monday morning. I could not wait to get away from the sights, smells and sounds of jail.

On my way out, Julie handed me a copy of the newspaper, opened to the Metro section. There was a short article entitled: *Former Patriot Arrested on Illegal Gun Charges*. Neither of us spoke until she drove away. I started to pour out the story before she held up her hand.

"Stop it," she said firmly. "I've got decades of education and training in psych and if you are guilty, then you must be an imposter." She held out a bag in her right hand. "The girls wanted to console you, so they sent you these cupcakes as a pick me up," she said, with a sly grin. "They want you to come over for lunch so they can cheer you up."

She knew about Erica and I filled her in about her husband. She asked if I knew any lawyers and I said I would have to rely on the court assigning one to represent me.

"How did you get Hooker to send you the bail money so fast?" I asked in a relieved voice.

She gave me a long look, then shook her head from side to side. "I couldn't reach him. So, this one's on me," she said, as I remembered he was in Oklahoma.

"I didn't want you have to front the money, Jewels," I said dejectedly.

"Should I turn around and take you back?" she asked lightly.

I asked her to drive me to the bank to confirm how soon the check would clear so I could pay her back. She told me to relax and take it easy. The funds would be there soon.

"Did you tell the twins about my situation?" I asked.

"I just said you had some trouble."

When we reached the hotel parking lot, I gave her a kiss on the cheek as I left. We arrived home twenty-five minutes later. Emily and Alexa answered the door and each one took an arm. They were wearing the tee shirts I brought them from Nashville, and disappeared right after Julie and I walked in.

A moment later, they returned. Lexi was carrying a shoe box which she extended forward.

"Here, J. W.," Emily said. "Mom said you're in trouble."

"We want you to take our puppy fund," Lexi said. A huge lump formed in my throat.

"We've still got almost seventy-two dollars," Emily said, and Lexi nodded vigorously.

I looked at each one before taking them in my arms and said I was okay. Julie told us all to sit and gave the girls a look like a proud parent watching them perform in their first school play, before she brought in a huge plate of brownies.

"Those two apples sure didn't fall far from my favorite tree," I said, and she shook her head.

I stayed for another hour until the twins had to leave for a birthday party. On the way out, they agreed to come over for a lesson the next day and I went in to call the lawyer Julie gave me. We hit it off until he said he needed ten grand upfront.

I logged onto the bank's website. My last deposit was recorded but had not cleared. I called the bank and they told me I should have the money by Tuesday.

* * *

At eight-thirty on Monday morning, I entered the district court and took a seat in the back row, next to a guy who was semi-dozing. He stirred and in no time, I got his memoirs.

"Hey, man, you here for a trial?' he asked. "I'm gonna be a witness later."

"No, I'm here on something else," I said.

"See that bald, skinny guy with the thick file in the front? He's my buddy's lawyer. His name is Ballantine Walsh and they call him 'Balls to the Walsh.' Neat, huh?" he asked. He slipped his palms face down under his ass and began to grin while rocking back and forth. "Walsh is a magician. Ever seen his ads?" he asked.

I shook my head.

"He had one that said, 'We don't care if you did it, we'll still get you acquitted.' Is he a wild, pissah dude or what?" he asked.

I heard the clerk call my name. "Next, case, Your Honor, is the People versus John W. Steele," said the clerk, before handing a file to the judge.

I walked to the front of the court where I was directed to stand next to a bailiff. The judge looked over the file before turning to me.

"Mr. Steele, do you have a lawyer?" he asked.

"No, Your Honor."

"Do you have the means to hire your own counsel?' he asked

"I do not, sir," I said respectfully.

"Is the bar advocate here?" the judge asked.

"She's at another arraignment on the third floor," the court officer replied.

"What's a bar advocate?" I whispered to the bailiff.

"Your free lawyer," he said, with a smirk. "Be ready to get what you pay for."

"I'm not waiting for her with a room full of lawyers right here," the judge snapped, as he looked over the packed courtroom.

"Is that Ballantine Walsh I see? Mr. Walsh, the Court thanks you profusely in advance for your willingness to represent indigent clients. Meet your new client, Mr. Steele."

Walsh stood up. He was disheveled and wore a checked coat, striped tie and plaid pants.

"Your Honor, may I respectfully decline? My

caseload is really full," he said, in a voice bordering on pleading.

"The Bar needs your services and will appreciate your willingness to help, as will this Court," said the judge, giving him a look that suggested it was not a volunteer effort.

Walsh glanced at me and nodded toward the back of the courtroom. The judge told me to follow Walsh, who escorted me down the hallway to a private conference room. Walsh opened my file and read.

"Talk fast. I have to get my witnesses ready."

"What do you want to know?" I asked, as he read furiously.

"Where'd you get the gun?" he asked.

"That cop planted it on me," I said.

He looked up at me and smirked. "Nice try. Who do you think you are, O. J. Simpson?"

"It's true. He found out I'm seeing his wife."

"You mean seeing, as in 'banging her till she screams for help'?" he asked caustically.

"Yeah, but they're separated."

"Did you resist arrest or fight with the cop?"

"Absolutely not."

"Were there any witnesses?"

"Not that I know about."

"Why were you at the hotel?"

"I work there. I'm a singer in the lounge," I said.

He looked up and stared deeply into my eyes before turning toward the door.

"Okay, I'll plead you not guilty. I want you in my office tonight at six o'clock to go over your case. Here's my card," he said.

* * *

I'd just gotten home about two o'clock, when my phone rang. It was Erica.

"Hey, what's up?"

"I just found out about your arrest. Are you okay?" she asked.

"Yeah, I made bail."

"My lawyer said my husband is using you to squeeze a settlement out of me."

"You know he planted the gun."

"I know. Listen, there's one more thing. Don't call me on my cell phone anymore. I found out it's been hacked," she said. "That's how he found out about us. If you need me, call me at work. I'm getting a new cell phone number."

A few minutes later, I heard a knock at the door and saw Timmy Cahill, the busboy, standing at my front entrance beside a man in his mid-forties. Timmy's face was somber.

"Hiya, J. W. I tried to call, but couldn't get cell reception from the lake," he said.

I remembered the unknown calls that never connected. "That's okay. I'm sorry but I have to go to a meeting, so I can't talk right now."

"Excuse me, I'm Don Cahill, Timmy's dad," the man said, extending his hand. "Timmy has something you might need."

I felt puzzled as Timmy took a deep breath and continued.

"I followed you out Friday night and saw you get busted by that officer. I took out my phone and recorded it," he said.

I felt my heart pound and my chest puff out.

"You're kidding," I said, fighting the urge to jump up and shout.

"I wanted to thank you once more, but before I could, the officer came up. When he hit you, I got out my phone. Here, look at the video," he said, extending his phone toward me.

I saw my arrest. It showed me being slammed against my SUV, the officer extracting something from his shirt and pressing it into my handcuffed palms. Then I was smacked behind the knees with his nightstick.

"I'm no lawyer," Don said. "But I told Timmy this could help you with your case."

I was breathing in spurts as I asked Timmy to forward the video to me. We shook hands all around as I told Timmy he had just won an all-expenses paid trip to my apartment for instruction on the guitar any time he wanted it.

* * *

Walsh's office was located in a suburban strip mall and had a sign over the entrance that read, "To get ahead in life, you need 'BALLS." After walking inside, I saw a waiting room full of people, several of whom were chatting in foreign languages. Many wore cervical collars or casts, while two were in wheelchairs. I took one of the few remaining seats and could hear Balls' voice, streaming out from behind the closed door with the frosted glass-panel.

I heard the receiver slammed down before the door opened and Walsh appeared. He nodded for me to enter, then addressed a family huddled together in a far corner. "Vlasic, give me a minute, okay?" he yelled. The entire family looked up grinning. Then Walsh turned and followed me inside.

Walsh was in his early sixties, about five foot ten, slightly underweight and had a ruddy complexion. The wall behind his desk was filled with newspaper accounts of cases he had won, each in a matching gold frame.

"I need your whole story. There's a thing called attorney-client privilege. That means I am bound by law to keep everything you tell me confidential so you can't hold anything back, no matter how many drug deals you made or how many arrests you've got for being a flasher," he said, smiling like a funeral director congratulating me for choosing the premier casket.

"Do they really call you 'Balls'?" I asked.

"Yep. I got the name Ballantine because my dad was an ale man. But, I worked my ass off to get the label Balls. It's better than some downtown preppie weasel named Skippy Tightass. And, it got me my summer house on the Vineyard and a condo in Palm Beach." He put his feet up on desk.

"How do you get away with your slogans and using that nickname?" I asked.

"Because it's free speech. The bar told me to knock it off and I refused. So, they sued my ass and I appealed all the way up. I said it was protected, like the band that calls itself Pussy Riot. The Supreme Judicial Court said as long as it wasn't used in a way that was fraudulent, unfair or deceptive, I could use it," he said.

I chuckled as he continued.

"That's why I moved my office here to this strip mall. I used to have an office in Cambridge, the haven for nut-job, left wing assholes. Finally, I moved here, and juries love me because they think I'm just like them, putting up with the same bullshit."

"Does my case go on the back burner because I didn't hire you myself?"

"Of course not. I'll make money from you. Besides, I have a saying from Johnny Cochran that fits: 'Everyone is innocent until proven broke,'" he said.

I grinned.

"Let's talk about you. What kind of a name is Steele?" he asked, hands behind his head.

"German, with a little Irish," I answered, as he sat up straight. "Not as Irish as you, but my grandmother was an O'Sullivan. My relatives from the other side are probably still hiding out in Paraguay, using some really deceptive alias, like Wolfgang de la Vasquez."

His face took on a pall, like I had just insulted him. "You're not some kinda Nazi whacko, are you?" he asked.

"Hey, lighten up, it was just a joke," I said, annoyed. "Why the hell would you ask me that?"

"Let's get something straight. Walsh is only a trade name. My real name is Wallenstein. I need to know... are you some kind of *schmuck* who's got a problem with a Jewish lawyer?" he asked.

I shook my head. "I don't give a shit if you're Benjamin Netanyahu's brother if you can get me off," I said.

His face relaxed. "I just want to make sure I don't have to put up with any bigoted crap. I grew up in Brooklyn and Wallenstein was fine there, but I went to law school in Boston and decided to stay."

"Why change your name?" I asked.

"Two reasons. There's plenty of members of

the tribe practicing here so I decided to call myself 'Walsh' to draw in all the political hacks. They can give me a check from the city treasury, then ask me to join them in a chorus of 'Ave Maria', even though I'll be croonin' 'Oy Vey' instead of Ave," he said.

"What's the second reason?"

He looked at me for a long moment.

"You're a musician. Do you know why Elvis was such a major sensation?" he asked.

"He was a great talent and got perfect songs," I said.

Balls shook his head. "You wanna know the real reason? Because America was knee deep in racism and Elvis was a white man who sang like he was black so his music oozed with soul. He had the best of both worlds, just like me now. I've got an Irish name and Jewish DNA. I'm Elvis with a law degree."

I started thinking of rhymes for "Ballantine" as he continued.

"Okay, tell me what really happened and make me a believer."

I told him my story, then pulled up the video from Timmy on my phone. He sat on the edge of his chair and whistled softly.

"Why would the cop do that? He would get fired and the city would be liable to you for damages. Plus, you could press charges against him."

I told him about Erica and how her phone was hacked. He asked if she knew about the video.

"Not yet. Does it matter?"

He brought his hands together and looked at me for a long moment. I sensed my next move would be a game changer.

"As I see it, you've got two choices. You can use this video as evidence to get the charges dismissed and then we'll sue the living shit out of the town. Or, you can give it to your girlfriend. So, it's either you or her, take your choice," he said solemnly.

"Why can't I do both?" I asked.

"If I use it, the city will fight to get it suppressed because it's illegal in this state to record someone speaking without their consent. If I convince a judge to keep it in, the cop will get fired, charged criminally and the city will get reamed. Your girlfriend will lose her job when the hotel finds out she was shacking up with you while she was on duty. Somebody is always the loser in situations like this. So, you have to decide if it's you or her. It's a no-brainer."

"Are you sure she'll get fired?"

Balls nodded vigorously and threw up his hands.

"This video will be on the six o'clock news faster than an Amtrak crash. No way she'll keep her job. But, my duty is to protect you, not her," he said.

"If it's illegal, how can a judge let you keep the video?" I asked.

"Only the audio part is illegal, you can use the tape without sound," he said.

"The cop says it's an automatic year in jail for having an unlicensed gun," I said.

"They'll never prove that. You can see him reaching into his shirt and putting something in your hands behind your back."

"What if he claims I had it before the video started?"

Balls looked at me for a moment and said,

"That might be a problem."

"I could go to jail for a year?"

"Don't worry, I'll get the gun charge tossed. Plus, you're a first time offender so I can get you probation on the other counts even if the jury sticks it up your ass like a Fleet enema," he said.

"I see why they call you Balls," I said.

He grew a hugely satisfied smile and folded his arms.

"The biggest compliment I ever got was when a prosecutor told me I could get a charge of sodomy reduced to following too close."

"I'll sleep on it and let you know," I said, as he walked me to the door before ushering Vlasic and his family into the office, while slapping each of them on the back.

* * *

I arrived home just as the sun was setting, and heard a text. Julie said the twins were going to a sleepover. After exiting the SUV, I saw two men get out of a black sedan and approach me.

"Mr. John Steele?" the taller one asked. "I'm Constable Lewis and this is my partner, Officer Connor. We have a certified document for you but we need a signature first."

He extended a clipboard and pen toward me.

"Who's it from?" I asked fearfully.

"The law firm of Corcoran and Bailey. Sign here, please," he said, pointing toward the sheet.

My hands were shaking as I signed. I was handed a large manila envelope before the duo left. The first line told me everything I needed to know.

"Pursuant to your arrest for illegal firearms possession, as well as other allegations of felonious conduct, this correspondence will serve as formal notice that Club Palladin is hereby invoking the previously designated 'moral's clause' and cancelling your obligations to perform there, beginning Saturday, August eight. The club is further irrevocably rescinding said contract because of such violation(s) on your part."

Feelings of fear and shame spread over me, as I ripped the document in half. I called Balls but he was gone for the day. As I hung up, I realized there was no longer any need for me to hold off on leaving until January. I could take off for Nashville any time.

Unless a jury decided to change my address to a local house of correction.

CHAPTER THREE

On Tuesday, I logged onto the bank's website after spending a sleepless night. Disappointment came over me because Sam's check still had not cleared.

Afterward, I met Erica at the hotel. She was sitting at a table in the rear left corner of a ballroom, engaged in a conversation with an employee in a hotel blazer, who left as I arrived.

"Okay, what couldn't you tell me on the phone?" she asked, nervously looking from side to side.

"This," I said, cuing up the video and handing her my phone.

"That bastard. What are you going to do with this?" she asked.

I laid out the options Balls had given me, including his recommendation of throwing her and her husband to the wolves. A few beads of sweat formed on her forehead.

"Are you going to take his advice?" she asked hesitantly.

I stared into that beautiful face that had grown into a shell of sadness.

"No. I'm going to give it to you. The only thing I care about is going to Nashville. Even if I get convicted, it might help me. Look at what San Quentin did for Merle Haggard," I said, as she stayed solemn. I pulled my hands up in front of my face, crossed my eyes, stuck my tongue to the side and simulated holding cell bars. That got a small grin from her.

"Why are you doing this after all the shitty things I said to you the other day?" she asked.

I stopped as I felt overcome with emotion.

"Two reasons. First, I had to show you you're wrong about whether I would give you CPR."

Tears began leaking and she dabbed her eyes with a tissue. "What's the other reason?" she asked.

"Your favorite TV show is 'House of Cards.' Your son goes to Suffolk University. Your ideal vacation spot is the Amalfi Coast in Italy, and the scene in 'Titanic' where Jack and Rose consummate their love, always brings you to tears. In short, I'm doing this because I really do care about you even if I never let it show."

She swallowed hard and her face contorted like she was in pain. "If I live to be a thousand, I'll never figure you out," she said finally.

After we parted, I again pulled up my bank account. Fear spread over my entire body as I kept jabbing at the screen and screaming. Sam's check was dishonored because it came from a closed account. Plus, my entire checking account had been wiped out.

I went into panic mode and spent almost an hour on the phone. I was told to expect a call from the FBI's fraud unit as a priority investigation would begin immediately.

"Have you given anyone your social security number recently?" the bank officer asked.

"Yes," I said, embarrassed as a vision of me filling out the W-9 form for Sam appeared.

After the call ended, I slammed the phone down and felt a sinking feeling, like someone had just died. I was more pissed than I could remember and began pacing back and forth.

I stopped. Rage would do me no good. Neither would self-pity. It was time suck it up.

* * *

Half an hour later, I arrived in the Mattapan section of Boston and found a space outside of the Imperial Loan Company. It was perched in the middle of a maze of multi-storied red brick buildings from the 1950s, highlighted with grimy, cream-colored stones framing the edges. Permanent bars covered the windows and sliding, chain-linked security gates turned stores into fortresses after business hours. I pressed the buzzer, heard the door release, went inside and asked for Morrie, the contact my ex-teammates used to recommend.

Rows of used Louis Vuitton, Fendi and Chanel bags were displayed. Signs in a few languages offered to buy gold. Diamonds and other precious stones filled the front-to-back display cases.

A huge row of guitars and other instruments covered the back wall. A troubled feeling came over me as I gave thanks it was the ring I was forced to give up, not my Martin. A moment later, a short, overweight man with thinning hair, chomping on an unlit cigar, wearing horn-rimmed glasses, dark Bermudas and a sweat-stained shirt, came over.

"I'm Morrie, what's up?" he asked.

"I need to get a loan on my ring," I said, holding up my right hand.

He pulled out a jewelers' loop, held the ring up and examined it.

"I can get you five grand," he said.

"Morrie, give me a break. The ring is worth at least fifteen," I protested.

"Maybe in Pittsburgh, but not in Boston. Not even if it had a picture of Gronk's ass on it, because this ain't Steeler country. So, its five grand. Take it or leave it."

I swallowed hard and thought for a moment before handing him the ring.

"And, so there's no misunderstanding, the point is a grand every six months. You've got six months to redeem it for six large, or a year for seven. If you're late, I'll have to charge you another point. And it's a grand if you head outside right now, walk back in and pay it off," he said.

"Jesus, that's like thirty five percent interest," I said, as I felt myself start to sweat.

"Welcome to my version of the Clinton Foundation," he said.

"Take good care of the ring, because I will be back," I said, as my voice broke.

He shook his head as he reached into his pocket.

"That's what everybody says," he replied, counting out a stack of hundred dollar bills.

* * *

Later that afternoon, Balls called.

"I just got a call from your girlfriend's lawyer. They're trying to settle her divorce case but there's one major stumbling block," he said.

"What's that?"

"Are you willing to sign a document that you won't press charges and will release the arresting officer and the city from all liability for your arrest?"

I thought for a moment before I replied. "You said a trial would ruin Erica. Plus, the husband will lose his job, right?"

"Yeah, but they would be considered collateral damage," he said, as I heard his irritation.

"But, if the video comes in, they'll both get fired. She can't get alimony from him if he's not working," I said.

"Look, I'm your lawyer, not hers. That cop deserves to have his ass kicked for what he tried to do to you. You're facing a year in jail because he's jealous? Give me a goddamn break."

"But, she doesn't deserve to have her life turned upside down because of him, right?"

"If you sign the release, it will be against my advice. You'll have to execute a document that I advised you against it," he said. "Why don't you take the weekend to think about it?"

"I don't need to think about it. Tell them they have a deal," I said, knowing that there was no need to ask about my termination from the club, because it no longer mattered.

As I hung up the phone, I heard him whisper, "Putz." I wasn't sure exactly what that meant, but decided it was not a compliment, even though it might be an award-winning song title.

Hooker called an hour later. He said he was ready to send Julie my bail money last week, but she said it was taken care of.

I told him how Sam turned into Bernie Madoff.

Then, he dropped his bombshell. "Son, don't get your hopes up but I may have found you a real job coaching quarterbacks. The head coach is checking to see if there are enough funds in the budget."

I felt my chest tighten.

"It's not a done deal yet. The chief finance guy is at a conference. I don't want to keep pursuing this unless you think you can put your legal troubles behind. So, I need some kind of commitment from you to head to Nashville."

"My lawyer is working out a deal right now. I should know in a couple of days."

"You can live with me as long as you want. Don't worry about paying rent," he declared, before he began to speak in a full-blown, Southern accent that was half cleric and half politician. "Son, Bill Clinton says you need to get down here now," he said, his voice taking on a lilt.

"Why? Is Slick Willie trying to turn the Capitol Building into a Hooters?" I asked.

"As our former president might say, 'It depends on what the meaning of is is.' You need to follow your heart. As we used to say in Little Rock, 'Puttin' wings on a pig don't make it an eagle,' and you ain't never gonna be no East Coast phony. Now, ah have to go pick up the latest love of my life, Tina, and tell her ah feel her pain as she unzips mah Oval Office."

"Somewhere, JFK is looking down at you and smiling," I told him, and we hung up.

I started to reflect on how lucky I am Hooker is taking me in without hesitation. I'm lucky but not shocked. It was right in character for him to think about a job for me. Generosity was always one of his strongest suits. I once gave him my last forty dollars when he was on his way to buy our tickets for the Sigma Chi

Sweetheart formal dance. He came back empty-handed because he met a woman at the store whose husband lost his job, so he gave her all our cash. We borrowed money from our dates to get a pizza and split a six-pack. We wound up wearing our tuxes and ball gowns to the university lake at midnight, where we joined everyone for a post-party moonlight skinny dip.

That memory made me smile. It also gave me an intense feeling of gratitude. Maybe Hooker needs some crazy laugh fests as much as I do.

Just after four o'clock, Balls called. My hands were shaking as I answered.

"Is this good news?" I asked.

"The short version is, the lawyer for the cop folded like a cheap ceiling fan after I gave him my *spiel*. He was trying to intimidate the wife's attorney, before I made things hotter than a tabasco fart at the equator."

"How?"

"I told them about my expert electrical engineer videographer. He enhanced the video and even without the sound, now it's clear what the officer did. Add your testimony along with the kid who took the video and we've got them by the short and curlys. The charges against you are dropped."

"What about the bail money posted by my friend?"

"The DA is pushing through a check as we speak."

"When will the deal be final?"

"As soon as you come in and sign."

"Outstanding. I'm leaving town as soon as everything is finalized."

"Where are you going?"

"Nashville, to write songs," I said as my mind flashed a picture of my ring floating away.

Balls' voice sounded like he swallowed thumb tacks drenched in gasoline. "Country music? Shit, that's the plot from 'Duck Dynasty' set to a twangy tune," he said. "Do you know what there is in Nashville that has two hundred legs and seventeen teeth?"

"What?"

"The first two rows at the Grand Ole Opry."

I laughed out loud as he continued.

"I'll call you when everything's ready. If you change your mind about suing, let me know."

"Balls, I don't care about the town or the money or anything except following my dreams."

"Fine, say hello to Hank Williams for me," he said.

"Hank has been dead for sixty or so years."

He cleared his throat and replied, "So has all that steel guitar wailing about Mamma tryin' hard while beating clothes on the river rocks, and Daddy drying out at the Betty Ford Center after propping up the chassis of a '55 Ford pickup on blocks in their front yard. Now, Jesus can tell them to be proud because they're poor, fat, illiterate hicks with no future," he said. My eyes grew wide as I pictured him saying it.

I told him to expect me as soon as the papers were ready while I mentally crossed him off my list as a possible collaborator, even though what he just described gave me at least half a dozen potential song titles.

* * *

Erica called the next day and said her lawyer talked the husband into signing over his share of their house instead of paying her alimony. Now, she never had to worry if he lost his job. His share of the house would make sure she could survive if a financial tragedy occurred.

I asked how the charges against me were dropped even though the video showed what a lying prick her husband was. She said the DA owed her husband a favor and agreed to destroy all copies of the video so the chief would never see it. That meant her husband could make up a story about how my arrest happened because of some interceding event and the chief would buy it because there was no evidence to refute it.

I told her I was leaving for Nashville and she said she looked forward to seeing me perform at a future concert. I told her I would miss her and suddenly felt myself getting choked up.

"Hey, are you okay?" she asked, after I paused for a long moment.

"I'll never forget the time we spent together. I thought holding my feelings back would make it easy to say goodbye. But, I still hurt as much as ever," I said, as a tear slid down my cheek.

"You can't turn your feelings on and off like a faucet. I hurt, too. But we both know this is the way it has to be," she said.

"I thought I could hide the way I felt. Now, I have to hope someone like you shows up again," I said.

"She will, and when she does, let yourself go and don't hold anything back. You can't fool your heart so it's better to love than lie," she said.

I said goodbye and realized her last words had given me one final gift. A song title.

After we hung up, inspiration struck and I began to write when my A string snapped. After browsing through my collection of strings for a replacement, I suddenly came across the letter the band left me at the hotel. In all the turmoil, it had completely slipped my mind.

I reread the letter and did a quick Google search. What I found made my smile explode. Their website was legitimate and contained scores of photographs, links and tour dates. Matt and Nick were the real deal and I sucked in a deep breath as I realized how I almost let this go.

Quickly, I dialed the band's manager, Mark Bliss. We spent almost an hour on the phone and I agreed to send him a few of my songs, cautiously optimistic that I was about to get a second chance.

Julie got home at the usual time and joined me for a late dinner. She said the twins decided to extend their sleepover and would be back tomorrow night. "When are you leaving?" she asked finally, her voice quavering.

"Saturday. It's my only option after Sam cleaned me out. Hooker said there might be a job there for me." I told her about the band, Power Sweep, and my conversation with their manager. I said getting connected with the band was a real long shot but I was convinced they were legitimate.

"What happens if you have to choose between Nashville and Atlanta?" she asked.

"It won't come to that," I said, suddenly on guard.

"I'll try to smooth things over with the girls," she said, putting her right hand on mine.

"I've been looking for a way to make my leaving a little smoother," I said. "What if I could get them a dog before I left?"

She shook her head. "That's tougher than you think. They want a retriever or a spaniel or a breed like that. The cost is anywhere from fifteen hundred to two thousand."

"Carol has a cousin who's a vet. I'll see if he can help."

* * *

The next morning, I had just left a message for Brad Lyle, the veterinarian, when my phone rang. My heart raced as I saw the caller ID.

"J. W., this is Mark Bliss from Power Sweep. I hope this isn't a bad time."

"No, it's fine."

"We've had a new development since last night. Our lead guitarist suffered a shattered pelvis when he lost control of his motorcycle and he's going to be out for several months. I'm calling to see if there's any way you could join the band for our upcoming tour." I felt my head pound and my chest quiver. Music was slapping me in the face and wrapping itself around my heart. I was so overwhelmed that my vocal cords would not cooperate. Then, I thought of Hooker as Mark continued. "I can get you eighty grand a year to start and you would only be a sideman until we could move you up to the front after one of your songs scores," he said. "You'd have to meet the band first to make sure they approve. But, Matt and Nick already know your work, so I don't anticipate any problems."

Somehow, I found my voice. "I'm really flattered," I said, as a vision of the coaching job flashed.

"After hearing the songs you sent, I can see our lead female singer joining you in a series of duets. It could be the second coming of Blake and Gwen," said Mark.

"I need a little time to think, because this is completely unexpected. Can I have twenty-four hours to give you an answer?" I asked.

"Sure. I'll round up the band if you tell me we can put a deal together."

"I'll have an answer for you tomorrow night."

I called Hooker but got his voicemail. I sent a text and asked him to call.

It was almost five o'clock when I got to Balls' office. We had a short conversation before he opened the manila folder in front of him.

"Sign this release for the city at the bottom," he said, shoving a pen forward. After I scrawled my signature, he handed me a document. "That's a letter from the District Attorney, formally dropping all charges against you," he said, before giving me a check. It was made out to Julie in the amount of five thousand dollars. "Getting bail back usually takes weeks. I told the DA we wouldn't sign without the check."

"Anything else?" I asked. as he shook his head up and down.

He shook his head. "Sign this letter saying I advised you not to settle, but you refused," he said. I complied, then stuck out my hand and thanked him. As we shook, he looked me in the eyes. "Stay out of trouble. If you don't, call me," he said, with a steely gaze.

* * *

As I left Balls' office, Brad Lyle called. He said a puppy could be very expensive, but he knew a breeder of Golden Retrievers. He also said the pet shelters were overloaded and lots of dogs were available, but it would require home visits, paperwork and be next to impossible if I was leaving.

I called the breeder, who said as a favor to Brad, he could get me a puppy for twelve hundred dollars. I declined and my phone rang. It was Hooker.

"Son, I've got great news. The head coach got approval from finance to make you the offensive backfield coach for the staggering sum of twenty-five grand," he said. I told him about my other offer from the band and could hear the disappointment in his voice. "Well, we gave it a shot," he said.

"Listen, this offer just appeared out of the blue. Let me sleep on this," I pleaded.

"Sure," he said. "This is a big decision." He took a deep breath and then we both became deep in thought.

"This reminds me of college when you talked me off the ledge after Melissa Sue Hoffman dumped me for that rich dipshit," I said finally.

"I know this is a life-changin' moment. Remember, I was also the one who stood beside you during all those bench clearing brawls. It was me who had your back in Beaumont when that asshole returned to the bar with his friends and they jumped you. We've stood shoulder to shoulder like brothers in mud, blood and beer, so let me put this to you in our terms. It's fourth and goal. The score is tied with one second left. Are you gonna run a play or take a knee?"

I stared straight ahead. Suddenly, I got really pissed at myself. Friendship was too precious to discard. I was going to do what I wanted, not what I should.

Then, my mind formed a picture of Jillian. I took a deep breath and made my decision.

"I don't need to sleep on it. I'm coming to Nashville on Saturday."

He let out a huge shout. "Outstandin'. I've never known you to settle for the tie before," he said.

The thought of Melissa Sue took me back to my junior year at Texas State. She was my next relationship after Ann dumped me in high school for being too "clingy." I vowed not to be so possessive with her. We had a great relationship until her folks came for parents' weekend. Two days later, she told me her father said all I was interested in was football and music. He said it was time to put childish things like me aside. That's exactly what she did, hooking up with some wealthy graduate assistant from Dallas.

I could hear the relief in Hooker's voice as he continued. "Son, we're gonna get laid so often you'll think we're wardens in a women's prison for ex-models and we both have a fistful of pardons. You still keep a tape recorder in the car in case inspiration strikes, right? Why don't you narrate your trip down here?"

I told him that was a first class idea.

"Us living together again reminds me of that song title you gave me a while back, 'Good Offning, Efficer. I Swear I Can Drive From The Back Seat,'" he said, and belly laughed.

* * *

Julie had the night off and I gave her the check when I got home. She went upstairs and returned with a stack of hundreds. She grew a faint smile when I told her I was considering keeping the money in my mattress so some prick like Sam couldn't steal it.

"When are you going to tell the girls about leaving?" she asked.

"Right now. I had no luck on the puppy so I'll just have to come clean."

I asked her to go outside with me and we found the twins playing on the swing set.

"J. W. has something to tell you," Julie said.

"When are you leaving?" Lexi asked.

"How did you know?" I asked, surprised.

"Because Mom has tears in her eyes and I heard you tell her about getting canceled at the club," Emily said.

"Saturday morning," I said, and they both teared up.

The twins asked if we could sing a few songs together and we jammed until after ten o'clock. After they went to bed, Julie stayed for a couple of hours longer.

She told me I made the right decision because I could always make money, but it was time to look for happiness. She said my friendship with Hooker was deep and compelling and this was probably my last chance to go to Nashville. Friendship and love are more powerful than anything else, and it was time to go out on my own, not as an obscure member of a band. Her last words were inspiring. "You're just floating here in a life jacket. That's worse than drowning."

After she left, I sat down with a pad and paper as her words kept running through my mind. After a long night of reflection, the silence looked me in the eye as dawn was breaking through the Eastern skyline and finally whispered the lyrics to 'Clouded Soul.'

* * *

Like a shepherd with no flock,
A key without a lock;
Or a beggar leaving nothing to bequeath;
Like an outcast with no name,
It's time to stake a claim;
Before the midnight sky can hang its wreath;
Chorus
My poet's soul will make me whole;
Treading water's worse than dying;
I'm a flame that's banked too long,
A muted voice without a song;
With gifts to give
That lead to rectifying

My own words were telling me there's a price tag on peace of mind. I could make money on tour but would probably be miserable with strangers, instead of having a ball being broke with my best friend.

Suddenly, a wave of sadness hit me like a hurricane force wind. Keeping my best female friend and only lover separated seemed like the perfect solution to avoid having my heart broken. Now that I was about to leave, I was terrified about losing both of them. It felt like my 'Clouded Soul' was about to be crushed.

A troubled feeling came over me. I wondered if I was in love with either of them, or worse, both. At once the answer appeared. It was time to claim music as my first love and take my place in that world. Then, I would look for another Erica to love, combined with a Julie I could adore.

Another wave of shock followed as an image of Jillian appeared. She was holding hands with music and flanked by the fading images of Jewels on her left, and Erica on her right.

* * *

It was just past 8:00 a.m. on Friday when I was startled by the phone. I had only been asleep for an hour. My brain felt overloaded and frozen, like I'd spent the entire night explaining the concept of work to the Kardashians, while binge watching a commercial with some geek selling me a pillow. The caller ID showed: Lyle Veterinary Clinic.

"Hey Brad, how are you?"

"Fine. Are you still in the market for a dog?"

"Sure, except I'm priced out."

"I got a call from a friend of mine whose mother just retired. He got her a puppy as a present last week and she only had it for a day when she had a massive coronary. She's in the ICU and the prognosis is not good."

"Jesus, that's too bad," I said.

"The doctors have put her on a 'do not resuscitate' protocol. Her son wondered if I knew someone who could take the dog. He said the puppy arrived already housebroken and that his mom hadn't even named it yet. Would you be interested?"

I felt my heart surge.

"What kind of dog?"

"A Cockapoo. You know, part Cocker Spaniel and part Poodle."

"How much?" I asked.

"Well, the son doesn't want any money. He said his mother is very generous and would want the dog to find a good home. I told him about the twins and he agreed. What do you think?"

"Let me ask the girls' mother and I'll call you right back."

I could hear the excitement in Julie's voice as she pulled up the breed online. Brad said to meet him at his office at four o'clock and he would have the puppy ready. He told me the son bought the dog a zippered airline carrier travel bag so the only thing I needed to buy was dog food.

I asked him for the son's name and address as well as his mother's in the hospital. I knew the twins would want to write and thank both of them and to wish her a speedy recovery.

Later on, I called Mark Bliss and explained that I was going to Nashville and had to turn down his offer. He said to call him after I got settled, to see where the band stood.

Afterward, I texted Hooker and said all systems were go. He sent a touchdown emoji. He said he was compiling a list of female fun candidates and would issue a full scale alert to all the bars, honky-tonks and liquor stores.

I arrived home just after five o'clock and removed the brown and white bundle of fur from the navy and gold carrier bag. He began to lick me and the sight of him was enough to make me collapse with laughter. He was covered with ringlets of fur, except for his deep brown eyes, nose and flashing white teeth.

Lexi almost pushed Emily out of the way to get to me, but Emily rallied like an Olympic sprinter so they arrived simultaneously. I handed them the dog and their squeals of joy lasted for over a minute. I went to stand next to Julie who put her arm around me.

"He looks like a shag carpet with teeth," she said and laughed.

The girls headed for the fenced-in back yard and took turns chasing the puppy for several minutes. Finally, Lexi turned and asked me what his name was.

"He doesn't have one yet. You and your sister get to name him."

I fired up the grill as the girls took turns holding the dog and setting up the picnic table. After dinner, they asked Julie and me to wait because they had a surprise. A moment later, they stood in front of us with their guitars and began to harmonize on the song 'Willing Heart.'

When they finished, I sang 'Clouded Soul' and told Julie if the song ever connected, she would get a writing credit. It was the perfect end to a special night and a gentle reminder that it was time for all of us to move on.

* * *

I was up at six-thirty on Saturday morning, and began loading the SUV. Julie came over and said the twins were having a tough time. I pulled the Martin out and followed her inside. The girls were sitting on the couch taking turns holding the puppy. Their eyes were red and teary.

"We have a name picked out," Emily said.

"It's Steeler. That's a combination of your name, Steele, and the fact that you're a dynamite songwriter. Plus, that's the name on your ring," Lexi said.

"I told you both there's a song for every moment," I said, as I looked into their eyes, then down at the lively ball of brown and white fur wagging its tail, took a deep breath and started playing the old Patty Loveless hit, 'How Can I Help You Say Goodbye?'

The song tells the story of a young girl, who becomes a woman, and turns to her mother along the way who always asks how she can help the daughter say goodbye. It starts off with the girl parting with a childhood friend, then watching her marriage break up, to finally sitting on her mother's death bed as her mom slips away. Each time, the mother says that it's okay to feel hurt and it's okay to cry. Then her mom holds her and asks for the last time how she can help her say goodbye.

When I finished, we gathered into a circle and shared a hug. I told Julie I could not have made it without her. I said I would be on a quest to find her again, this time as a long lost love.

I held the twins close and almost felt a sensation like they were my own children. For a moment, sadness overcame me as though a dam had broken in my soul. I told them to keep working on becoming musical savages, held each of them close, then got in behind the wheel. As I drove away, my sadness seemed to gently soften.

In less than ten minutes, I was on the interstate. For the first time in my life, I could let myself revel in my newfound freedom. Music was driving the getaway car.

Thank God the statute of limitations had run out on my past deeds with Hooker. I knew there was a song lyric somewhere in that thought. Unfortunately, the only rhymes I could come up with for "limitations" were "decapitations," "constipations" and "ejaculations."

A picture of Julie quoting Leonard Cohen appeared and I felt my face explode into a smile.

Fellow drunks and midnight choir mates, I'm finally free to come join you all, I thought.

Song titles inundated me as I headed west on the Massachusetts Turnpike. I was saying goodbye to the land of the Red Tides, White Brahmins and Blue Bloods. I blew past the green and white sign that read, "Leaving Massachusetts," and saluted.

I could almost see the credits start to roll as I heard George Strait sing the words of master songwriter Whitey Shafer. His lonesome voice told me this was where 'The Cowboy Rides Away.'

CHAPTER FOUR

As I reached the outskirts of Hartford, Neil Sedaka's hit, 'Oh Carol' came on an oldies station. It was the song I sang to her after the first time we made love. I changed the lyric about being nothing but a fool to, "Oh Carol, I am out of fuel," and we giggled like time took a sabbatical.

My mind became inundated with thoughts of my past life. I saw myself on a terrace overlooking Boston Harbor on the first night I met her friends, and visualized rich snobs in designer outfits sneering at me with sour looks like they just ate rancid king crab puffs. They peppered me with questions which I answered politely, until I got fed up.

I remembered saying the number of Nobel prizes awarded to Texas State grads was none, which coincidentally, is the same amount of Heisman trophies won by Harvard. When they talked about private clubs they were born into, I said the National Football League was an equal opportunity organization anyone could join, as long as they ran over people like a tank on steroids. A surly *contra-alto* from Cambridge said there were no legitimate Texas theater productions. I strongly disagreed because many Texans told me I should be on the stage, and there was one leaving in ten minutes.

Why did I stay so long? Two reasons—guilt and love making. For the first year Carol and I dated, she made my joy stick so hard it had to be pulled out of my pants by the Jaws of Life. When the passion wore off, I rehearsed my parting speech but couldn't find a way to tell her. I started sweating deeply whenever Carol was on my ass. Often, I changed shirts several times a day because they were soaked under the armpits.

Mostly, I stayed because I was raised Catholic, even though I stopped going to church when Jesus was still an apprentice carpenter. That's when I found myself at odds with almost everything the church taught and quit after I gave up waiting for an image of the Virgin Mary to appear on my grilled cheese sandwich. Still, my daily dose of childhood Catholicism sometimes dominates my thought process with feelings of guilt.

I grinned at a vision of me telling Julie that old Catholic guilt is as reliable as expecting Sean Penn to tear up while reading one of Hugo Chavez's speeches as a bedtime story to Joaquin *El Chappo* Guzman.

On the other side of New Haven, my phone rang. It was my unindicted co-conspirator.

"Vatican, Francis speaking," I answered.

The sound of a severe Irish brogue filled my ear.

"Aye, Holiness, Cardinal O'Sleaze here. 'Tis a fine day to be listenin' to your worthless arse waxin' a bit more chipper than the other day when you were on that goal line stand," he said.

"I'm ready to make peace with my demons. Writing songs always goes a long way toward my redemption."

"Begorra, there'll be a bedazzlin' good song title for yeh," he said.

"I'll write that as soon as I finish my latest work in progress."

"Will ya be tellin' me what's it's called before the Lord finishes clippin' the hedges?"

" 'Your Love Was Priceless, My lawyer Was Seven Hundred An Hour'," I chirped, as an image of Balls appeared.

"Son, you're ready to start coaching as soon as the co-chancellors give final approval."

My heart surged and my pulse raced as I thrust my right arm up toward the sky, stopping before I smacked the headliner in my SUV.

"What's your E-T-A?" he asked.

"I should be there the day after tomorrow."

"If you run into a lonely heiress, see if she's got a friend," he said.

I hung up the phone and saw an ocean of brake lights up ahead about to welcome me to New York City. I began to indulge myself by imagining song titles about the Great White Way that were sure to be immortal: 'I Guess The Lord Must Be in New York City But So Are Al Sharpton, Ann Coulter, Howard Stern and Joey Buttafuoco.' 'I'm Slipping Into A New York State Of Mind, So Bend Over.' Or, the show stopper, 'Excuse Me Sir, Can You Direct Me To The Statue Of Liberty Or Should I Save Time And Just Go Fuck Myself Instead?'

As traffic ground to a halt, I decided to stay vigilant. That was in case someone wanted to make friends by washing my windshield, in exchange for all my belongings, or Anthony Weiner showed up in the next lane and offered texting advice and family photo sharing in a much more colorful way.

* * *

I arrived in Nashville late Sunday night. Hooker helped me unload the SUV and offered me leftover pizza. My ass was dragging like a lead pipe and I fell asleep just before midnight.

In the morning, Hooker said the head coach wanted to meet me. He said he would text me the time later and asked what my plans were. I told him I was going to cash in the one black and gold chip I had, an entertainment lawyer named T. Edward Bryson.

I told Hooker that Bryson was the brother-in-law of an offensive guard I played with in Pittsburgh, Cody Davis. Cody told me Bryson is a dipshit but he knows everyone in the music business worth knowing.

"Shit, I figured you would have Navy Seal Team Six's task force escort you to Jillian's place first, especially after you struck out last time," he said, as we both chuckled.

"I have to work out a plan first. I won't make the mistake of showing up unprepared for her again."

Suddenly, he looked at my right hand.

"Where's your ring?" he asked.

I grew a chagrined look, then told him about the pawn shop. He shook his head and reassured me that we would find a way to get it back.

"Incidentally, J. W., how are you set for cash?" he asked.

"Fine," I said, reaching into my pocket. "How much do you need?"

* * *

I stayed in bed until after nine o'clock the next morning and left after a leisurely breakfast. The drive into the city was highlighted by a panoramic view of Vanderbilt University. The morning sky showcased the campus as sunlight streamed through the buildings and accentuated the architectural designs. The weather was perfect, low 80s with a cloudless sky.

Bryson's office building was located on the top floor of a high-rise structure a few blocks from the Hall of Fame. The facade projected an impressive high-rise office complex in the heart of downtown. After signing in with security, I took the elevator to the twelfth floor and arrived in front of a dark wooden door with a gold sign that read, "Law Offices of Bryson, Holden & Associates, P.C."

The office décor consisted of teak, marble and gentility. I approached a distinguished-looking woman seated behind a massive desk in a plush reception area. Original oil paintings covered the walls and the carpet was probably made out of old one hundred dollar bills. The receptionist appeared to be in her fifties, and gave me a look that almost made me check to see if my fly was open.

"May I help you?" she asked.

"Hello. I'm J. W. Steele. Forgive me for just stopping by, but I'm hoping that I can ask Mr. Bryson if he might have some free time after business hours."

She peered at me over her glasses. They were the reading type, the ones that can really piss you off when someone acting like a high school principal checks you out. "Do you have an appointment?" she asked.

"No, ma'am. I'm an old friend of his brother-in-law. I didn't want to take up his time during business hours, but was hoping I could meet him any time at his convenience," I said.

"Why do you wish to see Mr. Bryson?" she demanded.

"It's a personal matter," I said.

"I schedule all his appointments and also screen potential clients to avoid having him bothered or wasting his time. So either tell me what this is about, or I must ask you to leave," she said, in a tone of voice suggesting that she had been promoted to superintendent, and I had been caught writing 'fuck' on the wall of the girls' bathroom.

At that moment, a short, portly man in a white on white, French-cuffed shirt, dark tie and pin-striped pants held up by dark suspenders came out from the long hallway. He had a receding hairline and a belly that hung over his pants like an over-baked meringue topping. He looked like the kid who always asks the teacher a fifteen-minute question just as the bell rings.

"I'll handle this, Ruth. I'm Attorney T. Edward Bryson. Who are you and what do you want?"

Breeding forced me to extend my hand which Bryson gave a shake like it was a diaper he had to change. "I'm J. W. Steele. I played football with your brother-in-law, Cody Davis. I apologize for coming by without an appointment, but Cody said he would send you an email about me. I'm a songwriter, and was hoping we could have a drink at your convenience and you could give me some advice."

"I don't remember any such email and I don't have time for a drink," he said.

I continued my impersonation of Civil War General George Pickett, as I bull-headedly tried another charge up Cemetery Ridge, even though I already lost most of my division.

"I know you're busy. I need a little character guidance on how to get started."

"My character guidance is out of your price range. I have over two hundred clients to service. I don't do good ol' boy honky-tonkin' with anyone who's not on the charts with a bullet, or a CD that ships platinum."

This was a huge mistake. I stopped to let my irritation soften but he wasn't finished.

"My alleged brother-in-law, Cody, is an offensive—and I mean truly offensive—lineman who once attended a four-course banquet and called out, 'Who ain't got a fork? I've got four of them,'" he said. When I gave him a determined look, Bryson lost his patience. "You can leave voluntarily or we'll call security." He turned and walked away.

I stood there steaming for a short time before I left. As the elevator rumbled down to the lobby, I decided Bryson would be right at home on the East Coast. A whiff of fresh air filled my senses as I reached the street. Time to go to work.

* * *

I arrived at the stadium just before three o'clock. I passed a dusty football field where several groups of players in tee shirts, shorts and red helmets were doing various warm-up drills.

Immediately, the sight of congregating athletes caught my eye. The smell of newly mown grass filled my senses and I could almost see myself in uniform, calling cadence and feeling the shock of being tackled. An image appeared of me throwing a surgical strike fifty yards downfield and hitting my receiver in mid-stride as he sprinted into the end zone.

My breathing spiked as I saw Hooker. He turned around and a huge grin formed as he removed his cap and wiped his brow with the upper arm of his perspiration-soaked tee shirt, then headed in my direction.

"The head coach is waiting for you in his office." He led me through the tunnel and toward the coaches' enclave where I was introduced to Burl Sawyer. We talked about my playing days at Texas State and my time in the NFL. Burl said I would only need final approval from the chancellors and they were gone until tomorrow. I said I would watch practice to get an overview of the team and make a few mental notes.

When practice ended, I started to outline my thoughts on a huge flip chart when I was instantly struck with a plan for meeting Jillian. After leaving the stadium, I headed to an office supply store for poster boards and black magic markers. A bouquet of flowers and a bottle of dry chardonnay completed my gift assortment and I arrived at her condo complex just before six o'clock. Her parking slot was vacant. That meant she would have no chance to slam the door in my face.

I parked in front of the building, about thirty feet away. She would have to pass by me but at a distance far enough away so she would know I was not stalking her. I grabbed the Martin and the sign which I placed on the back bumper. Written in block letters were the words: "Will Work For A Lyric."

I paced for a while and wondered if she had a husband or boyfriend. What if she was a black belt and kicked my ass before I could introduce myself? Half an hour later, she arrived. As she looked up, I started to sing, in a soulful voice, the Kenny Chesney hit, 'You Had Me From Hello.' I considered changing it to 'You Had Me From Fuck Off,' but lost my nerve at the last minute.

A look of recognition appeared on her face. I sensed she wanted to smile but was apprehensive.

"Am I going to have to f-f-fight you off again? What do you want this time?" she asked.

A picture of Marlon Brando in a bathrobe appeared in my mind, as he gave orders to Robert Duvall. "I want no inquiries made. No acts of vengeance. *Consiglieri* of mine, I want you to contact the heads of the five families. This war stops now," I said, tapping my finger in a staccato-like manner on the Martin.

She laughed out loud. "That's my favorite movie," she said. "Even if my dad thinks it s-slanders all Italians."

"If you try any rough stuff, remember, I ain't no band leader. But, I do have an olive oil voice."

"Tell me your name again," she said, folding her arms.

"J. W. Steele."

"Was that line about w-w-writing a song for me this morning just another come-on?"

"No, it's perfect for you. At least, let me show you," I said.

She hesitated for a moment. I grew inspired and changed course.

"Would you feel more comfortable taking your own car and meeting me in a public place?"

"No. Anyone who'd go to this much trouble then keep s-s-s-suggesting ways to keep his distance is either the most considerate man in the world, or a eunuch," she said.

I directed her toward my SUV and told her about moving here to write songs.

"Show me your left fingers," she said.

I complied. She picked up my hand and examined the calluses on each fingertip. The evening light shining into her face showed me most of the fear in her eyes had melted.

"I guess the Martin's not just a prop," she said. "Tell me how you write a s-song."

"I usually stay up all night waiting for the sunrise, gulping stale coffee while watching coals die in a campfire, or sit in the darkness with a single candle and stare at the shadows, trying to smoke out the whispers. Most of the time, I analyze a song already written and try to improve it."

"You've got a great voice. Are you trying to break in as an artist, too?"she asked.

"Sure. A good manager can make Mickey Mouse into a country star, but a good songwriter is pretty rare."

"Here's a second opinion. In this town, ninety-nine percent of the songs cut are done because someone agreed to k-k-kill his own grandmother."

"What happens the other one percent of the time?"

"Somebody actually makes a good record." She laughed.

We found a space on the street three doors down from a restaurant with a sign in front that read, "Alfredo's," and got a front booth.

"So, your real name is Angela Trappani?"

"That's right."

"Why'd you change it?"

"Because I grew up in Texas and got s-s-sick of answering whether or not I was an Eye-Talian," she said, with just a slight drawl.

I told her about my time in Texas.

"Were you born there?" she asked.

"No, in California. We moved when I was ten years old."

"I'll bet that was a scintillating musical journey for an aspiring s-songwriter," she said.

I felt a huge grin spread over my face.

"I left behind 'California Dreaming' and 'I Love LA,' and hooked up with 'Galveston' and 'Texas When I Die.' I also discovered tender, poignant ballads, like 'Asshole From El Paso,' by the lovely and talented Kinky Friedman," I told her, as she chuckled.

"Is Steele a German name?" she asked.

"It is. I'm sure it was changed from Stiehlman or von Stiehl."

"Any other n-nationality in the mix?"

"Mostly German but with an Irish grandmother. I guess that means I get drunk with precision."

"What's the J. W. stand for?" she asked.

"John Wayne."

"Who n-n-named you?"

"My old man."

"Funny, you don't l-l-look like Bernard McGuirk," she said.

I chuckled. "What do I call you, Jillian or Angela?"

"Guys who think they can get me in the s-s-s-sack call me Jillian. My mother calls me Angela. My father calls me Angie. My friends call me Trapp."

"What about me?"

She looked me in the eyes and smiled. This was the first test for how well I was doing. I took a deep breath.

"It's Trapp."

My breath seeped out in a prolonged, sweet action.

"OK, it's J. W. and Trapp."

"Steele and Trapp is also good. Assuming you don't mind," she said lightly.

"Damn, that's it. We'll call our music publishing company Steele Trapp Mind," I said.

"That's really very c-c-clever," she said.

She seemed to have trouble with a word or two. Maybe it was because I made her nervous.

"Tell me about the song you've got for me," she said, as the waiter began sprinkling freshly ground pepper over her romaine lettuce leaves.

"It's called 'Whispers from the Silence of the Shadows'."

"Too long. How about 'Whispers From The S-S-Silence'."

"Get it sold and we can call it 'Sponge Bob Has A Gastric Bypass In Acapulco'," I said.

"What's the s-s-song about?" she asked.

"Songwriting. Staring into the shadows and strangling the silence until it whispers the words."

Trapp sipped her wine and suddenly burst out laughing.

"Speaking of song titles, I heard the best one from the guy at Panhandle's when I asked him if someone turned in my wallet. Know what he said?"

"What?"

She looked from side to side before she answered.

"'Hey lady, are you crazy? Who would turn in a wallet in this dump? The assholes who come in here would steal s-s-s-sawdust.'" She giggled.

I belly laughed. It was like reliving a party weekend.

"Your Martin looks brand new. Have you had it long?" she asked.

"A few years. It made up for the one I never got at eight when my dad said I was too small to control an adult-sized instrument. He even took me to a music store and showed me how I couldn't strum a full-sized Gibson with my pint-sized body."

She nodded like she understood, then reached for my right arm. After raising it like a traffic cop who was extending a white-gloved hand toward me and ordering me to stop, she placed her left palm up against my right. The size of my fingers dwarfed hers.

"Speaking of pint-sized bodies, try learning to form chords with short fingers like m-mine on a custom Les Paul electric," she said, as her eyes danced mischievously.

I grinned and continued.

"Are you saying I had it easier because of height privilege?" I asked.

"Well, I think President Obama would say I'm a v-victim of thin-thumb inequality."

Her wide smile told me she was beginning to feel much more comfortable.

"Why do you want to write songs?" she asked.

"Because there are things inside of me that I have to set free. The only way I can do that is to put them to music," I told her.

"That's the same way music gets to me," she said.

"Ever figure out why?" I asked.

She paused for a moment and gave me a look like I caught her hiding something.

"I'm afraid you'll think I'm weird," she said.

"Think of this moment as a confession from one weirdo to another. I have proof Willie Nelson was looking at my picture when he wrote 'Crazy' for Patsy Cline," I said.

"Okay, here's my theory. Writing a song is very close to making love. Every n-note and every word is like a kiss. It's using your mind to reach the most intimate release instead of your body."

I stared deeply into her gorgeous eyes. It was a perfect metaphor for music and title after title began to run through my mind.

"You probably think I'm either a s-slut or a nut," she said.

We were both silent for a moment as a picture appeared in my mind of us writing together.

"Why country music instead of something else?" she asked.

"Because it's rock 'n roll in a different format. My father was a musician, and he taught me that people never got enough of rock 'n roll. That's why it came back as country so it could become the bridge to other kinds of music."

"Why is it a bridge?"

"It extends to the masses. Early country was not widely accepted. You know why?"

"Because it was primitive, twangy and artists sounded like they had a s-s-s-sinus infection."

"That's why the music needed an extension to reach out to people."

"What's the b-b-bridge between country and folk?" she asked.

"Hank Williams and the old Nobel prize winner, Bob Dylan."

"Show me."

"Could Hank have sung about once upon a time, someone dressing fine, and tossing the bums a dime, while still in her prime?" I asked.

She thought for a moment before I followed up with part B.

"Could Dylan ask about a robin engulfed by sorrow, as soon as leaves start to die?"

"I think rock and roll linked R & B to country through suffering," she said.

"Some of it came from old Negro spirituals sung by the slaves, and merged with songs of poor white miners and farm workers who suffered through the Depression," I said.

"That's why a lot of the best musical sounds came out of black churches in the South. Of course, as soon as it looked profitable, some white guys came in and s-s-stole it from the black artists and composers," she said.

"Despite that, rock music did more for race relations than any Supreme Court decision," I said. "Poor blacks and poor whites needed something fun to sing about."

"Sex, right?"

I could only nod because my heart was trying to leapfrog over my tonsils and escape. I never talked to anyone about music like this because no one I ever met could understand.

"Kids in the '50s knew their fathers and grandfathers had been to war, and that sex was taboo. They began to realize how silly the music was. Country songs were still mourning crop failures and binge drinking."

She nodded. I was on a roll.

"That's why rock took off like no other kind of music ever had. Until that sonofabitch, Lyndon Johnson, escalated us into our fourth major war in forty-five years. Then, it turned dirty and ugly, and everything went haywire as the kids tried to put a stop to dying for some greedy politician. But not before some truly great songs were written."

Suddenly, she grew joyful, like she was having a spiritual experience.

"You know who the b-b-bridge b-b-b-builder..." She stopped as she teared up.

I got a sinking feeling as I watched her lips stop moving and she grew a sad look.

"I'm sorry, sometimes I have a slight s-s-s-stutter. It started when I was a kid and I still stumble over a word when I get uptight," she said, as her voice quivered slightly.

"All of us miss a word now and then," I said, watching her to make sure my response was appropriate.

"The biggest reason I s-s-started to s-s-sing is because I stop stuttering when I'm singing. That's why Mel Tillis was one of my first heroes," she said.

It was ironic that her speech impediment was barely noticeable, even though she must have thought it was a defect the size of a boulder.

"I spent a lot of time with doctors trying to overcome this. Now, it only happens once in a while unless I get really exhausted or stressed out," she said.

"I promise not to make you uptight, even when I bolt out of here and stick you with the check," I said, grabbing my armrests and posing like a sprinter ready to spring to show her I was kidding.

It worked. She laughed out loud.

"Okay please tell me who the bridge builder was who got you into country," I said.

"Patty Loveless. I saw her perform once and it changed my life. If I can ever t-touch someone through a song, in the same way she touched me, it will be worth everything," said Trapp.

"I've spent a lifetime thinking about music. It's the only thing that's ever gotten to me."

"Do you know why?"

"Two reasons. One, it lets me create."

"What's the s-second?"

I grew uneasy. Images from my childhood and the deaths of my parents appeared. I conjured up the sensation of hot tears on my cheeks and the provocative scent of funeral parlors.

"Naw, it's...uh, it's....uh," I hesitated, wanting to tell her, but deciding to wait for the right time.

"Maybe someday you'll feel comfortable enough to tell me," she said.

After we passed on coffee and dessert, she insisted on splitting the check. I knew I had to address the biggest obstacle she gave me.

"Uh, Trapp," I began, as my voice took on a slight vibrato. "You said you're involved and I don't want to get in the middle of that."

She grew a huge grin as though I had just given her a tagline.

"Don't worry, you won't. I'm stuck in a love affair with music."

"You mean there's no boyfriend or husband?" I asked, as my voice rose.

"No. M-M-Music and I keep running them off. The closest thing I have to a boyfriend is a lawyer at a firm where I work part-time. But, he's more like a brother."

"Are you a lawyer, too?" I asked.

She got a look of mischief in her eyes.

"I only became one because I'm not s-s-smart enough to do anything else," she said, as her eyes twinkled.

I smiled and felt my attraction to her growing more intense.

"Do you have any c-contacts in the music business?" she asked, on our way out.

I told her about Bryson, and the fiasco with Sam Presley. I didn't want her to think I was a total "dink bag," as the twins would say, so I left out the details of my encounter in Bryson's office. She said Bryson was pretty well-known in Nashville legal circles, but she had never heard of Sam. When we pulled up in front of her condo, I handed her the flowers and held up the wine.

"Did I earn the right to help you drink this chardonnay?"

She said no, and I began to feel dejected. "Not tonight. Sorry I can't invite you in, but I still have a project to finish and I'm on a d-deadline this whole week. We'll drink it next Saturday, when you come over with your guitar. Then you can show me yours, and I'll show you m-mine. I'll cook. Seven-ish?"

"Here's a title I've been working on for years. 'Love's A Gamble Based On The Promise Of A Lie.' See what you can do with it," I said.

"You're on," she answered.

I smiled broadly and asked if I could bring something to dinner.

"Yeah," she said seriously. "Our first platinum CD."

CHAPTER FIVE

The following morning, I met the school's co-chancellors for final job approval. Because TBC was first college in the state to integrate, the school's charter required one black and one white chancellor and each had to be a Baptist minister.

Hooker told me this meeting was necessary in order for the reverends to make sure they were not turning the team over to an atheist or a left-wing Commie vegan. I promised not to give my songwriters-of-the-world-unite speech and after a short confirmation meeting, headed back to the stadium.

After Burl introduced me to the team, I received looks of wonderment and awe while he talked about my background as a professional quarterback and special teams' gunner. I reminded them that getting knocked on your ass in the NFL was the same as college, only faster, harder, nastier and much more frequently.

After practice, Hooker wanted to go somewhere, but I opted out because my ass was dragging like a sack of wet cement. "Besides, my Coors prescription comes with unlimited refills," I said.

"I should probably give my body the night off," he agreed.

"In case I never said it, thanks for puttin' me up."

"I'm glad to have the company," he said.

"Judging from what I've seen so far, you sure don't seem lonely."

"You know I'll always be looking for a young lovely to have around. But every once in a while, I get sick of that. At least I can have a decent conversation with you."

That was code that he needed to vent and a therapy session was coming. I didn't know if it was for him, me or both of us.

I always thought Hooker's gregarious nature was a front even though his toughness was legendary. In the final game of our senior year, he broke his left forearm in the first quarter, but refused to come off the field, and wound up leading the team with eighteen unassisted tackles.

Our backgrounds were disparate, but strikingly similar. My parents' deaths led to my feelings of abandonment and using music as a coping mechanism. Hooker had a different kind of loss. His father worked long days and drank a case of beer most nights. He was an angry drunk and verbally abused Hooker's mother. She turned her wrath on him while favoring his older brother, Ronnie.

The only time I ever saw him cry was after his brother's funeral. Ronnie was killed when his best friend smashed an old Corvette into a tree while they were traveling over one hundred miles an hour. Hooker told me he was trying to find a reason his brother died. There was only one he could see.

"Maybe now, my mother will let me choose the dinner. When I came to school last year, I couldn't go home until Christmas. At dinner, my mom said, 'I made Ronnie's favorite dish.' I had been gone for six straight months, was homesick as a lost puppy, and he still lived there. Yet, she made his favorite fuckin' meal, not mine. Since I'm the only son left, maybe my menu choice will be honored now even though she wanted another girl," he said, looking down and angrily flicking the waistband on his underwear.

Despite his superior intellect, he dumbed down to be accepted. After a brutal encounter in English Literature class, anger made him rebel. The professor was a Meerschaum pipe-smoking, New York prick, in suede wing tips, sweater vests and corduroy elbow-patched, tweed jackets, who hated Texas, Texans and saved his most biting reviews for football players.

We were assigned to read *The Sound and The Fury* by William Faulkner, and Hooker was asked for his assessment. He began by describing one character, Mrs. Compton, who was portrayed as a hypochondriac, and nervously pronounced the word as "*hypo con dry ack.*"

"'Hypo Con Dry Ack'? I'm surprised your pigskin playbook didn't tell you that was the identity of someone who needs to consult with a 'Psy Chi At Rist.' Learn to speak trippingly on the tongue, or you are destined to reside in your peasant world where the immortal words, 'Hut One, Hut Two' are your only ticket to becoming a paragon of lingual *savoir-faire,*" said the professor, in a voice dripping with arrogance.

Hooker stood there seething, so I grabbed his arm. The incident inspired him to read everything he could get his hands on. The more he read, the more outwardly confident he became. He began to challenge the professor to call on him again. On the final day of class, it happened.

"We haven't heard from you for decades, Mr. Crowder," he began. "Perhaps you can give us your pedagogical review of why *The Pearl* by John Steinbeck is significantly more exciting than a running play when the guards pull."

Hooker rose and surveyed the class. Most studied their shoes to avoid being labeled a co-conspirator. "Well," he intoned. "Without tripping over my tongue, I believe this book is an allegory."

The professor reached for his pipe and adjusted his glasses. He did not smell a set-up.

"Regale us with your insight into the term 'allegory," said the prof. The condescension was thicker than our favorite gumbo. I knew a verbal ambush was coming.

"My pigskin playbook said it was the name of Bill Clinton's vice-president."

The professor's face turned ashen. He was so enraged, volcanic lava seemed to be spewing out of his ears. He removed his glasses and glared at Hooker like an exorcism was brewing.

"Can you spell the word 'flunk,' Mr. Crowder?" he asked finally.

Hooker looked thoughtful, rolling his eyes and shifting them from left to right like he was solving an equation. "Yes sir. It's Hut One, Hut Two," he said, as laughter exploded.

Hooker received an 'F' and appealed to administration. After his written assignments were reviewed, his grade was changed to a B plus. The professor protested and was dismissed. I knew it happened because our record was eleven and one and we went to the Sugar Bowl. An F would have made Hooker ineligible and we would have likely lost the game. That meant the school might have missed out on a couple of bank vaults loaded with currency from all that additional television revenue.

All I can say to that is: 'Hut One Million, Hut Two Million'. I'll bet the decision to reinstate Hooker was based on an audit that showed how much cash just one Saturday afternoon of pad-popping fun poured into the operating budget, compared to those hypochondriacs and allegories.

Still, Hooker had a serious, pensive side. The more he read, the more difficult it was for him to hide his analytical intellect. Later, he started working his knowledge into his impersonations. Imitations became his signature move, and I was glad to see he had not changed.

After dinner, I gave him the story on Jillian-slash-Angela and our date next Saturday.

"Tell me about her," he said.

"I've never felt so close to a woman so fast. She's also about to become my once-in-a-lifetime musical wife."

He stared at me for a moment. "Don't jump in too fast. Take it easy, okay?"

"I'm getting advice from a finalist for the love 'em and leave 'em award?" I asked.

"I'm only thirty-four. Way too young to have a permanent relationship. Especially since there's a bumper crop of twenty-two and twenty-three-year-olds out there."

I asked if he was afraid of getting Micronesian ball-rot or something equally colorful.

"A man's gotta go sometime and I don't plan on living long enough to sit on the front porch of a nursing home and piss in my pants all day," he said.

I found it challenging, if not downright futile, to dispute a statement saturated with that much crystal clear logic. "What about finding your soul mate?" I asked.

"How do I know the woman won't turn on me like Carol did to you? Finding someone who will stay with you is a real long shot," he replied.

"Maybe. Love is what keeps songwriters in business. You have to keep searching or all you have is emptiness."

"How can you spout all this crap right after your wife dumped you?" he asked.

"Carol's leaving was partly my fault."

He looked at me like a neurologist just told him I had no brainwaves left.

"But you caught her in bed with another guy, and you're taking the blame?" he asked.

"In part. I was faithful in body but my mind dumped her a long time ago."

He was in deep thought as I headed for the kitchen.

"You want another beer?" I called.

"Naw. You keep telling me about your musical ability reaching a higher level, and I'd like to hear a couple of your songs."

I felt my heart heave slightly and reminded myself this was my oldest friend, not a big-time record producer. I went into my room and returned with the Martin. Hooker shut off the CD player.

I finished tuning the guitar and suddenly felt nervous sitting in front of a man who had heard me play and sing more than anyone other than myself. I thought about the only other time I was this jittery and pictured myself ringing Trapp's doorbell for the first time.

"Okay, when I get to see a producer, I'm gonna lead off with this song," I said. I took a deep breath and began to sing, while he watched me intently.

* * *

Standing by the railroad tracks,
Listening for the train along the rail;
Thumbing on the interstate,
Caught a biker headed west to Vail
I flagged an eighteen wheeler
That was driving down along the desert floor
Turned my collar to the wind and rain,
That softly hugged the California shore
Chorus
Running from the memories,
And heartaches of trying to explain
Watching my tears falling
As they hit the ground
Like gentle drops of rain
I was afraid to find my freedom,
So all I am is free to find out why
I'll be sleeping with a stranger
While another night goes slowly crawling by

Finished, I felt my pulse surge as I waited for his review.

"Jesus, that's really good!" he exclaimed, as his eyes grew wide and sparkled.

I felt my breath seep out in even spurts and my pulse mellow. "Thanks. It's not 'Friends in Low Places,' but the right artist could do a lot with it."

"I can't get over how far you've come since college. What else do you have?" he asked.

"Well, I wrote this one for a female singer," I said, before hitting a C chord and stopping. I could not remember the melody. Thank God for my tape recorder. "I'll be right back," I said, rising and heading for my room. When I returned, I searched for the tune I had recorded on my trip down. We heard multiple excerpts of me engaging in the self-scrutinizing, therapeutic sessions he had suggested. When I finally found the song, he was curious.

"What was that monologue?' Hooker asked.

"A self-therapy recording session on my trip here."

His grin was wider than one of Carol's closets. Suddenly, he grew inspired. watching me intently. "Listen, I need a big favor," he said. "There's a professor in the Literature department named Sylvia Bernstein who I have been trying to hook up with. So far, no luck— probably because I'm a jock and she's a bit more ethereal."

"How does that involve me?"

"She loves to help people with their writing. I want to get the stuff on that tape typed up and tell her we're trying to write a book. I'll say we need her help."

"I didn't think the school would hire any twenty-year-old academics," I said.

He grinned before replying, "Let's just say she's a bit more mature than my usual partners."

"Don't forget I'm J. W. Steele, not Danielle Steel."

I found the tune for my song, refreshed my memory and began to play.

"Damn, that's a neat song, too. Got an artist in mind for it?" he asked, when I finished.

"Yeah, my potential musical soul mate, Trapp," I answered.

He picked up his empty beer can and waved it at me in a half-salute, then started speaking with a familiar Boston accent. "Son, in the immortal words of Ted Kennedy, "Let me, uh, say this about that. Now that I am, uh, dead and gone, I, uh, want to be reincahnated as the guy who, uh, hyahs the babes on Fox News. Trapp will be my, uh, chief analyst on a talk show about hot teachahs, called Tutahs with Hootahs. Now, have the, uh, bahtendah send those, uh, two blondes anothah round on my, er, uh, tab."

I looked at him in awe. That speech almost made me miss my roots in the Cradle of Liberty.

Suddenly, I got a picture in my mind of the scene in the movie *Titanic*, where Jack met Rose's fiancé, Cal Hockley. I saw Jack being told by Cal he could almost pass for a gentleman, then raised my beer and saluted Hooker before I shrugged and whispered softly, "Almost."

CHAPTER SIX

We had a short practice on Saturday and wrapped up just in time for me head over to Trapp's. After dinner, we adjourned to the living room and corralled our instruments. I was impressed that her Martin was a model D-35, the stunningly high-end version, made of rosewood and trimmed with white piping. My eyes twinkled as she handed it to me.

"When I was a kid, I never knew instruments like this existed," I said.

She asked about my first guitar. I told her money was really tight but my father still came through. He knew a guy at work with a cheap old acoustic. Dad agreed to work two shifts in exchange for the guitar. His buddy even threw in a book with pictures of chord formations.

"The thrill wore off when I tried to play. The body was damaged because it was left it in his friend's basement, too close to the furnace, and heat made it warp. The strings were so far above the frets it hurt to press them down. Still, it forced me to persevere so I finally learned how to play," I said.

I reached for my Martin, strummed and sang the song for her.

"Who was your inspiration?" she asked.

I told her my ex-wife, long before apathy was beaten by infidelity in a photo-finish. She asked how long I was divorced. I told her I was waiting for Carol to institute the formal action.

"Why don't you f-file the complaint?"

"I don't have time. She can't hurt me."

"That's where you're wrong. You might become a b-bigtime songwriter and she can claim she's entitled to a huge chunk of the royalties. And you take the chance of being, a, found liable by the Court, b, on the hook for any future earnings and c, obligated to provide for her in a manner to which she became accustomed," she answered, sounding like Nancy Grace scolding Judge Judy.

"What should I do?"

"Call a l-l-lawyer in Massachusetts. Do you know anyone there?"

"Just one guy," I said, then gave her the short version of my time with Balls.

"Why don't you contact him?"

"He told me divorce is to law what anal tumors are to medicine. Besides, you're my top choice as personal counsel."

"Not me. I'm getting out."

"You said your father is an attorney. Why aren't you practicing with him?"

She grew a determined look, like her eyes were on fire.

"I've wanted to be a singer since I was s-six years old. Yeah, my father wants me to join his practice in Houston, but that's not for me. He and I made a deal. If I became a lawyer, he would pay for everything, and I could write s-s-songs and perform on the side."

"Did he think you were just going through a phase?"

"Yes, so I agreed to come here, attend Vanderbilt, then join his practice in order to pay him back. I told him I reserved the r-right to become a singer, but I think he f-forgot that part."

"Don't forget that Bob Seger line about not needing it all," I said.

"I graduated several years ago and passed the b-bar in Tennessee and Texas. I joined Dad for two years, but now I want out. I moved back here a few months ago and got a p-part time position with a firm. A month ago, I told him I was going to quit practicing law completely. He hit the ceiling and c-c-claims I reneged. We haven't spoken for quite a while."

"Why are you so set against being a lawyer?"

She gave me a somber look, like she was hooked up to a polygraph.

"It's phony. My father is one of the best criminal defense lawyers in the country. He's had over one hundred first degree m-murder cases and never lost. Some of the s-scum he's gotten off need to be tortured. I would not do that."

"I thought lawyers say everyone is entitled to a defense."

"They are, but not one manufactured by sleaze, fantasy or outright fraud."

"Don't you want to make up with him?"

"I don't know. We both s-said some pretty hurtful things," she said, her eyes starting to grow slightly misty.

"I'll bet he feels as bad as you do."

"I doubt it. My dad is one of the t-t-toughest lawyers in Texas. He's used to having everyone do what he says, including his only d-d-daughter."

"Why don't you call him and see if you can reconcile?"

"I vowed I'd never speak to him again, until I s-showed him he was wrong about me making it as a singer."

I asked how. She said by getting a deal with a record label.

"You sound pretty determined," I said.

"We're Sicilian. P-Pride runs pretty deep. Well, I'll show him that he's not the only hardass Sicilian lawyer in the family. I'll make it on my own, and he'll have to admit he was wrong about me," she snapped, with a look like she was ready to settle all family business.

Instantly, my mind formed a picture of a father's king-sized bed in a masculine, wood-paneled bedroom; and in another room, a daughter's white, dust-ruffled canopy bed, surrounded by pink ducks-and-bunnies-frolicking wallpaper. Each bed contained a severed racehorse's head, lying at the foot, bleeding all over a different Hollywood producer, who was wearing silk pajamas and screaming at the sight of blood on his hands, while Don Corleone shrugged and sipped anisette.

"Did you ever get any grief about your father when you were a kid?" I asked.

"Always. The worst t-time was when he got a serial rapist's case thrown out because the police lied to a suspect about having a warrant. A week later, the bastard raped another victim and it got so b-bad my parents had to pull me out of school for a few days," she said.

"It sounds like you had a pretty tough childhood," I said.

"I can't tell you how many times I got asked if I was the daughter of that Mafia-connected lawyer who kept getting those g-g-guilty murderers off," she said.

"Did anybody stick up for you?"

"I only had one friend who made a difference, Michelle."

"Tell me about her."

"She was a real gem. Half black and half Hispanic. She knew the agony I was going through. Naturally, I went to an all-girls Catholic school. This little rich b-bitch, Elise, really gave me hell about my background and my stuttering," she said.

I saw her eyes become narrow, like buttonholes, as she continued.

"All of her cool, debutant friends, with their Bass Weejun penny loafers and Phillipa Guyton tailored knee socks, used to stand in a semi-circle, p-p-point at me and laugh. They nicknamed me the Garlic Guinea. They were mocking me one day after Michelle enrolled. She came over and told them to knock it off. Elise got in her face and Michie decked her."

"You're lucky you found her," I said.

"She's still like a sister to me. She played the violin and introduced me to contemporary and classical music. I got her into country."

"What ever happened to her?" I asked.

"She became a plastic surgeon in Los Angeles," Trapp said.

We both paused for a moment.

"You said you're practicing law part-time now?"

"I go to court a couple of days a week. The rest of the time, I try to f-finish my cases."

I asked if she had any contacts in the music business. She said no but she had a plan and needed my help.

"Count me in, even if the penalty's ten to life at hard labor."

Trapp shook her head.

"Just the opposite. The payoff's immortality," she said.

I asked what I had to do. She said first, I had to help her finish a song.

"What's it called?"

"'Reflections of Love'. I'm s-s-stuck on the chorus," she told me, picking up her Martin and hitting a G chord.

Trapp began singing in her beautiful, sultry voice.

* * *

I look in the mirror and I see your face
Night after night, alone in our place
Trying not to follow you, now that you're gone
Praying there's someone who'll help me hold on
Reflections of love, I see everywhere

She stopped, then turned to me. "That's where I'm stuck. Got any ideas?"

"Let me think about it.'

"I've also got an artist in mind for it, Wes McGovern."

"You're kidding. I thought he drank a tanker truck full of whiskey before his liver called in an air strike on its own position."

"He's d-dried out and making a comeback."

"How old is he, eighty-five or ninety?"

"Maybe he's forty-two or forty-three, but he's not too old. Country fans love comebacks, especially from alcoholics. It's like ex-cons becoming preachers. If you help me f-finish this song, you'll go on it as a co-writer."

"When can we get it to him?" I asked.

"That's the tough part," she answered, shaking her head.

"Why? We'll call his office and make an appointment."

Trapp stared at me like I just had 1500 cc's of dumbassedness injected into my right bicep.

"Do you know how many people have a song they're trying to pitch? Like a gazillion. Everybody is convinced that as soon as a star hears their homemade tape, s-s-she will fall to her knees in joyful thanksgiving. An artist can't go anywhere without being accosted by an idiot with an amateur-hour tape or CD."

I realized I was close to becoming a fellow of the Academy of Board Certified Dumbasses.

"Everybody can be gotten to. No matter how important they are," I said.

"Of course they can. Assaulting someone is easy. The hard part is having them invite you to s-stick around," she said.

"You mean like piloting a helicopter and landing in Johnny Cash's front yard, right?" I asked.

"I thought that was just a fairy tale," she answered.

"The story I heard was that Kris Kristofferson was working as a janitor at Columbia Records. He wanted music so much he turned down a teaching position at West Point to come to Nashville. He needed money so he joined the National Guard here and had access to helicopters. Legend has it he landed one in Cash's front yard, got out with a tape in one hand and a beer in the other. The song he delivered was 'Sunday Mornin' Comin' Down.' It became song of the year in 1970."

"Help me finish the song. Then, we'll find a way to see Wes," she said.

"When can we get together again?" I asked.

"How about next weekend? That will give us time to fool around with the words," she said.

Suddenly, I was struck by a block-busting idea.

"I just got a job coaching football at Tennessee Baptist. Our home opener is next Saturday afternoon. Why don't you come to the game, and we'll go out for dinner afterward?"

"I'll see if I can rent us either a, a helicopter, b, a landing craft, or c, an armored tank," Trapp said, after slipping her arm into mine and grinning.

I squeezed her tighter and gave her a short kiss. She looked at me for a moment.

"Can I tell you something that is very p-p-private with me?"

"Sure."

She stopped like she was gathering her words into a pile.

"The reason I put things in order preceded by a, b, and c is another mechanism I use when I feel I might have a problem with my s-speech. I learned it in law school and it lets me t-think and get a grasp of each word before I have to say it out loud."

This was another disclosure that was drawing us closer, maybe even toward me revealing details about those funerals I had such trouble talking about.

"You sound fine to me."

"I'm starting to get pretty tired and can feel my words s-s-slipping," she replied.

I felt myself drawing closer to her, had a vision of Erica and Julie watching me and instantly stopped. Until I was sure this was what I was searching for, I would hold something back to make sure my heart never got broken again.

A small grin formed as I realized I was fooling myself. My heart was ready to wrap itself around hers for one reason I had never found before. She was the first woman I ever met who was in love with music.

That was more than a song title. It was a preview of coming attractions.

CHAPTER SEVEN

On Saturday morning, I threw a change of clothes and my shaving kit into a gym bag. I couldn't stop thinking about how she compared song writing to making love. It was a metaphor so simple and picturesque, it was downright erotic.

TBC won the game on a last second screen pass I called. An hour later, we met Hooker and his date at a place called Wylie's Bar-B-Cue. His marquee guest for the evening was a woman named Tina. She was stunning and had the face of a teenager, even though Hooker told me she had just turned a ripe old twenty-three.

I introduced Trapp. She and Hooker were an instant hit.

"So, Jillian, I hope you broke that goof's feet at Panhandle's the other night," Hooker said.

"Thanks. When he grabbed me, I just snapped," she smiled.

Hooker folded his arms and began to speak with a thick Russian accent. "As director of Bolshoi Ballet vonce say, 'Ze last time I see moves like zat vas vhen Baryshnikov's feet catch fire. Now ve sail on Volga River and drink Stolichnaya toast to *detente*, yes, my leetle Bolshevik?" he said.

Trapp giggled as Tina seemed bewildered.

"Why'd you call her Jillian?" Tina asked.

"That's how I first met her. Jillian is her stage name."

Tina was curious about our musical choice.

"Billy tells me you two are professional songwriters. Why'd you all pick country music?"

"It's what life is all about," Trapp said.

"It seems so earthy," Tina said.

"Maybe, but some love songs dig a hole in your mind," I added, stifling a smile at the memory of Balls' tribute to country music.

We spent another hour talking about everything from love to politics. Trapp and Hooker seemed to be on the same glide path. After we paid the check, I looked at Trapp. "Well, reggae fans, we got some songs to write. You all have a wonderful evening," I said.

"Son, I hope 'Candle In The Wind' falls outta your pens tonight," Hooker said.

Trapp stared at Hooker for a long time before we left. It seemed like they were locked inside a telepathic chat room. "I really enjoyed meeting you," she said, extending her hand.

"Me too," he replied, nodding at Trapp. "Keep my buddy out of jail, okay?"

"Not only can I post his bail, but I can also get him r-reasonable doubt for a reasonable fee," she said.

"We could have used that in Vinita," Hooker said.

"What's Vinita?" Tina asked.

"A small town in Oklahoma," he said.

"In reality, it's almost heaven," I said.

"I thought John Denver said that was West Virginia," Trapp said, beating me to the lyric.

Hooker and I exchanged grins. We took turns telling the story.

"When we were sophomores at Texas State, we played Oklahoma State at Stillwater. My uncle told us

Vinita was the meanest, toughest town in the universe so we drove there after the game," Hooker said.

"We wound up in a classic redneck bar and got into a brawl with five guys who looked like they could make a convoy of Hell's Angels cower. The two of us kicked their asses all over the place. For a couple of nineteen-year-olds, this marked the highest high of our lives," I said.

"From that day forward, every challenge we overcame in life would be compared to the rush we felt after the major ass-whippings we distributed in Vinita," Hooker said.

"So far, it's on its own sheet of graph paper," I said.

Tina turned to Hooker and began to run her fingertips through his hair. "I think you'll find a night with me is a whole lot more stimulating than one in Vinita," she said in a sultry voice.

"We're interfering with the course of true love," Trapp said.

"I'll be real quiet when I come in," I told Hooker.

Hooker looked at Tina, then back at me. His eyes were filled with anticipation. "Son, if Jesus is still my pal, I won't be," he said.

* * *

Trapp and I stopped for a bottle of champagne on the way to her place. After we curled up together on the oversized, off-white sofa, she put her head on my shoulder.

"Hooker is a trip. He's also a very lonely guy. He's like the words to that old s-song by Jefferson Airplane, because he definitely needs 'Somebody To Love.'"

"How can you tell that after one dinner?" I asked.

"I minored in Psych to help me analyze juries. Deep inside, he has the kind of l-lonely written all over him that country music is all about."

"Maybe he can't find the right girl."

"He's too scared to try. Do you know if he had any issues with his mother?"

"Yeah, he did."

"That could explain why he c-craves affection and attention so much."

Suddenly I thought about Hooker's penchant for women's panties. I thought about asking her but decided to keep that detail private.

"He was my best man, but Carol hated him. That should have sent up red flags."

"Don't you think that people who love each other can s-sometimes disagree?"

"Absolutely. But if they're really in love, it will only be about things that mean something."

"Like what?"

"There are only three things worth a fight— gambling, drinking and adultery. Everything else is petty."

"I think l-l-lying, overspending and laziness rank right up there," she countered.

"Of course they do. But you'll find out about those before you commit to someone, and then you can leave. I knew Carol had trouble with the truth sometimes, but I still overlooked it."

"I've found most people can't change," she said.

"Have you ever been married?"

"No. I was engaged once but wanted to be a songwriter m-more than a wife."

She sipped her drink.

"No other serious relationships that swept you off your feet?"

"Just the usual school girl flings."

"How did you get into music?" I asked.

"I started as a child performer. My mother was an actress, and I wanted to be like her."

"Why music and not acting?" I asked.

"My uncle got me into the guitar. Every time the family came over, he entertained. I was a little ham, and he let me sing with him. I was hooked and wanted a guitar as much as most g-girls want a pony. My father bought me a Gibson for my next birthday."

I refilled our glasses.

"How did you start writing?" she asked.

"My dad taught me."

"Did he play guitar?"

"No, piano. When I was five years old, I picked out the melody notes to 'Happy Birthday' on our old piano and used that tune to write my first song when I was nine."

"What's the title?"

"'Billy Thompson's A Tub'," I said.

"I can't wait to hear it."

"It was about a pudgy little bastard who flung sand in my eyes. Remember, Mozart was only six when he wrote his first symphony," I said.

I picked up my Martin and sang:

* * *

Billy Thompson's a tub;
Billy Thompson won't flub;

Billy Thompson, Billy Thompson;
Billy Thompson's a tub.

"I knew I had a winner when Billy himself even sang harmony," I said.

She smiled and took a sip of her wine. "Was your dad in a band?"

"Yeah. He showed me what he could do on the piano while I sat next to him. A week before I turned eleven, he got killed when a drunk driver slammed into his delivery truck."

She flashed a look of sorrow. "That must have been devastating," she said after a long moment.

"I never got over it. The only good thing was when he died, I got his record collection. That's how I learned all the oldies."

"Did you take guitar lessons?" she asked.

"No, I had a book with pictures of chords. But, Dad could hear a song once and play it note for note."

"How did you learn to play the individual notes?" she asked.

"Dad made me listen to songs that emphasized guitar riffs, like Terry Kath on Chicago's hit 'Twenty-Five or Six to Four' or Don Felder and Joe Walsh trading licks on the Eagles smash, 'Hotel California'. He told me if I ever learned to play like those guys, I could do anything."

"Those riffs are really hard. How could you g-get them right without a teacher?"

"We couldn't afford a CD changer or cassette player so I had to listen to songs from vinyl records on his old turntable. I could slow down the sound from 33 and 1/3 to 16 and 2/3. That meant I heard the licks at half speed and kept playing them until I got the fingering right," I said.

"Did he also teach you how to write?" she asked.

"Yes. He even took me to the public library to get some books on poetry to see how poets used words. I told him I thought poetry was pretty lame, and I liked books about sports a lot more. When he told me the lyrics to some songs were discovered in books of poetry, I was floored."

"What did he show you about songwriting?"

"Dad had a mnemonic which stood for 'Please Stop This Heartbreak.' Those letters reminded him when he wrote a song to 'Paint' the picture, tell the 'Story,' pick the 'Theme,' come up with the 'Hook' and make the song come from a 'Bedroom, Barroom or Church.'"

"What does that last part about bedrooms mean?" she asked.

"He said they stood for love, pain and hope and I would understand when I became a man. I was at the age where being around girls was starting to make my pulse quicken."

"Is your mother still in Texas?"

I stopped and took a deep breath.

"No, she died of cancer when I was twelve."

She grew a look of grief. "That must have b-been awful."

"I got pissed at the world and tried to fight everybody. Until I beat up the wrong guys."

"What happened?" Trapp seemed mesmerized as I told her the story.

"When Mom and I went to Texas, we moved in with my grandmother. There was a bluff next to the highway, and I used to take my old guitar and try to write songs. A month after she died, I found two brothers, real badass bullies, there with a girl. One guy had her jeans and panties down with his hand between her legs. The other was trying to kiss her while she screamed.

I sprinted toward her and they let her go. She got away while the brothers turned and beat me to a pulp, smashed my guitar and said I was a dead man if I told anyone."

Trapp leaned forward on the edge of her seat as I continued.

"At school the next day, the girl begged me not to say anything. I agreed but vowed to even the score for myself. A week later, I found them downtown and broke one's jaw and the other's nose. That night, the sheriff came to my house and took me into custody.

I went before a judge, a tall, stocky African-American man. He took me back into his chambers and asked for my side of the story but I refused. He looked at me and said, 'Coach tells me you have one of the highest IQs in the school. He also said you could throw a football fifty yards when you were only thirteen. You have everything to make yourself into a star on the football field and get a scholarship, if you'd change your attitude.' I was still angry and sulked."

"What did he d-do?" asked Trapp.

"He asked if I knew who Bear Bryant was. I nodded and he said, 'Well, Coach Bryant once said, 'Angry players don't win football games; smart players do.' He said I couldn't fight everyone and told me in Texas, they had a saying from a fellow Texan named Dan Jenkins, that 'Laughter is the only thing that can cut trouble down to size.' He told me to save my passing hands and beat people up with a phrase instead of a fist."

"Did he convict you?" she asked.

"No. He continued my case and put me on probation. At school, I told my coach the judge was a con man who made up stories to scare me. He got pissed, shook me like a bale of hay and said the judge told me that story because he played for Coach Bryant and was All-Conference at Alabama in the seventies. Then, Coach said I could let my talent make me a legend or my temper could buy me a prison jumpsuit in Huntsville. He bailed me out like he did when I froze up singing in front of the whole school," I said.

"What happened then?"

"When I got to my locker, a book by Dan Jenkins called *Baja Oklahoma* was inside."

"That's about country m-music, right?" she asked, as I nodded.

"Attached to the dust jacket was a yellow Post-it note from the judge that said I had to read it as a condition of my probation. I had to put it down several times to catch my breath because I was belly-laughing. It taught me how to overcome my rage. Soon, I discovered another benefit. My lyrics went from drab and mundane to spry and clever."

"Sounds like he turned you around," she said.

"I became a board-certified observational smartass. The judge and my coach called to congratulate me after I was selected in the NFL draft, and I got pretty emotional when I extended my gratitude, before I treated them to an all-expenses paid trip, including sideline passes, to our home opener against Dallas."

She looked at me, paused and seemed more reflective. "Tell me about your marriage," she said.

"It was a short honeymoon period followed by years of being confined to a Turkish prison, with occasional time off to go to furniture and appliance sales with the warden."

"Why didn't you have children?"

"Neither of us wanted them."

"Don't you like kids?"

I told her about the twins, then said, "I love kids, but wasn't sure our marriage would last. She told me I wasn't a family man, but maybe I had the wrong family."

"Why'd you get m-m-married?"

"I thought I was getting a friend. She thought she got a celebrity. We were both wrong."

"How did she feel about music?"

"She never let it get in the way of Karl Lagerfeld trunk shows," I said.

She grew intense. I sensed something was coming and I was in line for a direct hit. "Let me ask you something serious, J.W. What would you do to make it in the m-m-music business?" she asked.

"I wouldn't kill anyone."

"Would you do s-something unethical or illegal?"

"I wouldn't burglarize a record producer's house, but I'd kidnap one and force him or her to listen to one of my songs," I said. That answer seemed to please her even though I was not through. "Music lets people know I was here. A song lasts forever. If I don't leave one behind, maybe I was never really alive."

"What about the people? They'll know you were here."

"That could be their imagination playing tricks on them." I picked up the Martin. "I have a surprise for you," I said as I started to strum. "'Reflections of love, I see everywhere....' That's where you're stuck, right?" I asked. I hummed softly for a moment. "How about this?"

* * *

Like visions of sunlight
That danced through your hair,
Making me wonder what I'm worthy of,
While I keep finding,
Reflections of love.

Her lips formed a huge grin, and I felt like I was at the top of a roller coaster, ready to start down. She leaned over and gave me a deep, heavy kiss. I responded, and moved my guitar out of her way. We kissed for another moment before she broke the embrace.

Trapp put her champagne glass on the table before she turned to me. "I just put the finishing touches on this song this morning. Tell me what you think," she said, and then began to sing:

* * *

I could see the sun arising,
As I finished my last beer,
And fumbled through the ashtray for a rush;
Did some pickin' on my six-string,
But I couldn't find the words
So I sat there in the comfort of the hush
I knew love was a gamble
When I held you in my arms;
That tomorrow could steal you away
But the loving was so easy,
I told myself some lies;

And now I see the price I have to pay
Chorus
You never said we had forever,
When you put your hand in mine,
Memories will comfort till they fade
If your mind is aching
From the strain of your heart breaking;
Love's a promise that starts dying
When it's made,

* * *

The Devil's sending cheers
As my eyes are forming tears
I guess you have to die before you heal;
But when you're feeling close to dying,
And nothin' seems worth tryin'
Love will make another promise that's not real
When the pain is over,
And you drink yourself sober,
Love will make you think forever can survive
As you live your life again,
Love will make you think you'll win,
When hurt and lonesome finally say goodbye.

"Jesus, that's pretty heavy," I said.

"Life has an ugly side. If you'd ever practiced l-l-law, you'd see that." She stirred against me.

"Do you know what the counterbalance to all the torture and sorrow is?" she asked. "Meeting you. Every time I'm with you, I forget another bad thing."

A lump the size of a softball filled my throat. I asked her to put her guitar down. I took her into my arms and felt her surrender. After several kisses, she drew back. "Did I get my signals crossed?" I asked.

"I've got to know one thing before I let you spend the night. Promise we'll k-keep writing songs together," she answered. She had a deeply serious look and I tried to lighten it up.

"Why don't you start pretending I'm Burt Bacharach and you're Carole Bayer-Sager?" I grinned.

"We may have to take a couple of Bayer. We're about to add a fourth roadblock to gambling, d-drinking and adultery."

"What do you mean?"

"If you think a drunk adulterer who gambled away his p-paycheck is worth a fight, wait until you see two collaborators argue over an augmented chord, or a single word in the chorus."

"There's something you should know before I spend the night. I don't sleep around. I'm a one-woman man," I said.

She slipped her fingers into mine. Her eyes seemed to suggest her passion was stirring.

"I don't sleep around, either, but let's take our relationship slow, OK? Don't ever forget that song by K-K-Kimmie Rhodes about love being one of those 'Hard Promises To Keep'."

Looking deeply into my eyes, she asked if I would like to join her upstairs. I nodded and felt myself trembling at the husky sound of her voice. When we got to the top of the stairway, the soft glow of a night light served as the backdrop for our only source of illumination.

She placed her hand in mine and we stood in front of her bed, pressed our lips together and captured each other's tongues. Her scent was like cinnamon and her taste reminded me of honey as I slid my arms under her blouse. Deene grew taut and pressed against my zipper.

We shed the rest of our clothing and the room filled with the provocative scent of a man and woman ready to make love. With lips locked together, our bodies plunged forward onto the bed, landing in the middle of the pearl sheets.

I forced myself to enter her slowly. She locked her legs around me and began taking me all the way inside. Her eyes glistened, and I kissed away a solitary tear before it could spill onto the pillow. Her breathing stabilized and she lay in my arms and nuzzled next to my chest.

We cuddled on the pillows resting against the headboard. In the middle of the night, she moved back over next to me and I felt myself harden. We made love again, wildly but not as frantically this time, as our silhouettes danced to the reflection of the night light.

When I awoke alone at seven o'clock, I could hear her downstairs and called out good morning, trying to think of the right song to sing to her. She answered in an excited voice and asked me to wait because she had a surprise for me. She came upstairs dressed in a burnt orange Texas Longhorns tee shirt that hit her at mid-thigh. I had slipped into my boxers and was sitting on the bed when she walked in carrying her Martin. As I followed her every move, she sat in the easy chair opposite the bed, winked and began to strum and sing the old Patty Loveless hit, 'Lonely Too Long.'

The first line starts by saying good morning and asking how I slept last night. Then, it shifts to how I'm still smiling so the two of us must have done something right.

My grin was as wide as a football stadium as I leaned toward her and joined her on the tag line about how "we haven't done anything that's wrong, but we've sure been lonely much too long."

"I've been d-dying to do that song since I first heard her sing it," she whispered. "But, you're the first man I've woken up next to in a long t-time."

* * *

We spent most of Sunday trying to write. Early in the afternoon, she told me she wanted to race me to come up with a hook. After pacing back and forth, then sitting cross-legged on the sofa for over half an hour, she suddenly stood, shouted the line and declared victory.

She told me to take off my Patriots AFC Championship tee shirt, because now it was hers. I stripped down to my shorts and tossed the garment to her. She took off her top, stood there bare-breasted, and slipped my tee shirt on. My heart jumped into my throat as our eyes met and Deene got ready to go on patrol. She walked over, raised my old tee shirt up and rubbed her bare bosom over my chest. I was out of my mind with desire when she pressed her lips to my ear.

I reached for her hand to lead her upstairs, but she nodded toward the couch. I took a deep breath as my shorts and her panties came off like they were ignited. We connected immediately, and our rhythm quickly increased until we finished. When we got dressed, she put my same tee shirt back on.

"It has your scent," she told me. "Every time I wear it, you'll be with me."

We wrote lyrics until it was time for bed. She snuggled next to me as we both drifted off. I was ready to fall in love with her, but knew that was risky, because she made it clear that nothing could interfere with our music, not even, as Dwight Yoakam once said, 'This Crazy Little Thing Called Love'.

Then, I thought of all my other romantic partners, and told myself to slow down. As I reflected how every past relationship of mine ended with a thud, I knew I had to keep something in reserve, some kind of hole card that would let me walk away only bruised and not broken.

A picture of Julie appeared in my thoughts. Trapp was slowly, carefully easing her way into my mind just like Jewels did. Next, an image formed of Erica nodding at me. It seemed like she wholeheartedly approved of Trapp becoming the romantic partner of my dreams.

As sleep overcame me, my thoughts turned to how I finally met the woman I was destined to find. She was my lover as well as my friend. If I was not in love with her yet, I soon would be. The hell with slowing down. I was falling in love, and there was no way I could stop.

CHAPTER EIGHT

Hooker was sitting in the living room when I got home Monday morning.

"You look like you just got carjacked by some high school girls," I said.

"I've been with Sylvia since yesterday afternoon. I've been laid in so many positions that John Henry feels like he needs to go to rehab."

"I've heard this story before."

"Not like this. We talked the whole time we were together," he continued. "With Tina and Bobbie and the rest of the pack, it's all I can do to find something to say."

"Are you two still writing my book?" I asked.

"Not exactly. She pretended to take a stab at it because she's too much of a lady to just jump right into bed with me."

"Out of curiosity, what did she think about my prose?" I asked, as he flashed a smile.

"She said your pen name should be Reed Dundant."

"At least you tried to trade the book for her favors," I said.

"The sex was only incidental. She's a woman who really makes me think."

I brought my hand up to my mouth, and pretended to speak into a two-way radio.

"Base to Hooker, and One Adam Twelve, be on the outlook for a freshly-fucked literature professor carrying bridal magazines and drape swatches. She is considered armed and dangerous. Approach with extreme caution. Acknowledge, over," I said.

"I know, my words are coming back to strangle me."

"Enjoy yourself, pal. You may discover that conversation is almost as good as sex. Especially when you can't get it on any longer."

'You should turn that into a song," he said.

"Shel Silverstein beat me to it with a tune called, 'Lord, Ain't It Hard When It Ain't'?"

* * *

Tuesday's mail brought a letter forwarded from my old address. It came from a Boston law firm, Darnell and Davis. They represented Carol and said if we could not work out a settlement, she would be filing for a contested divorce.

After practice, I rushed over to the condo. As we ate takeout, Trapp reviewed the documents.

"Am I in deep shit?" I asked

"Like most things in life, it depends on how good your lawyer is."

We stayed up writing lyrics until almost three o'clock. When she woke me at eight-thirty, my mind felt overloaded so I was not receptive to early morning chit-chat. I could probably have handled the chit, but the chat presented a huge problem.

"I just got a call from Carol's lawyer. They said she is planning on getting remarried to your old boss. That's why she filed now."

"Is she looking for alimony?"

"Probably. They won't b-budge on their demands. We'd better get ready for a b-battle," she said.

"Do we have a chance?" I asked.

"In divorce cases, it usually depends on the evidence and who the judge thinks is the most egregious party. We need evidence that s-shows she drove you away."

"How about a love note from Russ to Carol confessing he gave her a diamond ring?" I asked.

Her eyes twinkled. I gave her the details and she grew animated. "I'm not going to d-disclose it until it will have the most impact."

"Is that note really strong evidence?" I inquired.

"If handled right, it could be a nuclear bomb."

* * *

Trapp and I continued to engage in a passionate love affair with both our minds and bodies. Love-making was still intense, but less frenzied. The next night, after we snuggled together with her head on my chest, she began to run her fingers over my arm as she whispered softly.

"There's something I have to know," she said. "Why do you t-think our relationship is so strong already?" I thought for a long moment. Her next question sent me reeling. "Do you think we're in love?"

I felt a wave of fear rumbling through my entire body. Somehow, I had to find a mid-point between being "clingy" and "stoic." And, I had to find a way to protect myself from heartbreak.

"I think I am," I said after I turned on my side to face her.

She raised up on her elbow and brought her hand up under her head for support, then leaned forward slightly as she spoke. "We need to talk before this g-g-goes any farther," she said, as her voice quavered. "You may not want to see me again after you hear this s-story."

Her tone made me sit up straight.

She took a deep breath and continued. "When I was sixteen, I met a boy named Jay at a Catholic school dance. He was a musician and we started d-dating and singing together. He even posted one of our s-songs on Youtube, and it became a sensation. One day, an agent contacted us about coming to Nashville."

My eyes were glued to her as she spoke.

"Of course, my parents wouldn't let me go b-because of my age. Jay was a year older and said we should get married so I could leave without their consent. I was too young to marry in Texas, so we decided to r-run away. My father found out, ordered an Amber alert and had the cops stop us at the state line." She stopped and looked away for a moment. "Well, Jay left for Nashville by himself as soon as he t-turned eighteen. I was only a few months away from my eighteenth birthday and my f-father and I made a deal. If I graduated from high school, he'd give his consent for me to go. I left the d-day after graduation and moved in with Jay. Reality knocked on my d-door as soon as I got there. Jay lived in a dump and money was tight. But, Eddie, our agent, got us some gigs so I f-figured things would improve. A month later, Eddie pulled me aside and said Jay was dragging the act down and I needed to go out on my own."

I watched her face contort like she was making a deathbed confession.

"I tried to d-defend Jay but knew Eddie was right. I wrote most of our songs and J-Jay's contribution was minimal. I was a seventeen-year-old kid who was away from home for the f-first time and got the idea I was special, so I dumped Jay and moved in with Eddie. Solo gigs started coming and I was headed to the t-top."

She paused for a moment. "After Jay left, I fell madly in l-love with Eddie. We stayed together for a little over a month. One day I woke up and he was gone. No note, no call, nothing. He just m-moved out and left for LA. He even stole a s-song I wrote and sold it to a new band."

I felt transfixed as a picture arose of her as a kid, before she became so strong, confident and steady.

"I had been doing hard drugs with Jay and Eddie since I got to Nashville. By the t-time Eddie left, I was addicted to heroin. Tracks on my arms and thighs. Deep sweats. I started missing gigs and was about to p-pawn my Gibson, when I broke down in the shop and they called an ambulance. I left before it arrived because if I went for treatment, it would have s-shown up on my father's health insurance. I was at a crossroads. It was bad enough g-going home as a failure, but being an addict was d-devastating. I panicked."

"What did you do?" I asked finally.

"I called my friend Michelle. She was at Duke in pre-med and had a house off c-campus with two other girls. She used her credit card to pay for my bus ticket and told me to c-come down and stay with them until we figured out what to do. When I got to North Carolina, she got me into rehab and borrowed the money from her mother so I didn't have to use my insurance," she said evenly, as she choked up.

I stayed silent and watched her.

"I was conflicted because of my Catholic upbringing, my g-guilt over dumping Jay and Eddie leaving me, but Michelle talked me down off the ledge. She was a rock and I n-never forgot her for it. A few weeks later, I was well enough to go b-back to Houston and face the music." She looked at me and shrugged.

"What happened to Jay?" I asked.

"He hung around for a while and then went back to Texas. His sister came to see me in college and said he died from a d-drug overdose because he never got over me leaving him."

I took her in my arms and held her.

"So, that's what love did for me. I swore would never let myself fall for anyone again. I feel like it's my f-fault about Jay dying. That's why I always hold s-something back," she said.

I wanted to reply but couldn't find the words as she continued.

"The whole thing taught m-me something else. I told Michelle I still wanted music and she said the only way I could protect myself was to become a lawyer. As soon as I told my d-dad I wanted to go to law school, it seemed like all the past was forgotten."

"That's an incredible story," I said.

"I felt you had a right to know before this r-relationship went any further," she said, in a half-whisper. "If you can't handle the drug part, I understand, but I n-needed to tell you so you could decide."

I wondered if I would have been as strong as she was. Suddenly, I was overcome with a sense of belonging. Trapp was the woman I wanted to spend the rest of my life with but, like before, I still had to hold some feelings in reserve.

I took her in my arms and felt my eyes water. She was clinging to me like I was a life raft pulling her out of rip tide.

"Did you ever hear the Vince Gill song, 'Love Never Broke Anyone's Heart'?" I asked.

She nodded.

"There's a lyric that talks about how losing love is what causes the pain. Maybe music will give me the chance to show you I'm not Eddie and you're not to blame for Jay," I said, as her tears washed over my skin.

"Love can't interfere with our writing," she said.

I held her again and whispered, "It won't."

"Lyrics can only pop out when we have an unobstructed m-mating of our minds," she said.

"That's because we've each acquired a Steele-Trapp Mind."

She looked into my eyes for a long moment before she spoke.

"That's a song title," she whispered, before locking her lips onto mine.

* * *

On the Tuesday after Columbus Day, Trapp was talking on the telephone as I waddled into the kitchen.

"Good morning.... Because your client was a material witness and I need to take his deposition.... If you do that, I'll m-move for sanctions under Rule eleven...Why don't we meet at his home.....No, only about forty-five minutes.....That's fine, next Wednesday at ten o'clock. 105 Willow Tree Lane," she finished.

"OK, Judge Janine, what was that about?" I asked.

"The answer to part A is Wes McGovern's lawyer. Part B is that McGovern's deposition is scheduled in a f-fictitious case."

"I still don't get it."

"Do you know what a deposition is?"

"It's where someone testifies under oath outside of a courtroom."

"Right. I'll be taking Wes's deposition next Wednesday. He has to show up and talk to me, or he'll be in c-c-contempt of court."

"Deposition for what?"

"Nothing. We'll get him there, and I'll play our demo tape for him," she said, smiling.

"Why would he show up if it's phony?"

"He thinks it's real."

"Wait a minute, isn't that illegal or something?" I asked.

"It's pretty shaky but there's no other way. Remember, I told you it's easy to assault someone, but the t-trick is getting them to remember you? Well, I guarantee you, he'll remember us."

"But won't his lawyer contact the court and have you fined or something?"

"Yeah, but I've got that f-f-figured out."

I scooted my chair closer.

"I never filed a lawsuit with the court, so I didn't violate any rules there," she said.

"But you sent papers to McGovern, right?"

"Yes, I did. But all I did was m-m-make up the title and details. The only thing he will be out is some time. This is what I meant when I said we had to do something unethical."

"What do I have to do?" I asked.

"Show up and pretend you had a car accident."

"But, doesn't McGovern have to pay his lawyer?" I asked.

"I'm taking my checkbook. I'll write his lawyer a check for fees and expenses right there on the spot. So nobody gets hurt, everybody gets p-paid and we can pitch our songs. And maybe we get our big break."

I was still skeptical. "Yeah, but don't you have some kind of code of conduct that says you won't send phony documents and such?"

"Sure I do, but this is the only way I know to make him listen. His lawyer won't check it out and by paying his legal bill, I'm off the h-h-hook. Great plan, don't you think?" she asked.

"To quote the brightest and most beautiful lawyer I know, I think that if this doesn't work, we are a, fucked, b, screwed, c, both of the above."

* * *

The following Wednesday, we headed south on Interstate 65, arrived in Lebanon and came to a long driveway. We found a closed gate with an electronic box and Trapp pushed the intercom button.

"Yes?"

"Angela Trappani. I'm here with my client for the deposition."

The electronic gate swung open, and we drove through.

"I thought this guy lost everything when he hit the skids," I said.

"I guess he managed to keep a little from the vultures."

We drove up into a circular driveway and parked behind a sleek, black Mercedes sedan and a white Cadillac Escalade. Trapp exhaled deeply and rang the bell. A man wearing a cowboy shirt, jeans and boots answered. He reminded me of a younger George Jones, without the white hair.

"You mus' be Ms. Trappani. I'm Wes McGovern. Why don' y'all come on in?" he said.

"Thank you. This is Mr. Steele," Trapp said.

"Let's go in the back room. Mah attorney is waiting there," Wes said. He led us past some empty rooms until we entered a dining area, where a man wearing a pin-striped suit was seated next to a woman. She sat behind a black recording device, propped up on a metal stand in front of her. In the next split-second, I almost sank to my knees. Of all the lawyers in Nashville, Wes went out and hired T. Edward Bryson.

"This is my attorney, Mr. Bryson. This here is Ms. Trappani and Mr. Steele," said Wes.

Bryson seemed preoccupied, barely glanced in my direction and did not offer his hand. "Let's get this over with. I have to be back in my office by eleven-thirty," he said, after looking at his watch.

Suddenly, Bryson stared at me. I sensed a light just went on for him.

"Wait a minute, weren't you in my office a while back?" he demanded.

"Yes, I had the displeasure," I answered, after deciding it was too late to lie.

"What are you two trying to pull?" Bryson asked.

"Mr. Steele is the plaintiff in this suit. We're not trying to pull anything," Trapp said.

She turned to me and whispered, "Why were you in his office?"

"I'll tell you later," I said, regretting I had not told her about my meeting with Bryson because I was so embarrassed after the fiasco with Sam Presley.

Trapp turned back to Wes as the stenographer swore him in.

"Please state your name for the record."

"It's Wesley McGovern."

"And where do you live?"

"Why, right here, darlin'. This is mah home."

"What's the address?"

"105 Willow Tree Lane."

"What is your profession?"

"Ah'm a country singer. Everybody knows that," Wes answered.

"Would you consider yourself an expert on country music?"

"Objection. That's irrelevant," Bryson said.

"This is a deposition. I'm entitled to establish the witness's background," she countered.

"Well, start asking appropriate questions. So far, every question you've asked would need a search party to try to find some relevancy."

I could see Trapp's nostrils flare as she snapped back. "If you want to testify, Mr. Bryson, we'll be happy to a, swear you in, b, take your statement, or c, prepare an affidavit," she replied.

"Don't get smart, Counselor, or we can see how clever you are in front of a judge."

Trapp pressed the question. "Would you consider yourself an expert on country music?"

"Why, ah guess so," Wes answered

"You'd know a good country song if you heard one, wouldn't you?" Trapp asked.

Bryson lumbered out of his chair. "That's enough," he said.

"Why, ah guess ah would, sure," answered Wes.

"I only have two more questions, Counsel, so sit down and we'll finish up," said Trapp.

Bryson glared at Trapp, then finally sat down.

"Mr. McGovern, calling your attention to March 26th of this year, did you w-w-witness a collision between Mr. Steele and another man on Broadway in Nashville?" Trapp asked.

"No, ah didn't," Wes replied.

Trapp reached into her briefcase, took out a tape recorder and placed it on the table. "I'm going to play a statement from one of the witnesses, and I want you to see if you recognize the voice," she said to Wes.

"Wait a minute. I object," Bryson said.

"Let him authenticate the voice, and then we are finished," Trapp said.

"This is worse than a brief from a first year law student," said Bryson, folding his arms.

"All right, sir, tell me if you recognize this voice," Trapp said, hitting the 'play' button.

The room became filled with Trapp's and my voice singing, 'Reflections of Love.'

Bryson grew red in the face and grabbed for the tape recorder.

"Sorry, I must have grabbed the wrong tape," Trapp said.

Wes was listening intently as Trapp snatched the recorder away from Bryson.

"Goddamn you, this was a ploy to have him hear the tape. I'm going to the Bar Association. I'm gonna pull your ticket," Bryson roared.

Trapp turned to Wes, as I stepped in front of Bryson. "Is this a good country song, Mr. McGovern?" she asked.

Wes seemed to be listening over the ruckus. He looked into her face and said, "Yes, it is."

Trapp grinned as she turned to the reporter. "I want that on the record. The witness stated under oath this is a good country song," she said.

Bryson pulled out his cell phone and rapidly dialed a number. "Ruth, have one of the associates file an emergency motion for sanctions against a lawyer named Angela Trappani. Have it marked up for a hearing right away," he barked.

Trapp shut off the recorder, and turned to Wes. She seemed a little shaken by Bryson's threat.

"If I leave you a CD, will you l-listen to it?"

"Ah don't know. Ah'm confused," Wes replied.

Bryson ended his call as Trapp put the tape recorder back in her briefcase. "This was nothing but a goddamn ruse. This deposition was phony. These two are a couple of hucksters who wanted to slip you a recording!" he shouted.

Trapp pulled out an envelope and slid it toward Wes. He stared at it. She spoke to Wes, as I moved in front of Bryson, who was trying to grab the envelope. "That's a new CD, lead sheets and a brief biography. P-P-Please listen to the whole thing when we leave," she said.

After reaching into her briefcase for her checkbook, she turned back toward Bryson. He was huffing and slamming papers into his briefcase. "I think that song is p-p-p-perfect for you, Wes. Mr. Bryson, tell me what Mr. McGovern's bill is, and I'll p-p-pay you right now," she said.

Bryson flew into a rage, grabbed the envelope from McGovern and flung it at Trapp. It struck her in the chest. I felt my outrage spike. "You incompetent little bitch, you'll p-p-pay all right because I'm gonna run you out of town for the stunt you just p-p-pulled. Now take this dumbass jock and get out of here before I have you arrested for trespassing," he hissed.

I reached for the envelope and slid it toward McGovern. Bryson gave me a vicious shove and I was knocked backward against the table. I was pissed now and decided enough was enough. "Trapp, how much do you charge to defend someone for assault!" I yelled.

"For s-s-simple assault, a thousand dollars."

"What's simple assault?"

"One p-p-punch, instead of a beating," she replied.

That was all I needed to know. I turned to Bryson, and prayed silently that my high school coach or the judge never found out what I was about to do. "Here's a fistful of due process, you fat bastard," I said. I smacked Bryson right in the mouth, knocking him down. I was ready to beat the living shit out of him, when I realized that I'd already spent more than I could afford. "I'll pay you out of our first royalty check. Now, let's get out of here before I consider running a tab," I said to Trapp. I turned and bent over toward Bryson who was on the floor rubbing his mouth with a silk handkerchief. "If you ever mock her again, I'll rip your head out through your asshole," I snarled. Then I headed for the door. Trapp looked at me as we reached the car.

"Tell me the truth, are we in serious trouble?" I asked.

"Probably. There was no other way to do this. Maybe B-B-Bryson is b-b-bluffing. I hope McGovern will convince him to take the money and drop the case."

"Are you worried?"

"No. I knew this could backfire," she said.

"I shouldn't have punched him. But he gave me no other choice."

"Maybe we can petition the court for a change of v-v-venue to V-V-Vinita," she continued, trying to smile.

* * *

At seven o'clock, Trapp called and said she had just been served with documents that summoned us both to court. Bryson filed criminal complaints against both of us for fraud and conspiracy, and against me individually for assault. I told her about my run-in at Bryson's office.

"Trapp, could you lose your license over this?"

I could hear panic in her voice as she answered yes.

"Why don't I say I lied to you about the phony accident? That would get you off the hook."

"That won't f-f-fly. I filed the fake deposition notice without the proper court documents, not you. If they disbar me, I'll deal with it. Dammit, I'd still rather sell one song than win a thousand jury trials," she said.

That's just what a real songwriter would say, I thought.

"I'm really pissed because Bryson made my stuttering more intense," she said. "I won't let that happen again, especially with a j-j-jerk like him."

I meditated for a moment on how I had been in Nashville for barely two months and in that short time, I was about to get my girlfriend disbarred, charged with assault and I was being sued for divorce. All because of my obsession with music. My mind began singing the old Bobby Fuller song, 'I Fought The Law.'

The feeling of terror intensified as I realized that in the song, the law won.

CHAPTER NINE

The following morning, Hooker came home after another romantic interlude with Sylvia. I told him about the hearing and he agreed to tell Burl I had an emergency. I drove to Trapp's place shortly before noon and we left for the courthouse.

After our arrival, we went to the last courtroom on the first floor and sat at an oak table to the right of the bench. Bryson was already at the other table, sitting next to a young man and woman. All wore navy suits, hands-off attitudes and sullen looks. A man in a tan, tropical worsted suit emerged from a door next to the bench.

"Court, all rise. Superior Court is in session. The Honorable Randolph W. Barksdale, presidin'," he called, as the judge walked to the bench.

"Please be seated," he said.

"First on the list, Ya Honah, is a motion for sanctions against Attorney Angela Trappani, by Attorney T. Edward Bryson," called the man in the suit.

"Ah've read your allegations, Mr. Bryson, and these are very serious charges," the judge said.

"I felt it necessary to call them to the court's attention. This was egregious conduct on the part of Ms. Trappani. It caused my client undue hardship and was a flagrant misuse of the legal system by an officer of the court for her own personal promotion," Bryson said.

"If these charges are true, they would certainly involve censure and could possibly lead to disbarment. Does the punishment fit the crime?" the judge asked

"I believe the court has to put others on notice against a similar course of action. This is not a matter that can be taken lightly," Bryson said.

"Ah am troubled by the potential for disbarment. Is there any other way to resolve this?" Barksdale asked.

"Not as far as I am concerned. Don't forget, I was also criminally assaulted by Mr. Steele. Without any provocation, I might add," Bryson said.

I jumped to my feet as Trapp grabbed my arm.

"That's a lie, Your Honor," I said.

"Ms. Trappani, control yoah client," the judge said.

Trapp told me to knock it off as Bryson continued.

"I believe the only fair disposition of this matter is the stiffest punishment for fraud by this attorney, and the appropriate fine and incarceration for the criminal activities of her client."

Bryson sat down and shot us a defiant look. I saw a dark-bluish discoloration under his eye.

"Very well, then. Ms. Trappani, what is your response?" the judge asked.

"Your Honor, I am truly sorry this matter has come before the court. All I can say in my defense is that I have offered to reimburse Mr. McGovern for any fees and expenses," she said.

"Am I to undahstand you do not deny these charges?" the judge asked.

"There was no intent to defraud and therefore no deceit. I still stand before this court ready to pay Mr. McGovern for any a, costs, b, expenses, or c, fees," said Trapp.

"In that case, I have no choice but to hold a full evidentiary hearing. This court considers Mr. Steele's previous outburst as a denial. The parties will appear in this court a week from today at one o'clock. At that time, a hearing will be held to determine if you, Ms. Trappani, shall be subjected to disciplinary action, including possible disbarment, and whether you, Mr. Steele, shall be subject to indictment for assault. Ms. Trappani, Mr. Steele, I advise you both to retain counsel in this matter," Barksdale said and the next case was called.

Bryson closed his briefcase and a wicked smile formed. Trapp and I left in silence.

* * *

I arrived at the stadium shortly after two-thirty. Burl told me to report to the co-chancellors. I went to the administration building and was escorted into the conference room where Reverends Chantelle and Bartlesville were waiting with two security guards.

"Thank you for comin', Coach Steele. Ah'm afraid we have received some disturbin' news. We have received a Federal Express letter detailing how you have deserted your wife in order to move to Nashville. There were also allegations about sordid sexual details in your private life that could reflect poorly on our decision to bring you on board here," said Reverend Chantelle, as I felt my forehead flush.

"Who sent you the letter?" I asked.

"A Mister Allister W. Lyle," said Reverend Bartlesville.

I grew livid as I stared across the table. What an asshole Boomer was.

"That's my father in law," I said.

"Suh, do you have anything to say about these charges?" Bartlesville asked.

"Well, gentlemen, with all due respect, my relationship with my wife ended when she ran off with another man. I think the details should remain private," I answered.

"Ah'm afraid that's not true. Everything you do or fail to do reflects on this institution. Desertion of your spouse is a wicked act. Therefore, if you cannot produce sufficient evidence to refute these charges, we have no choice but to terminate your employment," Chantelle said.

I started to get more pissed, then stopped. I needed this job even if the money sucked. "How can I prove it if you don't believe me?" I asked.

Chantelle responded, "Suh, you cannot work for the Lord with these sinful charges staining your soul."

"Ah'm afraid you have left us no othah choice, Coach Steele, if you are not prepared to produce evidence at this time," Bartlesville said.

They were firing me for leaving Carol after she cheated. I could tell they had already decided I was guilty so I shook my head.

"You are dismissed, Mr. Steele. These gentlemen"— he said gestured toward the security guards—"will escort you out of the building. You will be paid through today. May God forgive you your transgressions, sir."

I was steaming as I reached the parking lot. I called Trapp on the way home and gave her the details, then told her about Boomer contacting the school.

"Sit tight for a while. Maybe I can float you a loan until you get b-back on your feet. Why don't you come over now and let's talk?"

When I arrived, there was a red and white Federal Express envelope in front of the entrance. I handed it to her when I got inside.

"Do you know the name on the return address?" I asked.

"Jake Skylar, Attorney-at-law. He's a big-time entertainment lawyer who handles a lot of stars. He's also one of Bryson's biggest competitors. What do you suppose he wants?" she asked. Suddenly, Trapp threw the papers skyward, and then began to scream. She turned and jumped into my arms, planted a huge kiss on my lips and wrestled me to the couch.

"Sonofabitch, now I know how running backs used to feel. What's going on?"

"Wes McGovern retained Jake Skylar as his new lawyer. After we left the other day, Wes dumped Bryson. He also listened to the tape—and get this! I took the wrong one with us. I thought it only had 'Reflections of Love' but it also had 'The Promise of A Lie.'"

My chest started pounding as I began to pace. "What's the next step?" I asked.

"Meeting with Wes and his lawyer." Her face lit up as she grabbed my arms. "We have to start putting an act together right away. I think you should go get your stuff and move in here. We have a l-lot to do to get ready."

"As long as we have an understanding between us."

"What's that?"

"I love you. This time, I mean it like a man and not just a songwriter."

"I love you, too," she said.

I had one more thing to say. She placed her hands in mine and looked into my eyes.

"I need to tell you the real reason why country music gets to me. After my dad was killed when I was ten, music and I became estranged. Sad songs reminded me of him and made me break down. I felt ashamed because crying was not the way a man should act. About a year later, my mother got sick and we were forced to move to Texas to live with my grandmother. One day, Mom called me in and said before my father died, he told her I had more musical talent than anyone he had ever seen. She made me promise to honor his memory by becoming a songwriter."

I stopped and swallowed hard. "A week later, she died. I refused to show any emotion, telling myself that my broken heart should stay hidden. As I sat in church, an image appeared of Dad and Mom. One sad song after another started torturing me. After the funeral, I broke down in the car and almost bit through my bottom lip trying to stay strong, but hot bitter tears kept flowing like raindrops trickling down a windowpane."

I looked off into the distance. "When the car stopped, I jumped out and vowed no one would ever see me lose control again because it was a sign of weakness. Then, music appeared and I grew angry. I went on the attack and shouted that country songs were harsh and cruel. When I finished, the silence whispered in my ear for the very first time."

"What did it say?" Trapp asked, as her voice trembled.

"It told me to write my own lyrics so I could cry inside," I said, as tears flowed freely.

"So no one can see you?" she asked. I nodded and rubbed my thumbs up under my eyelids, as she gripped my hands tighter.

"Every time I write a song, it lets me shed a huge lump of sorrow, and no one will ever have to know."

She took me in her arms and I wept. My feelings for Trapp were starting to leak out. The fortress I built around my heart was collapsing, one brick at a time. There was nothing I could do to stop it.

* * *

The following morning, I drove over to pick up my stuff and found Hooker sitting at the table. I told him about our musical triumph. He jumped up and shook my hand, said he was thrilled and was not surprised. I told him Trapp invited me to move in and also felt a need to tell him about my legal problems.

"You said Bryson shoved you and threw a paper at her. Doesn't that help?" he asked.

"Maybe."

"What did Trapp say?"

"She tried to convince me she's not worried, but I think it's just an act."

We shook hands and gave each other a short hug.

"Son, remember me when you hit the big time," he said.

"I don't know how to thank you," I said, as he slid his hand into mine.

"It was great having you around. Even if you were a bad influence on me."

"How?"

"By telling me love really does exist."

"Not Sylvia?"

"I can't explain it. She's forty-eight years old, certainly not the youngest or most attractive woman. But if you ever saw her with her hair down and a little makeup, you wouldn't believe how good she looks. Of course, she's a single woman stuck at a religious college, so she has to keep a low profile on campus," he said, as a picture of Erica flashed.

"That doesn't matter. You've dated starlets, and I've never heard you say you couldn't wait to get back to any of them."

His eyes grew as round as dinner plates.

"I can't get enough of being with her."

"I figured you would have dumped her now that the novelty has worn off."

"This is the longest I've stayed with someone."

"How does she feel?"

"I don't think she's head over heels in love, but glad she found someone who respects her and explores her mind."

"Run with this for as long as you want. When the time is right, you'll know how to handle it."

"Burl sends his regards. Says he's sorry those two morons gave you the axe," Hooker said, folding his arms.

"Give him my best, OK?"

"Keep in touch. Let me know when you make the cover of 'Rolling Stone'."

"Glad you found Vinita one more time," I said.

* * *

Trapp and I met with Wes McGovern and his lawyers the following Tuesday. We were escorted into the conference room where two men—one black and one white—were waiting. They rose to meet us. The black man needed a cane to steady himself.

They were both tall, about six foot four and muscular, even if time had added some softness. The white man looked like a Medicare version of Mark Harmon, except that he wore a grey moustache. The black man reminded me of a graying Denzel Washington. His face was very familiar even though I was sure we had never met.

"Hi, I'm Jake Skylar," the white man said, extending his hand. "Wes is running late so I thought we might get acquainted."

"And, I'm his law partner, Aubrey Evans," the black man said, shifting his cane left so he could shake our hands.

Suddenly, the link clicked and my eyes lit up. We were in the presence of greatness. Aubrey Evans, as in Hall of Fame running back.

"Also known as Ace, from the Dallas Cowboys," I said, as my voice rose and shook slightly.

"Oh my God, my father said you were the greatest running back the Cowboys ever had, b-better than Calvin Hill, Tony Dorsett, or even Emmitt Smith," Trapp said excitedly, bringing her hands up to her face.

"Your father is obviously a man of unbound eloquence and extreme intelligence," Ace said.

"Emmitt Smith would have eaten his lunch,' Jake said, as he winked at us.

"My dad is Joseph Trappani, a lawyer in Houston. Do you know him?" she asked.

"Sorry, I don't," Ace said.

"When I saw the firm name, I never put it together. How did you become partners?" I asked.

"We go back to the 1960s. We played football at Texas Central University, lived together in college and reunited in Boston in the early 1990s. We still have an office there but we moved the bulk of our practice to Nashville in 2000 to do entertainment law," Jake said, as I pictured Hooker and me thirty years from now.

"I played quarterback and on special teams for the Patriots and lived in the Boston area for nine years," I said. "Until knee problems forced me to retire."

"I thought I spotted that kickoff commando look that Jake and I lost centuries ago," Ace said.

"Wes McGovern was originally Ace's client. We work on all the cases together. That's why I wanted to meet you," Jake said.

"How did you get the name Ace?" Trapp asked.

"It's an acronym. Aubrey Charles Evans," he answered.

"Ms. Trappani, I understand you're also a lawyer," Jake said.

"I'm a member of the bar here and in Texas," she replied. "By the way, please call me Trapp."

"How about first names all around?" Ace asked.

"Do you have your own practice?" Jake asked.

"No, I'm doing some per diem cases with Whitmore and Whitmore," she said.

"Are you a Nashville native, Trapp?" Jake asked.

"I'm from Houston originally and came to Nashville to go to Vanderbilt."

"We started to collaborate a few weeks ago," I said.

"Wes is sure glad you did," Ace said. "He thinks you two are about to become a hot property."

"Incidentally, I envy the two of you," Skylar said.

I looked at Trapp and felt my whole body tingle.

"Why's that?" Trapp asked.

"Because you have so much talent and you have done some great work," he replied.

"That's very flattering. We thought these songs were perfect for Mr. McGovern," she replied.

"Oh, Jake's not talking about your songwriting. It's good, but it's not at the Tom Douglas or Lori McKenna level yet. It's all over town about the deposition and how each of you knocked Bryson on his overabundant ass. Trapp with her mind and quick wit, and you, J. W., with your fists," Ace said.

"Ace and Bryson have mixed it up in court a few times. Eddie is still looking for his first win," said Jake.

"Trapp and I have our own battle coming up with Bryson," I said.

"What do you mean?" Jake asked.

Trapp told the story of our legal troubles because of the fake deposition.

"I know I shouldn't have sent him a d-deposition notice, but I was out of ideas. I've offered several times to pay his fees and expenses. Bryson won't listen," she said.

"Don't be offended, Trapp, but that was not the most prudent move," Jake said.

"I know," she said. "But I c-couldn't think of anything else."

"Bryson is no Boy Scout himself. I've seen him pull some things that could only be described as sleazy.

Jake, remember the time he flat-out lied to the court about having no documents and I checked with a lawyer on a previous case and we found everything we needed? He told the judge we misunderstood him," Ace said.

Skylar shook his head and grew agitated.

Ace suddenly took on an impish grin.

"Why don't I represent you?" he asked. "I can't guarantee we'll win, but Jake just gave you Eddie's dismal record against me."

I looked at Trapp. She knew what I was thinking.

"That's very kind but I don't think we can afford you," I said.

Ace shook his head."Don't worry about that. This one's on me," he said.

"We'll even get Wes to agree to it. That way, there's no conflict," Jake said. "Besides, Ace only gets this excited when he knows he's going to slap Eddie around like a piñata."

At that moment, Wes McGovern was escorted into the conference room, followed by a waiter wheeling a continental breakfast. After a few more moments of small talk, Skylar handed each of us a proposed contract for the sale of all rights to 'Reflections of Love' and 'The Promise of A Lie.' Trapp reviewed each provision, while my participation was cosmetic. When we finished, she asked for a private room to discuss the terms.

"OK, this seems like a standard deal," she began when we were alone. "But, I'm not sure I want to g-give up all rights to the songs."

"Don't we have to do that to get a deal?"

"Maybe. But once we do that, we relinquish any royalties."

"How can we avoid that?" I asked.

"I'll t-t-tell them we want to open Wes's show," she said.

I shot my fist up into the air.

"Mother, get the deed to the ranch. I think I'm dreaming."

"Don't get too excited. Offering the deal is easy; getting them to agree is the hard p-part."

"Trapp, I don't care about the rights. I'll do whatever you say."

We broke for lunch and Trapp hammered out the provisions she wanted in the new contract and presented them when we returned. McGovern balked.

Trapp gently reminded everyone that Wes needed a huge boost to start his tour and that our songs were made for him. Jake and Ace both smiled and left the room to speak privately with Wes. They returned and the deal got a lot sweeter.

It took almost two hours, but finally, we came to terms. We would open for Wes on his Houston tour in January, in exchange for a writing credit for Wes. We were limited to three songs for each show and Wes retained the option to sign us for the balance of the tour. The best part was that we kept the writing and publishing rights.

"The contracts will be ready for signature tomorrow afternoon at two o'clock," Skylar said. "I believe you two are destined for stardom. However, I have to tell you I'm a little envious because I once tried to write songs, but gave it up, so I guess I'm still a songwriter trapped in a lawyer's body."

"Let's meet tomorrow after the contracts are signed, to prepare for the hearing," Ace said.

We shook hands all around. After we left, Trapp and I were flying.

"I'll bet those two have some tales to tell," Trapp said. "And most of them have a nasty ending."

"What do you mean?" I asked.

"A black man and white man living together in Texas in the '60s. My daddy said those were horrible times when he was growing up."

A day later, the contracts were signed. Afterward, we met with Ace. He said we didn't have many options. Even though Bryson provoked us, what we did was unethical and an abuse of the system. Ace said he would call Bryson to try to negotiate a deal but he was not optimistic.

On the way out, I wondered where Balls was now that I really needed him.

CHAPTER TEN

That night, I called Cody Davis, Bryson's brother-in-law, in Minneapolis. After hearing my story, Cody had an idea.

"I know things about Bryson that will drive him wild. You can't do it like me. I need to come to Nashville. I'll be there in the morning and fly back the same day."

"Aren't you getting ready for a game?" I asked.

"Sure, but back spasms made me physically unable to perform. So, I'm out until Sunday when I have to knock somebody's dick into his gym bag," he said.

"That will be the time for you to start whipping out some old-fashioned, red, white and blue encephalopathy," I said.

Cody was the toughest interior lineman I ever saw. He would knock a guy down repeatedly until he was stopped by the officials.

I grinned as I thought about the medical reference. That was the bond that cemented our friendship, after a wiseass sports writer wrote a negative article about Cody. The writer was a pseudo-intellectual weasel who detested athletes, because he was consumed by envy. He got his kicks through denigration because he felt an erudite superiority to jocks. Cody became a target because the guy thought he found a patsy who was too big and stupid to compete with the power of the word processor.

The writer called Cody a "Bullying Behemoth," who was the product of a "Hero-Worshiping Culture that coddled the biggest brutish beasts, in a game for mental midgets." He blasted Cody for his aggressive licks and sustained blocking, and nicknamed him "The Concussion Concierge," because of all the late hits he dished out. Cody got pissed because he was obsessed with playing like a champion on every play, but never delivering a cheap shot.

Cody asked me for help and I told him to do the unexpected. Knock the prick down with words like vacillate, egregious or Draconian. The medical term for brain damage from repeated concussions was chronic traumatic encephalopathy. Work that into the conversation, to keep the guy off balance. At our next home game, Cody customized my advice. The writer certainly had balance issues.

Cody found the writer on the sidelines. They spoke for barely ten seconds before Cody picked him up by his neck and shook him like a box of Frosted Flakes. Cody said if he kept "vacillatin'" and wrote any more "shithouse slander" like that again, he would jam a Winnebago full of encephalopathy so far up his ass, he would have to unbutton his shirt collar to relieve the pressure on his sigmoid colon. He twisted the guy's iPad into a cone and tried to bite his smart phone in half. Cody said if he wanted to do something about it, to "go get help from some fuckin' egregious editor or dipshit concierge dressed up in a suit made of Dacron." Instead of flipping a coin, Cody said he should come back with "whoever could bench press the most."

The writer was so scared he pissed his pants and became a no-show for the rest of the season.

The league fined Cody twenty-five grand. He said he got off cheap. I became his best buddy and permanent medical confidant. We nicknamed him the "Emperor of Encephalopathy."

I offered to pay for his airfare to Nashville. No need, he told me, because he had just signed a huge contract.

"I never knew there was such huge fuckin' money in parcelin' out encephalopathy," he said.

* * *

The following day, we met Ace at the courthouse just before one o'clock. He said Bryson would not budge on a deal to dismiss the charges, so the hearing would go forward.

The hearing began with Bryson presenting his case. When he finished, Ace started to speak when the bailiff walked up and tapped me on the shoulder. I turned around and saw a tall, enormously-built man at the rear of the court.

Cody had arrived, wearing a dark suit and a wide-mouthed grin. Bryson was looking at Ace and did not turn to see Cody. I tugged at Ace's sleeve, nodded to the rear of the courtroom and told him some new evidence arrived. He turned to the bench and asked for a short recess.

We left the courtroom and entered the hallway. Cody was leaning against the opposite wall. Since he's about six foot eight and weighs close to three hundred and twenty pounds, it was hard to see where he ended and the wall began. I introduced him to Trapp, and then to Ace. He was captivated by Trapp. I told him on the phone about Ace's Hall of Fame background and he was awestruck by him.

"My God, it really is Ace Evans. I'm honored and moved, sir," Cody said with a gasp.

"Well, that's very kind, but I'm not sure why you're here," Ace said.

Cody grinned and outlined his plan. Ace belly-laughed while Trapp seemed unmoved. Cody and I high-fived before Ace and Trapp quickly walked back inside to get Bryson.

"Eddie, we need to see you in the hallway," Ace told him.

"What for?" Bryson asked.

"To settle this case," Ace answered.

"The only settlement I want is your clients' asses hanging from an oak tree," said Bryson said and sneered.

"Either come outside, or I'll tell the judge you refused to try to resolve this. He'll throw this case out of court," Ace said.

"Read your civil procedure rules, counselor. A party refusing to try to resolve a matter without the court's intervention is s-s-subject to having the action dismissed. With prejudice," Trapp interjected.

Ace nodded.

Bryson thought for a moment. "All right, let's go outside," he said. His face took on a look of horror when he saw his brother-in-law. "Cody, what the hell are you doing here?" Bryson asked.

"Visiting my least favorite relative. Why are you being such a butthole to these two fine people?" asked Cody.

"This is between me and them," Bryson told him.

"Either you drop this horseshit complaint, or suffer the consequences," Cody threatened, folding his arms and looming over all of us like a crane.

"What do you mean?" Bryson asked.

"As soon as the season's over, Amy and I will come and stay with you for a couple of months. And we'll bring the boys," Cody said.

"You can't do that. That's extortion," Bryson wailed, holding up his arms as though pleading.

"I like to think of it as family bonding. Especially when my two sons, your lovable nephews, turn your house into Six Flags Over Nashville. Drop this case, or you and me will have a nice spell of country clubbin', where I can tell all those pussy aristocrats you hang out with about how I once got arrested in Dallas for waving my dick at a carload of Cowboy fans."

Ace was on the verge of laughing out loud even though Cody was not through painting this family portrait.

"Or, maybe they'd like to hear about the time we played in Detroit, and the game went into overtime. After we won, I led all the offensive linemen to the fifty yard line, where we dropped our pants and mooned every sonofabitch in the stands. I know how much you love those stories. We're gonna have us a couple of months' worth of fun, and a lifetime of memories," Cody said, rubbing his hands together. Then he turned to Trapp. "Pardon me, ma'am, for the graphic descriptions of body parts and vulgar language. But this flamin' asshole don't understand nothin' else." He bowed slightly. I was almost giddy.

"Damn you, Cody, this is so unfair," Bryson said, sounding like he was trying to pay for dinner with an expired credit card.

"Naw, unfair is ruinin' this lady's career, and giving my pal, J. W. here, a criminal record just for using their wits to get ahead. We both know what they did isn't half as bad as some of the stunts you've pulled and bragged about. So, either do this my way, or start lookin' for an architect to build another level onto that pisshole of a mansion you live in with my social climbin' sister. Of course, it would sure be nice to see her again, so I could watch her face take on a snooty look like someone shoved a rusty razor blade up her ass ten years ago."

Bryson started to answer but stopped. I knew I couldn't look at Trapp.

"Tough maintainin' an edge as a perpetual prick, ain't it, Fast Eddie?" Cody asked.

"You win, Cody. I'll drop the case," Bryson said, finally, throwing up his right hand, before turning and stomping back into the courtroom.

"Ain't family values the cat's ass?" Cody said, after shaking hands with me, Trapp and Ace.

"Cody, I'll never be able to thank you for this!" I exclaimed, giving him a short hug.

"No, this was truly my pleasure. Thank you, J. W., for letting me slap Bryson around," he said.

"Why'd you call him 'Fast Eddie'?" Ace asked.

"Well, before he knew I was a Neanderthal, he once told me his favorite movie character was that guy Paul Newman played in *The Color of Money*. You know, that pool shark, 'Fast Eddie Felson.' Well, ol' T. Edward nicknamed himself 'Fast Eddie' because of the way he did his work so fast. I thought that was so goddamn stupid, I was ready to gag," Cody said.

"Can you stick around for a couple of days?" I asked.

"Naw. They need me for a little encephalopathy against the Broncos this weekend." His face grew a huge smile as he thought about just another day at the office.

"Cody, it was a real pleasure. I wish I would have had you blocking for me a thousand years ago. The biggest linemen we had were barely two-sixty," said Ace, as his eyes lit up.

"Mr. Evans, it's been a pleasure," said Cody.

"Please, make it Ace. I'm not old enough to be called 'mister'."

"Maybe not, sir, but you are a superstar. And you deserve to be treated like one."

They clasped hands and I could see Cody was moved. It was almost as if he was taken back in time by one of the legends who paved the way for today's sky-high salaries and media attention.

I shook Cody's hand and Trapp reached up and gave him a giant hug, even though she needed a stepladder. After he left for the airport, Ace, Trapp and I walked back into court.

"Where do we stand on this matter?" the judge asked.

"Your Honor, this matter has been settled. I am withdrawing my complaints against Ms. Trappani and Mr. Steele," Bryson muttered through clenched teeth.

Trapp gave me a soft elbow in the ribs and then squeezed my hand.

"I'm happy it could be resolved. Court is adjourned," the judge said.

We stood as Bryson angrily closed his briefcase, turned and headed for the door. He stopped in front of us for one parting shot. "Evans, you must think you're really something for pulling that stunt. Well, these two better stay the hell out of my way in the future, or they'll find more trouble than you can handle."

"We'll keep our distance, if you remember one thing," I replied.

"What's that?" Bryson asked, sneering.

I arched both eyebrows and tried to sound like Dwayne "The Rock" Johnson.

"Don't ever walk into a big time pool hall again, 'Fat Eddie.' Or we'll have Minnesota Cody come back and break all your knuckles."

Trapp let go with a howl. Ace grinned widely as he shook his head while Bryson's face grew a look so hot I was afraid the paint would peel.

After Bryson stormed out of the courtroom, Trapp and I looked at each other. Suddenly, my mind was flooded with a musical rush of inspirational lyrics. I began to sing softly to the tune of 'Happy Birthday.'

* * *

Eddie Bryson's a tub;
Eddie Bryson won't flub;
Eddie Bryson, Eddie Bryson;
Eddie Bryson's a tub.

Trapp harmonized with me on the last line and we explained the song to Ace. He was laughing and singing it as he used his cane to hobble out of court while we followed.

A few seconds passed before Trapp and I both got the same idea. I looked into her eyes and they were sparkling like a pair of polished diamonds. Thanks to Cody, we were neither a, fucked, b, screwed nor c, a combination of the two.

"D, none of the above!" Trapp and I shouted in unison, before high-fiving.

* * *

We stopped for a celebratory dinner and got home at seven o'clock. After dinner, Trapp began to read the newspaper while I picked up the Martin and started to create. Instantly, she sat up and called me to her side, gesturing like she had a nervous tic as she spoke.

"You're not g-gonna believe this. Your old pal, Sam Presley, was just arrested. Here's his picture," she said, pointing and shaking her finger.

I jumped up and moved behind her. A photo of Sam and Darla being escorted out of a hotel in handcuffs, covered the right side of the page. The story described how they were taken into custody after they tried to pass another phony check to some unsuspecting mark.

The FBI was quoted as saying they'd had a wiretap in place for months. Sam and Darla had multiple aliases and were being charged with identity theft and conspiracy, along with Amanda Parsons. Amanda's job was to make contact with aspiring artists all over the East Coast, gain their trust and let Sam clean out their accounts. They were all facing the prospect of long prison terms.

"You were caught up in a scam. No one could have seen this coming," Trapp said.

I nodded as a fantasy of Cody twisting Sam, Darla and Amanda into matching iPhones, appeared in my mind. Again, I wondered how I could have let myself fall for this scheme when Sam's initial reference to the Presley name thundered in my sub-conscious. A sorrowful look spread over me as I realized it could all be explained by the title of an old number one hit for Elvis back a couple of thousand years before I was born, 'Now And Then There's A Fool Such As I'.

CHAPTER ELEVEN

The next few weeks flew by. On Veterans' Day, Hooker called and asked if I could meet him for a beer. I told him it sounded serious. He said women problems always were.

As I was leaving, Trapp asked why they never met us for dinner or a drink. I told her he always had an excuse. She asked Sylvia's age and I told her late forties. She nodded and said Hooker finally found his mother figure.

He was sitting at the bar when I arrived. I motioned to the bartender and pointed toward Hooker's beer.

"Hey, man. It's been a long time," he said. "It sounds like you and Trapp are still going solid."

"We are, I'm thrilled to say."

"Sylvia and I are on the rocks," he said. "She wants to go back home to New Jersey."

"What did you say?"

"I hinted that I could go with her."

"How did she react?"

"No response. She skirted the issue."

"Did you press her for an answer?"

"I tried. She said it wasn't working for her."

"OK, tell me why you feel like you're being destroyed."

He leaned back on his barstool and interlocked his fingers.

"I love her. I've never gotten involved before because I didn't want to go through this."

"She's not the only woman in the world. Aren't you the original one-night stand guy?"

175

"Yeah, that was bullshit, too."

"Why?"

"I wouldn't admit it, but I was out of my mind with fear."

"What were you afraid of?"

"Being alone."

"That's what life is all about. There's no guarantee of happiness or pain-free existence."

"I could have stopped this by not getting involved."

"And then what would you have accomplished?"

"I wouldn't have to go through the heartache."

I shook my head.

"She needs to move on, because this isn't right for her. Would you want her to stay if her heart wasn't in it?"

"Of course not. I love her too much for that."

"Then you have to try to let go. Maybe not today, but gradually you'll come to grips with the fact that it's time to put this behind you."

"What if I can't?"

"You have two choices. You can sit around and drink yourself into a coma or you can join the rest of the world and realize that you will learn to love again," I said.

"There's a third choice. I could go back to my old different-girl-every-night ways with women. At least, that was safe."

I sipped my beer for a long moment before I answered.

"Maybe so. But only until another Sylvia comes along. Then, we'll be back here having another self-help therapy session."

"As I've heard you say a thousand times, isn't that what country music is all about?" he asked.

We were leaving the bar when I saw a sinister-looking man waiting by a tree off to the side. He walked toward us in a hurry.

"Mr. John W. Steele?" he asked.

"Yeah, that's me."

The man grabbed my wrist, and pushed a document into my hand.

"You're served, sir," he said, before quickly leaving.

I examined the document as Hooker looked over my shoulder.

"What is it?" he asked.

I stopped reading, and looked up at the sky for a moment.

"Son-of-a-bitch, Carol just filed for divorce," I said. "There's a court proceeding scheduled for the middle of December in Massachusetts."

"I got blind-sided and now you get firebombed. Well, fuck love and every heart it's ever broken," he said.

I took out my phone and called Trapp. She asked me to read the first page to her.

"Fortunately, I'm free that day," she said.

"What if I don't show up?"

"Then I suggest you hang onto your wallet, J. W. Because Carol may get custody of that, too. She's also c-c-claiming she was the inspiration for some of the songs you wrote so your future as a songwriter is in jeopardy."

"But I don't have anything to get. I can't even pay you."

"Don't worry about that. I'll add it on to what you owe me for r-representing you on the assault charge."

"Wait a minute. Cody and I got that dismissed."

"Then I'll take it out in sexual favors," she said lightly.

* * *

The holiday season arrived. I invited Hooker for Thanksgiving, but he passed. He seemed depressed, but ready to make peace with losing Sylvia. Trapp and I continued working on our act. She had several conversations with Carol's lawyer. Each one seemed to make them dig their heels in deeper. We made plans to go to Boston and appear in court.

The week before the hearing, we got a surprise in the mail. It was the crucial piece of evidence that formed the basis of their most contentious claim that Carol contributed to my song writing.

It was a Valentine's card that I gave her right after we started dating. In it was written, "Our one-night stand could stand a whole lifetime. I love you, J. W."

Trapp said they were arguing that was proof she was my inspiration. I was so pissed off I could barely see. Now I knew why Trapp hated lawyers so much.

I asked Trapp if she sent them a copy of Russ's note to Carol about the ring. She told me she was holding that in reserve until she knew when it would do us the most good.

As soon as I knew the hearing was likely going forward, I called Julie. We agreed to meet for dinner after we got out of court. It gave me a small shot of relief when I thought of Trapp finally getting to meet her and the twins.

* * *

A weather front moved into the East Coast the day before we left. Our flight was cancelled and the first plane available was at seven o'clock the following morning connecting through New York City. The next day, we left Nashville on time and landed at LaGuardia Airport fifteen minutes late, before claiming the last two seats on the shuttle to Boston.

After arriving, we caught a cab and sped through the center of Salem, past the Christmas lights and decorations, before we pulled up in front of an ancient-looking, gray-brick building. The sign read, "Essex County Probate and Family Court."

We entered the crowded courtroom, and walked to an empty table on the right. I looked at the spectator section and saw some familiar faces—my soon-to-be ex-wife, Carol, my ex-boss, Russ Hartley, and Boomer. I pointed them out to Trapp.

"Counsel, was the other party served in this matter?" the judge asked.

A man in a navy suit rose from the table to our left.

"Yes, Your Honor," he answered.

"Have you spoken with Mr. Steele or his counsel?" the judge asked.

"We were told they would both be here today but they are not. The grounds of our complaint are desertion. He abandoned Ms. Steele months ago in a most egregious manner, and moved to Tennessee. If there is any hardship on the defendant, he brought it upon himself. Therefore, I am requesting that the court proceed, as the defendant obviously intends to default, just like he did at the 209A hearing," Mr. Blue-suit replied.

Trapp and I reached the opposite table. Carol's face dropped, and Russ took on a scared look, like I still had him pinned in a throat lock after I caught him and her in bed. Boomer's face became flushed.

"Very sorry to be late, Your Honor. Our plane was delayed. I'm Angela Trappani, attorney for Mr. John W. Steele. I am licensed to practice law in Tennessee and Texas, but not in Massachusetts. I have a certificate of good standing from each of those jurisdictions, and would respectfully request that I be admitted *pro hac vice*," said Trapp.

Darnell examined the certificates handed him by Trapp, then looked at Boomer who shook his head.

"I object, Your Honor," he said after removing his glasses. "My client does not have the obligation to pay for the education of an out-of-state attorney to accommodate Mr. Steele. They had plenty of time to retain local counsel."

"Ms. Trappani, how do you respond?" the judge asked.

"Frankly, Your Honor, I'm puzzled why counsel would object. Mr. Steele has obtained the only attorney he could for these proceedings, and dropped everything to fly fifteen hundred miles to be here today," she said.

Out of the corner of my eye, I saw Carol surveying Trapp with a look of pure hate. My spirits rose as Trapp continued.

"While it's true that I have only been in courtrooms in Texas and Tennessee, I would be flabbergasted to find out that the Commonwealth of Massachusetts would deny a man the right to be represented by counsel of his choosing. I assure this Honorable Court that my education is more than sufficient to allow me to zealously defend my client's case and also pursue the multitude of counterclaims he has regarding the plaintiff's flagrant violations of the law."

"Ms. Trappani, that is a very cogent argument. You are hereby admitted to represent Mr. Steele," the judge agreed.

Trapp was not finished.

"Your Honor, at this time, I am filing a counterclaim on behalf of Mr. Steele against Ms. Carol Steele. Mr. Steele is requesting a divorce from Ms. Steele on the grounds of adultery, desertion and mental cruelty. I will also be seeking a civil complaint in Superior Court, against Mr. Russell Hartley for alienation of affections and criminal conversation. Mr. Steele is claiming that Ms. Steele and Mr. Hartley were lovers, and that Mr. Steele caught them *in flagrante delicto*, which triggered his leaving the marital home."

I looked at Carol and Russ, whose mouths dropped. I reached a feeling of euphoria when I saw that Trapp, like Karen and Richard Carpenter, had only just begun.

"Is there any evidence this alleged adulterous affair occurred behind Mr. Steele's back?" the judge asked.

"We have written evidence of a romantic note from Mr. Hartley accompanying a luxury gift to Mrs. Steele long before the couple separated," Trapp said. Russ's face blanched. "We also intend to reopen the restraining order case because we have evidence Mrs. Steele perjured herself when she sought to have Mr. Steele removed from the marital home."

Carol brought her hand up to her mouth and took a deep breath as Trapp continued.

"Mr. Steele will be seeking an equitable division of the marital assets, and an award of alimony from Ms. Steele, because he is now unemployed. In addition, I will be filing suit against Mr. Steele's father-in-law, Mr. Allister W. Lyle, for defamation, tortious interference with contractual relations, violation of civil-rights, false-light invasion of privacy and intentional infliction of emotional distress, because his actions caused Mr. Steele to lose his job and suffer significant monetary damages. We will be seeking punitive damages on each of these counts, and moving for an attachment of all real and personal property of Mr. Lyle, plus corporate assets."

Boomer's face took on a horrified look as he leaned over and whispered to Carol. Darnell leaped to his feet like he was goosed by a poker covered in hot bacon grease.

"Your Honor, this is an outrage. There is nothing to support these..." he thundered, before being silenced by the judge.

"You'll have the opportunity to respond in time, counsel. Please continue, Ms. Trappani," Judge Tracy said, motioning for Darnell to sit.

Trapp did not miss a beat.

"The reasons behind this cause of action are the unconscionable acts committed by Mr. Lyle, when he contacted Mr. Steele's former employer, and made scurrilously false allegations that defamed Mr. Steele and caused him to lose his job."

Boomer looked at Trapp fearfully as she continued.

"What's particularly outrageous is the way Ms. Steele, Mr. Hartley and Mr. Lyle have caused damage to my client. And may I respectfully suggest to the court, that these things I am alleging were uncovered in a relatively short time of representation. I can't wait to see what I find when I really start digging," she said.

Darnell rose, then sat back down.

"Of course, Your Honor, we are certainly amenable to trying to settle our differences. A compromise, so to speak. May I request that counsel for the plaintiff and I be given some time to see what we can work out?" Trapp asked.

"Mr. Darnell?" the judge said.

Darnell looked at his clients, then cut his losses.

"That's agreeable to us," he replied, moving for an immediate cease-fire on all fronts, at all parallels.

"I'll see all the parties back here at 2:00 p.m. We'll recess for lunch."

Trapp told me to kill some time while she talked to Darnell alone.

After I left the courtroom, I saw Carol, Russ and Boomer standing off to the side. I approached them, and they backed away like I had a bomb strapped to my back and was waving the detonator at them. I didn't care. There were a few questions I needed to ask.

Carol couldn't wait to pounce. "Isn't that little suth-run belle just so precious? She's only been in courtrooms in Texas and Tennessee. Well, shut mah mouth and pass them grits," she hooted.

"She can't help it, she went to Vanderbilt, not Princeton. Isn't that where you learned how to cheat with a married man who buys you a bigger diamond ring than his wife has?" I answered.

Russ started shifting nervously while Carol sizzled. Boomer huffed. I asked Carol to speak with me alone. Finally, she agreed.

"I don't understand what you have to gain from this fight. You wound up with all the money and everything else. Why are you doing this?" I asked.

"Because marrying you was a huge mistake."

"It was a mistake for both of us. Why couldn't we just part without the anger and deceit?" I asked. "Especially with you taking all the money we had saved."

"My lawyer told me to do that," she said.

"How could you dump me for Russ?"

She stopped and looked at me for a moment. "You made me feel like I was second to music," she said.

Neither of us spoke for several seconds.

"I was wrong about you, J. W., and I shouldn't have blamed you for all my problems. I'm going to tell my lawyer to settle this thing. I'm also going to make shuah you get back yoah share of our joint account," she said, before walking away.

I recoiled and watched Carol as she pulled Boomer aside and engaged in a heated debate for several minutes. I looked at her and felt no anger, only confusion, and wondered why she had the change of heart.

Trapp came over and outlined the terms she had proposed to Darnell. I agreed with everything and thought how, after all these years, today was one of the few times Carol and I had a real conversation.

Goodbye Carol. This time I really am out of fuel, I thought.

* * *

At exactly two o'clock, the judge retook the bench.

"I'll hear from counsel for the plaintiff," she began.

Darnell rose."Your Honor, we are willing to amend our complaint to no-fault grounds of irreconcilable differences. The defendant will agree to drop his counterclaim. Mr. Lyle is considering an agreement to pay Mr. Steele a year's severance pay, plus attorneys' fees and expenses to settle the tortious interference and other claims. We also reached an agreement regarding a division of marital assets and future expectations for each party," he said.

"How do you contemplate the division of marital assets?" the judge asked.

"We have proposed a fifty-fifty split of everything the couple acquired during the marriage. Ms. Steele will pay Mr. Steele one-half the value of all the housewares and furnishings that she retained. Neither party will have a claim on any future acquisitions or income of the other. That includes songwriting, performing and related activities by Mr. Steele," Darnell answered.

"You said Mr. Lyle is considering an agreement. Are you saying that he is not in complete agreement with the terms you have proposed, Mr. Darnell?" asked the judge.

"Mr. Lyle has some reservations," Darnell said and looked at Boomer.

"I see. Well, if he is unwilling to agree, that is certainly his choice. All parties are here now and Mr. Steele and his counsel have made every effort to appear and defend. So, if you cannot agree, we will hold a full hearing in two weeks. If that is Mr. Lyle's decision, be advised that I am prepared to order him to pay Mr. Steele's attorney's fees and travel expenses for the next hearing. And, I can promise you, he will not like the results of that proceeding," Judge Tracy said.

I stifled a smile as Darnell turned, looked as the others and held a brief, spirited conversation. Finally, Boomer took on a disgusted look and nodded. Darnell faced the judge.

"My clients are all in full agreement," he said. "We are ready to resolve this right now."

* * *

Trapp and I met Julie and the twins at the duplex before we all went to dinner. We were invited to stay overnight, but our return flight was at 7:00 a.m., so we took a room close to the airport.

Julie and Trapp were an instant hit. The twins were shy at first, then immediately loosened up after they showed Trapp the Yamaha and told her that I bought it for them. Steeler was the biggest hit of the night as the twins talked about the name on my ring. Trapp asked about the ring and I spent an uncomfortable moment telling her about it without disclosing that it was in hock. I vowed to reclaim the ring when I finally got the divorce settlement money from Boomer.

The twins could not wait to perform for us. Trapp and I were blown away at their harmony, as well as how the chords seemed to flow and mesh. When they finished, they handed each of us a guitar and said it was our turn. I gave Trapp the Yamaha and took the older, warped instrument.

'Clouded Soul' was our first song and Trapp told Julie she looked forward to the day they joined us in Nashville. The twins beamed and gave her a hug as Steeler barked and we all belly laughed.

We did four more songs before they let us stop. We told them about opening for Wes McGovern in Houston and invited them to come as our special guests.

Dinner turned into a full-blown party. Trapp and Julie seemed to connect like sisters. As we were leaving, she pulled Julie aside and engaged her in a long conversation. Since I wasn't invited, I corralled the twins and talked to them. Afterward, we all said goodbye before Trapp and I piled into a cab.

"Julie and the twins are everything you said they were, and more," she said.

"Those two are really talented," I said.

"What's the deal on your r-ring?" she asked.

I told her the story but said I'd misplaced it. She pressed a little but I changed the subject. She gave me a long look that said she was not fooled.

"What did you and Julie talk about?" I asked.

"How you were such a great influence on the twins. And, some girl talk," she said.

"We were never involved, you know," I said, wondering why I had the need to defend myself.

"I know. We just t-talked about your friendship. She also told me your lonely side seems tucked away and it was p-probably because of me. I was really flattered."

          * * *

We were headed home from the airport when music from the radio began to play softly.

"There's a place down in Printer's Alley that..." I started to say, when she stopped me with a furious shout.

"J. W., listen. Quick! Listen!"

"*You never said we had forever, when you put your hand in mine, Memories will comfort till they fade; So if your mind is aching, from the strain of your heart breaking, Love's a promise that starts dying when it's made,*" sang a man's voice from the radio, before the song finished.

The announcer broke in when it was over, as my skin began to tingle while my mind raced like it was under contract to NASCAR.

"Yessir, all you Wes McGovern fans, that was the ol' songbird himself, with a tune that was jus' cut last night. We sent our own Dan Wayland out to talk with Wes, and here's a part of that conversation," the announcer said.

"So Wes, you're gonna start tourin' again real soon, right?" another radio voice asked.

"Ah shore am, Dan. We'll be startin' off in Houston in a few weeks," Wes said.

My mind began processing a wild, kaleidoscopic spectrum of thoughts. I was too nervous to look at Trapp. Out of the corner of my eye, I saw her staring straight ahead, her lower lip dropped almost to her chest.

"Tell us about this new song you just released, 'The Promise of A Lie.' Did you write it?" Dan asked.

"Naw, that was written by a couple of young'uns I just met. A fine-lookin' lady named Angela Trappani, and her collaborator, J. W. Steele."

I felt the hairs on the back of my neck begin to pinch like small gauge needles.

"You must have a lot of faith in the song if you released it before your tour," Dan observed.

"Ah shorely do. Ah think these two have a wonderful future ahead of them, and I look forward to maybe kickin' around a few ideas of mine with them," Wes replied.

"We'll look forward to that, too. From the lobby of the Opryland Hotel, this is Dan Wayland. Back to you in the studio."

Trapp looked up. She had streamers of tears running down her cheeks.

"J. W., this is the happiest m-moment in my entire life," she shouted.

"Welcome to Vinita. Population six thousand five hundred and sixty-six," I answered.

For the first time since my mother died, I shed some tears myself. Instead of the usual pain-inspired flavor, these tasted sweet and cool, like the unbeatable combination of love and success.

"I'm glad I'm here to share it with you," she said, holding me tightly.

CHAPTER TWELVE

Christmas Day arrived. Trapp and I invited Hooker but he went to visit a friend in New Orleans. The phone rang after dinner. Trapp spent several minutes listening. At one point, her entire body stiffened as she carried on a short dialogue before issuing a terse 'Merry Christmas'.

"That was my mother. She put my d-dad on the phone at the end. We didn't exactly reconcile but he did say he missed me," she said.

"What did you tell him?" I asked.

"The only thing I could think of without b-being pissed. I wished him a happy holiday."

"Why didn't you tell them we're coming to Houston?"

She looked at me with her eyes blazing. I sensed I had gone too far.

"That's not the same as a recording c-c-contract," she said, as her scowl told me to let it drop. I watched her fidget and could have sworn her eyes became cloudy. For a moment, I almost envied her. I had no family to call on Christmas since my grandmother died three years ago.

* * *

Our act peaked right after New Year's Day, a week before the shows were scheduled to go on. We arrived in Houston on January ninth. After we unpacked, we had a long drink with Wes. He said if people liked us, he would book us as the opening act for the rest of the tour.

The next morning, we ate a light breakfast, rehearsed for an hour and tweaked an arrangement. Just before three, Trapp said she was ready, and wanted to take a short walk alone to clear her thoughts. We agreed to leave for the concert at five-thirty.

After setting up our equipment and rehearsing our numbers one final time, Trapp said she was satisfied that things were as close to perfect as they would get. I sneaked out and peeked through the curtain to watch the crowd filing into their seats. Trapp was sitting in front of a mirror, humming and singing our tunes softly, while finishing her makeup, as I returned and retuned my Martin for the thousandth time.

"You're gonna knock 'em dead," I said.

"You mean we're gonna knock 'em dead," she said, as I shook my head from side to side.

"You're Wynonna, I'm Naomi. This act could fly without me, but it would fold without you."

She looked over at me and beamed before returning to her eyeliner brush.

"Not if you keep putting words in my mouth. We've w-written some quality tunes, J. W. Everybody says so. And I'm talking about A & R guys and producers. If we do well on the tour, we have a chance of getting a recording contract."

There was a knock at the door.

"Come in," we both called.

A stage hand, dressed in cutoffs and a tee-shirt, entered carrying a huge bouquet of balloons and a dozen red roses. The balloons were from Julie and the twins, who were absent because of final exams. The caption read: *'Congratulations and break some hearts, not legs,'* and a stuffed puppy, a dead ringer for Steeler, was attached.

The roses were from Hooker, who called us his only famous friends and best drinking partners. Trapp reached up to dab at her eyes and my emotions were ready to boil over. We continued to admire our gifts when the stage hand returned a moment later.

"Ms. Trappani, there's someone here to see you," he said.

"Who?"

"He didn't say. He said it wouldn't take long, and it was very important."

"Maybe it's someone from a record company," I told her, as my whole body stiffened.

"OK, s-send him in," she replied.

A moment passed before a short, distinguished-looking gentleman in a dark, expensive-looking pinstriped suit, entered. He had a head full of silvery-dusted hair, a deep tan, a lean, sinewy build and a sad smile. He carried a huge bouquet of white roses.

Trapp looked at him for a few seconds, before dropping her eyebrow pencil and bringing her hands up to her face. Tears began to fall, causing her mascara to run. She rose and ran toward the man. They embraced tightly, and he reached up to brush away a year from his left eye.

"Hello, D-D-Daddy," she said.

"Hi, Angie. Welcome back to Houston."

"What are you doing here?"

"Well, I came to offer my services in case you need a lawyer."

"Thank God you didn't come because you n-need my services as a lawyer."

"I'd rather have your services as my daughter," he said, and I felt my throat trying to process the football that a huge linebacker seemed to be stuffing into my esophagus.

"Where's M-M-Mama?" she asked, drying her eyes.

"In her seat. She said it was bad luck to see you before you performed."

They continued to embrace, as I remained standing.

"Daddy, I w-want you to meet someone," said Trapp, clasping his hand and leading him over to me.

"J. W. Steele. Patriots' gunner and quarterback. Songwriter. Suitor. The man who called my office and told me that you two were coming. I'm Joe Trappani."

He extended his hand toward me, as Trapp gave me a look that said she disapproved of my interference in her family business. I couldn't tell if she was aggravated at me or not, but presumed that I would suffer her wrath later, even though I was convinced I did the right thing.

"Pleased to meet you, sir," I said, shaking his hand.

"I can't thank you enough for calling," he said sincerely, gripping my hand tightly while shaking it firmly.

"You sounded like you were reading from an investigator's report about J. W.," said Trapp.

"Do you really think I abandoned you? Forgive me, but you know how hardheaded we Sicilians are. Naturally, I asked some people in Nashville to keep an eye on you to make sure you were safe—not to invade your privacy, but only to know you were all right."

She tried to feign outrage, but wound up smiling instead. "I s-s-should have known," she said.

"I'm very proud of you, Angie. In fact, I'm proud of both of you," he said.

"That's quite a vote of confidence, sir. Especially since you don't even know me," I answered.

"I know you care for Angie. And you treat her with respect. You respected me enough to let me know my daughter was here, without telling me what a fool I was. Now, I'm going out front with your mother. If she saw us together, she'd get so mushy, we would have to bring in the flood control people." He hugged Trapp and shook my hand again.

"T-T-Thanks, Daddy. I love you," she said.

"It takes a lot for me to admit I was wrong, Angie. But this time, I was wrong."

I turned to her when we were alone, as she sat at the table and quickly redid her makeup.

"I'm sorry, but when he called on Christmas, I saw how much it affected you. I figured I would let him know you were here and he could decide if he wanted to see you," I said.

She nodded and wiped her eyes.

"Are you mad at me for sticking my nose in?" I asked.

"I should be," she answered. "Why did you do it?"

"I thought of an old proverb that sealed the deal, 'It's better to seek forgiveness than ask permission.' This is a once in a lifetime event. Somehow, I didn't want you to go through life kicking yourself because you didn't invite your parents tonight."

She watched me carefully as her eyes began to show a look of peace.

"I know what it's like to lose a father. Mine can never come back, but yours is still here. That's why I interfered, because of that old Kristofferson song about how I'd rather be sorry for something I've done instead of something I didn't do," I said.

She looked at me for a long moment. I felt myself letting my feelings go. This time, I had no control and knew that for the first time, I was falling head over heels in love with a woman who had also turned into my best friend. She was Erica and Julie fused together, with a dash of the best qualities of Ann, Melissa Sue and even Carol added for good measure.

"Even if I were mad, I'd have to get over it, because you were right. If I let this night get away after everything I d-did to get here, I would have never forgiven myself."

She stopped and chuckled.

"Speaking of proverbs, you f-forgot the one that says, 'The only way to cure one stubborn Sicilian is to make her r-r-reconcile with another stubborn Sicilian.'"

The stagehand knocked again, then stuck his head inside the door. "Five minutes, you all."

I held out my hand. Trapp took it. Together, we exited the room, guitars in hand and walked to the stage.

"Houston, I'm thrilled to say we don't have a problem," I told her giddily.

"Thank God I get to sing. Now, I'll s-stop s-stuttering," she said.

I looked at her and saw her satisfied grin. Our time came as the announcer spoke.

"Good evening, ladies and gentlemen, cowboys and cowgirls. Hidy to you all, and welcome to the show. We're gonna start off with a hot new duet that will soon be making the rounds. So, put your hands together now for Steele Trapp Mind."

The band began to play as we walked onto the stage. The applause, camera shots and bright lights were like a mainline injection of several hundred cc's of calming, frenzied euphoria. After a few moments, the band broke into the beginning of our first song.

I tried to stop shivering from sheer joy, without success, as I stood there looking at the crowd. The floor under my feet felt wobbly, as though it was about to collapse. At once, I realized it was only my legs struggling to stay steady, just like the times I stood on the forty-yard line, waiting for an opening kickoff in front of a hundred thousand fans and a national television audience.

For my entire life, I wondered if this day would ever come. Now that it had, I tried to compare it to the way I had imagined it would unfold. My imagination told me I would be nervous and scared but, instead, I was shocked to feel a soothing gentleness, like there were no more battles to fight, no more wars to win.

I looked at Trapp. She glanced back, and I saw a look on her face that told me she was feeling the same emotions that had captured me. It was a moment of symbiotic fusion, one that could never be shared by anyone else, only the two of us.

"On behalf of Patty Loveless, I'd like to welcome us both to heaven," I said to Trapp.

"A suburb of Vinita," she whispered, her eyes glistening.

She turned back to the audience and put her guitar in position, before strumming and beginning to sing in her magnificently soothing voice. I played my Martin in time with the band and waited to join in on the harmony.

I was surprised that my mind was suddenly filled with thoughts about my parents. Before my part in the song came up, I looked out into the sea of dimmed lights and saw music at the back of the arena. It stood next to my father, who had one arm around my mother. They were all grinning like proud family members watching a problem child making a debut in a recital. Music's face was beaming broadly and it was nudging my dad while sending me a huge wink, as he gave me the thumbs-up sign.

Suddenly, my entire high school assembly appeared, stood and cheered as I saw my old coach and the judge saluting me and smiling. A vision of Ann, Melissa Sue, Julie and Erica appeared in my mind, and they were all clapping wildly.

"Welcome to the club," music whispered, as everyone else beamed. "We've been waiting for you."

* * *

After the show, Trapp's parents invited us to dinner. A limousine took us all to a four-star seafood grill and steakhouse.

Despite the reunion between Trapp and her father, a slight tension was present as dinner began. Everyone was on their best behavior, but it seemed like we could all use a drink. The captain came to the rescue with two bottles of wine, one white and one red.

Her parents insisted that I call them Joe and Marion. I needed time to adjust to that level of informality and being with potential in-laws, especially a father in a twenty-five hundred dollar *Canali* suit, and a mother with enough jewels to open an outlet store for Tiffany's. They seemed like wonderful people, the kind I used to meet when I was a semi-celebrity, but continents away from my current usual crowd consisting of diverse variations of Burl Sawyers and Hookers.

"That was the best concert I've ever seen," said Joe.

"The opening act is what carried the show," added Marion.

"After that standing ovation they gave the two of you, Wes McGovern must be patting himself on the back," said Joe, grinning at both of us.

We all took a minute to settle down. Trapp sipped her wine faster than usual.

"So," began Mrs. Trappani, "Tell us how you met."

"I was performing in a dive, and J. W. helped me out of a j-j-jam," said Trapp, giggling.

"Actually, she didn't need my help. She basically told me to leave her alone," I amended.

"I'm glad you helped," said Joe. "Or this night may not have happened."

"How's the p-p-practice, Daddy?" asked Trapp, with a slight quiver.

"The same. Still no shortage of criminals or people who want to sue each other."

"When do you have to go back to Nashville?" asked Marion.

"We have a show t-t-tomorrow night and leave the day after," said Trapp.

I desperately wanted to enter the conversation but was still struggling with addressing them as Joe and Marion. Finally, I decided to test the waters with a simple request.

"Excuse me, Joe, but I'm not a wine drinker. Would you mind if I ordered a Pearl?"

"That might be a problem," he replied, signaling the waiter. "The brewery closed a few years ago or I would have joined you."

We ordered two Coors and I could feel the tension ease as everyone started to relax and enjoy the party. Soon, Trapp and Joe were swapping stories that had us laughing out loud.

"Remember when we were in the elevator at the c-courthouse?" she asked, as Joe nodded.

"Yeah, it was filled with lawyers and I said I locked my keys in the car," Joe started.

"And this old guy in the back barked out, 'Don't worry, I've got some clients who can get them out for you b-before you know they were inside,'" Trapp said.

"Or the time my defendant didn't show up for a hearing and the judge said, 'Mr. Trappani, I'm going to issue a warrant for your client's arrest,'" said Joe.

"And you said, 'Your Honor, my client is a schizophrenic with dual personalities.' And the judge replied, 'In that case, I'll issue t-two warrants'," said Trapp.

"Nothing could top that divorce case with the two eighty-five-year-olds who were married for over sixty-five years and told the judge they had been miserable for a long time," said Joe.

"The judge asked them why they w-waited so long to split up if they weren't happy and the wife said, 'we wanted to wait until the k-kids were dead'," Trapp said.

Joe loosened the knot on his *Ermenegildo Zegna* tie and Marion removed the diamond earrings that were so big, Harry Winston must have delivered them in a wheelbarrow. Before dessert came, Trapp and Marion went to the ladies' room. When they were out of earshot, Joe turned to me, raised his beer bottle and saluted. "I'm going to invite you both to lunch. I have a present for each of you. So, back me up in case Angie doesn't want to come," he said, as the women returned.

After dinner, we had a final drink in the lounge. Trapp sat next to Joe and I sensed that a cease-fire was in place and the cannons were headed for storage.

"Will you come back soon?" asked Joe.

"We'll be back and s-stay for a while next time," said Trapp.

I exhaled slowly and celebrated in silence.

"Why don't we meet for lunch tomorrow? I'm in court in the morning but should be back by twelve-thirty," said Joe.

Trapp and I exchanged glances. I was thrilled when she nodded along with me.

"Why don't I pick you up at eleven o'clock? We can give J. W. a tour of your past life," said Marion.

"C'mon, Mom, that will be a r-r-real snore," said Trapp.

"No, I'd love to see it all," I said, as Marion nodded.

CHAPTER THIRTEEN

Trapp's phone rang shortly after eight-thirty the next morning. Her end of the conversation consisted of mostly nods, thank yous and okays, before the call ended.

"Who was that?" I asked.

"Wes McGovern. He said we did a w-wonderful job last night and invited me for coffee this morning."

"What time do we meet?" I asked.

"He asked if I would m-meet him alone."

"Are you afraid about going?"

"No. We're meeting in the coffee shop. I would be on g-guard if he asked me to come to his room."

I grew uneasy. She seemed to sense it.

"I don't think it's sex he's after. Wes might be able to out-drink me, but I don't think he's the type that wants to b-bang me on top of the omelet station," she said.

After Trapp left, I called Hooker. I needed to share the wonderment of last night. After nine rings, I was ready to hang up, when he answered.

"Hey man, are you still alive?" I asked.

There was no answer. I kept asking questions and assumed the call was dropped so I called back. He answered on the fourth ring.

"Hooker, are you there? Can you hear me?"

After a long pause, he responded.

"Zat you, J. W.?"

"Hey, man, have you had a few already?'

"Yeah, and I'm about to have a few more. Sylvia left last week."

"I've seen you handle tougher times. Don't let this get you down," I said.

No answer. I tried again.

"Hooker, I won't give you any bullshit about how you have to stay strong and move on. But, I promise you, nothing lasts forever."

"I can't get over the fact that I let her go. The first woman who ever broke my heart," he said.

"Things were stacked against you from the beginning. There was the age difference. She detested Nashville. Maybe the things she hated were a lot stronger than her love for you."

"How did you get to be such a goddamned expert?"

"I'm not. I'm just a poor ol' country songwriter."

"Yeah, well fuck music and every life it's ever ruined."

"I'll be back tomorrow. Go easy on the sauce. That stuff won't help, you know."

"Yeah, okay," he whispered before the line went dead.

* * *

It was almost eleven o'clock, when Trapp returned.

"There's no easy way to say this. Wes offered me a permanent spot with his b-band as the lead female singer."

"Great," I said. "We can open the show and you can close it."

She looked at me for a long while. "You don't understand. They only want m-m-me, not you. We won't be opening after tonight."

It felt like a screwdriver was being plunged into my flesh. We both knew what the next question was that neither of us wanted to answer. "What did you tell him?" I asked, my voice breaking despite every effort to keep it stable.

"I said I had to t-t-talk to you," she said. Trapp sat on the couch and stared straight ahead. I pulled up a chair opposite her.

"What happens to us if you turn him down and leave?" I asked.

"He said we won't be his opening act any more. We both knew this is one of the risks of being p-p-p-partners. I won't give you that fairy-tale nonsense about how if it were you, I'd s-s-step aside and wish you the best."

Suddenly, a feeling of frustration appeared. "If you go, it will be your choice. Don't ask for my blessing so you can leave with a clear conscience," I said.

Her eyes flashed as she stared at me.

"This has nothing to do with p-p-power-washing my conscience," she shot back. "It's not like I'm dumping you and r-r-r-riding off with Wes. I wish you were going with me, but the plain truth is, that's not p-p-part of the deal." Then, as the lawyers say, the burden of proof shifted to me. "Tell me what's in your heart, J. W.," she said.

"Why am I out?"

"Wes said he doesn't have a spot for you."

"Do you believe that?"

"I don't know. Maybe he w-w-wants to get rid of you so he can try to get in my pants."

"Did he say I'm not good enough?"

"Not in so many words."

"What does that mean?"

"He said you were g-g-good but not memorable."

"What did he say about you?"

"He said I was unique."

I started to get pissed. I was on the verge of losing Trapp as well as my shot at making it big.

"So it's time for you to move on with him as your unique partner, right?"

"That's not f-f-fair."

"Fair can kiss my ass. I guess I could start emailing Pete Best now, because I know he's not unique either."

"Who's Pete Best?" she asked, looking puzzled.

"The drummer Ringo Starr replaced right before the Beatles came to America. He wound up loading loaves of bread onto trucks and then became a civil servant."

She stayed silent.

"Are you basing your decision to leave on how I react?" I asked.

"In part, yes."

"Why?"

"First of all, I won't believe you if you t-t-tell me you'll go to pieces if I leave. I love you, J. W., but I won't stay because of that either."

"You know if you leave, it's over between us."

"Why?"

"Because we won't be together. Like Kristofferson said, 'You'll find yourself another.'"

"He also said 'But I'll be r-r-right here if you need me.'"

"Only lyrics, not reality," I said.

"We could still write together," she said.

"How, by email or Twitter?"

She stared at me. Her eyes began to glisten as a tear slowly trickled down her cheek. "Whatever h-h-happens, I love you," she said.

I shook my head. "Love's a promise that starts dying when it's made," I said.

I began to pace while she sat on the sofa.

Her phone rang. "It's my m-m-mother," she told me. She said Marion was downstairs waiting.

I walked over and took her in my arms. "Just think of me and you'll stay steady and cool," I said. "We need to put this problem on hold."

* * *

Shortly before noon, we went on a tour of Houston and saw all the landmarks. Afterward, we went to Joe's office. I was overwhelmed at the artifacts that covered the walls. To the right of his massive desk, there were pictures on the wall of famous sports stars. I saw Joe between Bum Phillips, ex-coach of the former Houston Oilers, running back Earl Campbell and quarterback Warren Moon. Another showed Joe flanked by Rockets stars Clyde Drexler and Hakeem Olajuwon. In another, he stood between Nolan Ryan and Tom Seaver at the All-Star game. There must have been over sixty pictures and all were inscribed.

I was mesmerized by the last picture on the bottom. It was over forty years old and showed a much younger Ace Evans, in his Dallas Cowboy's jersey, while receiving his All-Pro award from Coach Tom Landry. I furiously motioned to Trapp.

"Why didn't you tell me about Ace's picture on the wall?" I asked excitedly, as she gasped.

"I never paid attention to that wall. Most of those guys p-played before I was even born so I never heard of them. I only remembered my dad talking about Ace."

On the opposite wall, there was a group of inscribed photographs of country music stars. Reba McIntyre and Tricia Yearwood were in the middle, flanked by Larry Gatlin and the Gatlin Brothers. Garth Brooks, George Strait, Kenny Chesney and Patty Loveless were on the opposite side. Among the others were Brad Paisley, Miranda Lambert and Brooks and Dunn.

"I didn't know Joe was such a country music fan," I whispered.

"He is, as long as I'm not the one singing," she replied, shrugging.

Behind the desk were citations for being a distinguished alumnus from the University of Texas, recognition as a past president of the Houston Bar Association and numerous awards from various defender organizations. At that moment, Joe arrived. He was carrying two packages that were covered by bubble wrap. He smiled at us, kissed Marion and Trapp, then shook my hand.

"Joe, do you know Ace Evans?" I asked.

"I met him years ago when I first started," he said.

I looked at Trapp and we both laughed.

"Dad, Ace is one of our attorneys. He helped put this d-d-deal together with Wes McGovern."

"Really? I didn't know he became a lawyer. I'll look forward to seeing him again," said Joe.

"What's in the packages?" asked Trapp.

"The two greatest additions to my walls. Fortunately, I have a photographer for a client and he owes me a favor or two. I had him take this one at the concert and get it ready this morning."

He unrolled the bubble wrap. Inside was a photograph of Trapp and me, onstage last night after we finished our set and were waving to the audience. It was so real it made you feel like you were there, waiting for the encores to begin. My body began to tremble ever so slightly.

Trapp brought her hands up to her face and I saw her eyes moisten.

"This is the best way I could think of to show you I was wrong, Angie. I'm really proud of both of you," he said, as they embraced before she pulled out a tissue.

"What about the other picture?" asked Trapp.

"Well, I had this one made a while back. I didn't know if I would ever get a chance to hang it. I had to see if you two were serious first. It looks like I finally can put it up, especially after I saw you both on stage last night," he said.

He unveiled a photograph of me, in my Patriots uniform. I was floored.

"I'm putting the picture of the two of you right in the center, between Reba and Tricia. I had your picture made a little larger so it would stand out," said Joe, slipping his arm around Marion.

We stared at the picture for a long moment. Our eyes kept darting from the other photos back to ours and I felt like I was going to explode. Joe said his client was sending us our own copies and also told me my football photo was going on the wall next to Ace.

"I hope you don't mind," said Joe.

I felt a surge of pride. "I just hope Ace doesn't mind," I said.

* * *

After lunch, Trapp and I invited Joe and Marion to that night's show, but he was a keynote speaker at a dinner and they were unavailable. We said our goodbyes and went back to the room.

"That's a side of my father I've rarely seen," she began.

"It shows how much he loves you."

"I feel awful over some of the things I said to him. Remember when I t-told you about the huge fight we had?"

I nodded.

"He asked me to reconsider joining him and I said, as sarcastically as I could, 'Dad, trying my best to get Hitler clones community service and p-probation, will never come close to having a guitar in my hand.' I knew that would hurt him deeply but I was really pissed."

"We all say things we regret."

"I know, but it was his skill as a lawyer that made all the best things in my life possible. My father's a legend in the defense bar. He never loses. He's so good, his fee for defending a first degree murder case is everything you own," she said.

I almost had to catch my jaw as it dropped. "How can he do that?"

"Simple. He tells the client if he wants to get acquitted, it's worth it."

"What if they ask about being convicted?"

She grinned. "Then he tells them where they're going, they will have no need for their worldly possessions."

I silently gave thanks that I had never plugged anyone, even Russ, Carol or Boomer.

"Joe is a really good man. Those photographs he had made have to tell you that," I said.

"I know. But the message I got was singers made people feel g-good and lawyers caused pain."

"Maybe it's the system, not your father."

"I guess I'm starting to understand why he's like he is. He always said the prosecution tries to convict no matter what the evidence is. Doesn't the guy in the street deserve the same treatment?"

She told me that picture of us was incredible. It was also a panacea. "Every time I get uptight in front of my father, I'll think of that photograph of us hanging on his wall. I think my speech problems might totally be cured someday."

* * *

When we took the stage that night, I knew this could be the last time Trapp and I performed together for a while, maybe even forever. I added some extra zing to my playing and singing. When we finished, the crowd was on its feet. They called us back for two encores. The second time, I clasped her hand in mine. "Go ahead and try this with Wes," I told her. "You'll have to fight to get him to drop the Jim Beam bottle so you can hold his hand."

She gave me a slight kick with her right boot. I took that as a sign of acknowledgement.

We went for a seafood dinner. Conversation was light as each one of us tried to avoid the decision. Finally, I could wait no longer. "It's almost crunch time. Have you decided?" I asked.

"Not yet," she answered. "I'll call him in about an hour after he finishes his show."

"Are you going to share it with me first?"

"As soon as I figure it out."

We went back to the room. Conversation was stalled as she got up and headed for the door.

"This is the biggest decision in my life. I have to take a walk and try to figure it out," she said.

She was gone for half an hour. The moment of destiny arrived. I felt myself stiffen and also felt annoyed at Wes for putting us in this position. She looked deeply into my eyes. At once, my anger softened.

"I have to do this. It's the b-break of a lifetime," she said.

I pulled myself together before I answered. "I know. There's no other choice," I said.

She nodded and dialed Wes's number. "Wes," she began, "I've made a decision." She looked at me, smiled, and blew me a kiss. I waited for the lightning bolt to tear through my soul, as she took a deep breath. "Thanks for the offer, but I want to stay with J. W. and be part of Steele Trapp Mind," she said, as a look of comfort and contentment spread over her face.

When she finished, I took her in my arms. "Why did you turn it down?"

"Because all those arguments I gave you fell f-f-flat. I couldn't imagine leaving you. That would have been the end of us," she said. She stopped for a moment and locked her fingers onto mine. "I couldn't let myself do t-this again like I did to J-Jay," she whispered.

I glanced into her eyes and saw she was still mine. Like all of the greatest love stories, she gave up everything for me. "We'll get another chance, I promise," I said.

She gave me a look like she just lost a recording contract. "I doubt it. I think I'm fresh out of d-depositions," she replied.

CHAPTER FOURTEEN

I was wide awake at 6:00 a.m., when the sound of Trapp's phone startled us. She got out of bed and began to pace around the room. Over and over, in a voice shrouded in panic, she kept repeating the word "no." Her call lasted for over an hour. Her last words were, "We'll b-b-be there as soon as we get our things together."

"We have to check out as soon as possible. My father has a c-c-crisis," she began.

"Is he sick?"

"Worse. A huge s-s-scandal is erupting. My Uncle Jack is married to my father's sister and has been the family stockbroker for years. The police found him south of the city where he crashed his car into a t-t-tree. He had a loaded g-g-gun in his mouth and an empty bottle of whiskey on the passenger seat. They stopped him before he could pull the trigger."

"Where is he now?" I asked.

"Hospitalized. He left a trash bag full of documents outside my father's office. There was a n-n-n-note inside the bag where Jack confessed that he was bilking his clients for years. He was f-f-forging signatures on transfer orders and s-s-stealing money."

"Does he want your father to defend him?" I asked.

She burst into tears and shook her head.

"Not this time. Dad was one of his b-b-biggest victims. That dirty sonofabitch stole all of my father's money. My family is r-r-r-ruined," she said as I held her close.

"Let's get a cab. You just concentrate on helping your father."

* * *

Half an hour later, we checked out and headed north.

"What do you plan to do?" I asked, as we pulled away from the hotel.

"I've got to stay here for now. I have to take over for my f-f-father so he can investigate."

"Do you want me to stay with you?"

"I have too much to do that can't involve you. Attorney-client privilege and all that. I have to see what the m-m-monetary picture is and find out what court cases are pending. I will be w-w-working eighteen to twenty hour days for quite a while."

"What should I do?" I asked.

"Go back to Nashville. I'll be h-h-home as soon as I can."

"Should I wait until tomorrow?" I asked.

She shook her head. "No. I don't mean to be cruel, but I need to s-s-spend all my time with my mother and father."

"I'll see if I can get a later flight today," I said.

We rode for almost forty-five minutes before we arrived at the house. While I certainly did not expect them to live in a modest one-bedroom bungalow, I was not quite prepared for what I saw.

The house was set on what seemed like twenty-five million acres. At the end of the driveway was a massive Georgian Colonial, with enormous white columns, situated at the apex of a cobblestone boundary. The grounds were so massive, it seemed like it was a two-day ride to the pool.

Joe and Marion came out to greet us and we went into the breakfast area for coffee. After a few moments of forced small talk, Joe and Trapp went into his private office while Marion and I tried to make conversation.

"I'm sure Angela told you about our situation," she began tentatively.

"She told me a little about Jack," I replied.

"Joe is crushed. He and Jack were as close as brothers."

"Do you know what happened?" I asked.

"Jack called in the middle of the night, sobbing about what he'd done. He talked about huge gambling losses and the papers he left outside Joe's office. He threatened to take his own life and hung up. Joe called the police, then went to the office. He started to review the records Jack left and then realized they were evidence he had to preserve."

"When did Jack call?"

"About four o'clock this morning. Joe's first thought was that Jack needed a lawyer. He was going to find him when the police said Jack was taken to the hospital."

A moment later, Trapp and Joe emerged.

"We have a plan in place," said Trapp. "I'm g-g-going to stick around and help Dad."

"I'm sorry we can't spend some time together, J. W.," said Joe. "But, Angie and I have our work cut out for us for quite some time."

I got a seat on the 7:00 p.m. flight. The airline said I could try to go standby at two-thirty. I decided to gamble and ordered a ride to pick me up at eleven o'clock.

Everyone embraced me when the car arrived. Joe and Trapp were dealing with this event with typical lawyer-like stoicism. Through the back window, I saw all of them standing side-by-side with their arms around each other and continued watching them as the car started down the driveway. I had a sinking feeling, as though my life with Trapp was going to change for a long time.

* * *

When I landed, Hooker was not there to pick me up. After several unanswered calls, I gave up and took a taxi to Trapp's place. After texting Trapp that I was home, I toppled into bed and slept for twelve hours straight.

In the morning, I called Hooker but kept getting his voice mail. I had a quick breakfast, then headed for the post office to get our mail. There were two surprises. The first was from the record company and contained my first royalty check in the amount of three hundred and sixty-four dollars. My hands shook as I stared at it, and then I pumped my fist into the air and vowed to have its image turned into a poster for the wall.

The second letter was addressed to Trapp and me from Dan Wayland, the reporter who broke the story of Wes McGovern's comeback. I smiled as I read.

Dear Ms. Trappani and Mr. Steele:
Congratulations on your association with Wes McGovern. The songs you wrote are truly outstanding. I am managing a new band that needs help with songwriting. Please call me at 555-6452 to discuss a meeting.
Best, Dan

* * *

Another call yielded no answer from Hooker, so I decided to drop by his apartment. Knocking failed to get a response from him, so I used my key. What I found scared me.

The apartment was in shambles. Empty liquor and beer bottles covered the floor. Dishes were piled in the sink. Several pizza boxes containing scraps of crusts and tomato stains, littered the countertop. The kitchen smelled like a musty campsite and looked like a tornado tore through it.

I found him in the bedroom, face down on the floor, lying next to a puddle of vomit. I covered my mouth and nose, then went through a series of dry heaves, before I stabilized. I felt like a cop escorting a prisoner into the drunk tank.

It took several attempts, but I finally got him awake. Trying to get him up and off the floor was the next challenge. Because of Hooker's size, I almost needed a backhoe to move him. I prodded and probed his body until he responded and half-stumbled, half-crawled, into the bathroom. It took a series of tries before I was able to get his head over the commode right before another wave splattered into the toilet.

"Son-of-a-bitch," I muttered. "There's a country song hiding somewhere in this experience. I just need a rhyme for puke."

Ridiculous song titles about multi-diverse topics began to flash through my mind as a way to deal with the mess and odor. After pinching my nose with my left thumb and index finger, while steadying him by holding the nape of his neck with my right, I began to create memorable names for tunes that were sure to be immortal.

'I'm So Drunk I Pissed In Someone Else's Pants,' 'The Kindness of Strangers Led Me To A Week on Penicillin,' and 'I Wanted a Girl, Just Like the Girl That Married Dear Old Dad, Till I Saw What Dad Had On the Side,' were the finalists.

Finally, with one hand covering my nose, I pulled him back and let him pass out on the bathroom floor. Then I dragged him by the feet into the bedroom and left him in a heap.

I went out for food and cleaning supplies, knowing there was a long day ahead of me. I returned an hour later and could hear Hooker moaning in the bedroom.

"J. W., is that you?" he wailed.

"Yeah, it's me. Now tell me who the hell you are."

"I'm in a world of shit, man. I don't know what to do."

"Well, to quote Don Corleone, you can act like a man!" I screamed.

"I know," he said meekly. "Give me a little time and I'll get up."

"Take all the time you want. I'll pick up the trash and clean the kitchen, but I draw the line at puke. That will be waiting for you no matter how long it takes."

* * *

An hour later, I managed to clear places to sit at the kitchen table after removing three huge bags of trash. The kitchen was on the verge of being transformed from squalor to sterile. Hooker stumbled out of the bedroom in shorts and a tee shirt.

"You're not getting any coffee or food until you clean. I don't want you throwing up again," I said.

Without a word, he ambled toward the bathroom. I could hear him gagging as he tried to force his body to greet the day. Twenty minutes later, he emerged and sheepishly asked for coffee. While it was brewing, he sat at the kitchen table and held his head in his hands.

"OK, what's up with you?" I began.

No response.

"Hooker, I'm not gonna play twenty questions. Either level with me, or figure this shit out by yourself."

He looked up and I was astonished at his face. Deep, corrugated creases surrounded his nose and eyes. His teeth looked like old Life Saver Peppermints that turned the color of stained porcelain. His eyes were red and swollen and reminded me of two mushrooms that just released their liquid.

"I can't get over the fact that Sylvia's gone," he said finally. "We were together for over two months and she just up and dumped me. I've been out of control and even got drunk and called her at 3:00 a.m. once. What a stupid mistake."

"You have to find some kind of coping mechanism," I said. "Some way to get through this until the torture starts to ease. That's why I use music."

"What good is that?"

"Why do you think country songs tear your heart out, send it through a wood chipper, and then put it back together?"

He got up and walked unsteadily toward the coffee pot. He started asking questions when he returned, a sign that I found encouraging.

"What does music have to do with it?"

"It's an ointment to put on the wounds and help in the healing. Finding people to help you deal with the turmoil of life is how we survive. It's rare that we find someone who will stick with us forever and until you do, you can use music as a plasma to hold your mind together."

"I thought love was the answer to every problem," he said, as he rubbed his eyes.

"Love is just a vaccine that wears off unless you get a booster shot. Poets also tell us we have to love ourselves before we let someone else in."

He stared for a moment.

"How can country music fix this?"

"It lets you deal with it while having a few drinks with your barroom pals and a sympathetic jukebox, instead of a large caliber, semi-automatic pistol."

He got up, than plopped back down. Equilibrium had not yet made a full commitment to the rest of his body. I had one more teaching point.

"There is one song that's in a class by itself," I told him.

"Which one?"

"The old Garth Brooks hit, 'The Dance,' written by Tony Arata. "It's about a guy who lost the love of his life. One day, they were in paradise; the next day she was gone. So he wallows for a while before it hits him."

He looked at me through red, tear-stained eyes and asked, "What?"

"He talks about a dance they shared. That's a metaphor for their relationship, symbolizing a life together that finally ended. He realized that he could have avoided all the torment, but the price was too high."

"What do you mean?"

"He would have to skip the dance," I said, as he stared blankly ahead. "Tony found a stroke of genius when he wrote that song."

He sipped his coffee and looked back. I thought I saw an imaginary light bulb illuminate over his head. Then, I realized it was probably only three or four watts.

"Does that mean the agony of parting is the last thing we go through at the end of a relationship? And that we focus on the heartache and overlook the love?" he asked.

"It does. Love has a shelf life. When it dies, you can't heal until you lose the sorrow."

"Why does love have to die?" he asked.

I told him songwriters and poets have been on a quest for an answer to that question since time began. "Sometimes, there is no reason why it wears off. We just get replaced by someone else."

"That means the guy in 'The Dance' figured out that love will let him go on, as soon as he lets go of the heartache," he said, looking like he just solved a puzzle.

"You can vow to never love again and build a wall as high you want. It just means when all those stones you used to fortify your defenses crumble, you'll simply have a lot farther to fall next time you let someone in," I said. He looked at me like I was a prophet knocking on heaven's door. I grinned and told him, "Those are Kenny Chesney's words."

"I'm never going through this again," he said, running his hand through his hair.

"There's only one way you can guarantee it," I told him, as he looked perplexed. "Stop dancing."

Hooker tried to mount a comeback by letting his comedic side emerged from hibernation.

"Son, having this talk doesn't mean we're going to hold hands in side-by-side bathtubs, like in those Cialis commercials, does it?' "

My answer appeared after a long moment. It was precise, insightful and directly on-point, while eliminating all confusion. "Naw, but it means you're still all by yourself on puke patrol."

CHAPTER FIFTEEN

I spoke to Dan Wayland about the band later that afternoon. The conversation was colorful, to say the least.

"What's their name?" I asked.

"Don't have one. They're considerin', 'Third and Long' or 'Hard Whiskey and Soft Women,'" he said.

"Tell me about the members."

"The drummer, Dez Cassidy, has done some minor recording. The bass player is Toby Kendall. He's the brains of the outfit. Garcia Chambliss is on lead guitar. They can all play like Keith Richards but they ain't exactly Carerras and Pavarotti when they open their mouths."

"What are they like to work with?"

"A bit temperamental. Dez is usually stoned. Shit, I think he'd smoke anything from adhesive tape to World War II Jeep tire shavings."

"What about Garcia?"

"He's basically a real sociopath, but he can really burn it. He's got riffs they ain't imagined."

"Garcia is an unusual name."

"He said his mamma was a big fan of the 'Grateful Dead' so she named him after the lead guitarist, Jerry Garcia."

"Tell me why he needs a personality transplant."

"He grew up as a tough little bastard who was always in a scrape of some kind. When he was seventeen, he set off a stick of dynamite in the town square. The judge told him he could either go to jail or the Marine Corps."

"What happened?"

"He joined the Marines. He was back less than a year later with a bad conduct discharge. A month later, he crashed his Camaro into a tree. Cost him his right leg below the knee. It made him even nastier."

"How did music enter into this equation?" I asked.

"He picked up a guitar during his rehab. Him and his Fender are like a pair of bookends."

"Why do you think he's such a prick?" I asked.

"He's supposed to have an IQ in the 140s."

"If he's so smart, why is he anti-social?"

"He told me he thinks he was put on this earth to get rid of phony bastards. He said everybody in charge of something was an asshole who either knew someone or bought his way in."

"I'm sure there's a scientific paper about to be published on this topic," I said.

"He used professors and judges as examples. He said professors were surreptitious—his word—insects who couldn't function in the real world, so they spewed specious—again, his word—theories to students held hostage, who they knew could not argue with them."

"What about judges?"

"Garcia said they made decisions based on sheer stupidity, cloaked in pretentiousness—another of his words—and never take into account whether the son-of-a-bitch on trial needs his teeth kicked in."

"Can't argue with logic like that," I said, picturing Justices Sam Alito and Elena Kagan, heading north to Columbia University, armed with hockey sticks and ready to pummel the piss out of a tenured PhD in aeronautical engineering, who was completely guilt free, because he definitely needed his teeth kicked in.

"Tell me about the bass player," I said.

"Toby is the silent one. He's been writing the band's songs. I guess he's their answer to Jerry Lieber while Garcia is Mike Stoller with a rap sheet. Mostly, he writes this petunia shit about losing yer paycheck and stayin' faithful through the foreclosures and the sheetrock plant closing. You know, stuff to make you think when you really want to chase some honeys in short skirts."

"So you think we're what they need?"

"Exactly," Dan continued. "You and Trapp on lead vocals."

"I'll bet you Garcia will be a problem. He sounds like someone whose idea of fun is to slip high fructose corn syrup into Splenda packets at awards banquets for diabetics," I said.

"He wanted to call the band Cluster Fuck Sygyzy. We had to talk ourselves blue to get him to drop that one," said Dan.

"Sygyzy?" I asked.

"He told me it was a straight-line configuration of three celestial bodies, whatever that means."

"Like him, Dez and Toby?"

"Yeah. Next was the name Metastasis. Even offered to change his name to Lem Phoma."

I took a minute to mull that one over because I never heard of anyone exploring the fun side of cancer before.

"But you two will win him over, J. W.," Dan continued. "Especially with Trapp. Damn, she's prettier than a swimsuit model."

"Dan, I'm not sure I want to win him over. And last time I checked, Trapp was not doing a graduate thesis in anthropology either."

"But both of you are the catalysts this band needs. It's your ticket to stardom."

"Sounds more like an introduction to plea bargaining. And you think the three *amigos* are going to let us take over the songwriting?"

"Hell, yes, son. It's a perfect marriage."

"So was Kim Kardashian and Kris Humphries."

"Damn, boy, you kill me." Dan chortled.

I made a quick decision.

"Trapp's out of town for a while. Introduce me to the boys and I'll see where we are."

"I'll call you tomorrow."

"Tell Garcia we'll consider naming the band Obstruction of Justice or Resisting Arrest. That way, he could change his name to Gil T. S. Charged," I said.

I could hear Dan howling as the phone went dead.

* * *

Trapp and I were on the phone for over an hour that night.

"Tell me what you're up against," I said.

"My uncle was a Bernie Madoff wannabe," said Trapp. "He would send t-transfer orders out to my father. After my father signed the order, Jack would change the instructions and s-steal the funds."

"Why didn't your father question him?" I asked.

"Dad never suspected anything was wrong. My dad is ruthless and tenacious as a lawyer, but he's s-s-soft as hell when it comes to family ties and never questioned Jack."

"What a scummy bastard," I said. "Are you making any progress keeping everything afloat?"

"Yes. I'm staying until the weekend. I have to be in court every d-day."

My heart sank. I had foolishly hoped this was just a short ordeal.

"Let me know what I can do to make this easy for you."

"I guess I made the right call not going with Wes. I'd have to pull out of that gig now."

"When are you flying back?"

"Friday afternoon. I'll come back here to help from time to time, but for now, I can buy Dad some time to work with his clients and still go after my uncle."

* * *

I met the band the following afternoon. One had his head down on his arms spread over the table. After checking for a toe-tag and seeing none, I presumed it was Dez, the drummer, who might be comatose but was at least, still on life support.

I guessed the serious-looking one was Toby, the bass player. He wore an old shirt and cutoffs and was on his cell phone. The one who looked me up and down like he was ready to ask if I had a search warrant, had to be Garcia. He wore a stained tee-shirt with an infinity sign. Underneath the sign was the caption, "Amy Winehouse Lives So Fuck Off."

Dan started to outline the agenda when he was cut off by Garcia, before he could gavel the meeting to order and ask for a quorum call.

"I don't think we need anybody else in the band. I only agreed to this meeting because Dan said you could give us a new sound," he said.

"Yeah, well I heard you boys don't exactly have a full Excel spreadsheet when it comes to gigs," I said.

"Ah goddam...where them thru hunnert fuggin' pizzas loft curchin, gravy shit..." muttered Dez, barely lifting his head before it fell back to his arms.

"We think Dez smoked genetically altered flu vaccine wrapped in parchment paper," said Toby.

"I want to hear why Mr. Songwriter here is our savior," Garcia said.

"Now, that ain't what I said. You boys are great musicians, but there ain't exactly a back order for them in Nashville. We just need tunes that will sell," Dan said.

"Why don't we have J. W. play one of his songs?" Toby asked.

"Aw, shit, grunga...son of barfin' with a balsamic Jeesus...longhorn scramblin' zitty sidewalk freezin' so I could stoned...," Dez muttered before sitting up and turning his head to his right, and then laying it back on his hands.

"I think the next question should be for Donald Trump from Megan Kelly," I said, as Dan snickered.

"OK, Mr. Hot Ticket, show us what you got," Garcia said, sneering.

"Not yet," I answered. "I hear you're Billy Gibbons on steroids with a guitar. Show me."

Garcia stared at me for a long moment, rose and walked to the bandstand. He corralled his guitar and came back to the table. Before I could take a breath, he did a riff that started at low E and ended up just south of the seventeenth fret.

"Follow that, asshole," he said, enormously pleased with himself.

I grinned as I remembered a story rumored to be true, about Jerry Lee Lewis and Chuck Berry, at a concert in the late fifties. Both wanted to close the show and their managers got into a huge beef. Finally, Lewis relented and agreed to let Berry close.

When it was Jerry Lee's turn to perform, he got the audience worked up into a frenzy. Women were screaming, guys were shouting, cops were calling for reinforcements. With the audience at a fever-pitch, and police donning riot gear, Lewis got ready for his last number. He took out a coke bottle filled with gasoline, drenched the piano and set it on fire. The building went nuts as firemen rushed in to fight the four-foot high flames leaping skyward from the Steinway baby grand, while Jerry Lee banged out his final tune, causing the finale to turn into a classic rock and roll inferno.

Afterward, Jerry Lee walked off the stage to where Chuck Berry was standing, open-mouthed and wide-eyed, stopped, put two sticks of Juicy Fruit gum in his mouth, looked him directly in his terrified eyes, snickered and whispered, "OK, follow that, asshole."

I did a series of songs. Toby nodded but Garcia sat there mute while Dez tried to freebase his wristwatch.

"That's some really good stuff," Toby offered.

I looked at Garcia. His face grew a look that reminded me of a convict on death row who didn't like the fat content of the rib-eye he ordered for his last meal.

"You can write but I can play," he said finally.

"By God, I knew this would work!" Dan shouted.

"I want to hear some of Toby's songs," I said. "Maybe he and I can do some writing together."

Toby's eyes grew wide as he nodded briskly.

"OK, enough of this geranium shit. This ain't a fuckin' love-in for Occupy Music Row. I plan on doing some of the writing too," Garcia said.

I started to get hot, then decided to try a softer approach.

"Look Garcia, I know you're the leader of the band. But why not let Toby and me try to come up with some material first? When we get done, you can take a look at it and give us your input."

Garcia looked at me, and I could sense he felt victorious because I called him the leader.

"Ok, we need some hits, boys, so you better turn yourselves into Brooks and Dunn," said Garcia.

"When do you want to start?" I asked Toby.

"Tonight, right after I get off work at two."

"Where do you work?"

"Right here. I'm the head bartender."

* * *

Trapp called me just before ten o'clock.

"How's your father?"

"As well as can be expected. I did some r-research and we have a good case that my uncle's brokerage house is on the line for what Jack did."

"How is he personally?"

"I think he's aged ten years. Dad will be broke if we can't f-f-find a way to get his money. He's looking for someone to sue the brokerage firm. No luck, so far."

"Why not? A huge recovery should make someone step up."

"Politics, J. W. The brokerage house is well connected. They'll claim Jack was acting on his own and they n-n-never knew about his activities."

"Can't you beat that theory?"

"It's too soon to tell. I've gotten Dad's c-cases almost up to date so I can come back to Nashville."

I asked Trapp how she was doing.

"I keep looking at our picture on Dad's wall a thousand times a day and that gets me higher than a shot of morphine," she said.

I told her about Dan and the escaped chain gang known as the band.

"This guy Garcia sounds like a real whack job who ought to be in an institution," she said.

"He can play like Chet Atkins with hyperactivity disorder. He's bright, but I don't know why paranoia has to complete the mix."

"Do you see us having a f-future with them?" she asked.

"I'm not sure. I'm meeting Toby, the bass player, tonight when he gets off work to see if we can write together," I said.

"Our writing s-sessions always ended up with us in bed. Be careful that Toby doesn't get you inspired."

"I'm pretty sure Toby has the wrong equipment."

* * *

I met Hooker shortly after eleven o'clock. We got the last empty table in a corner and actually had a conversation, as the house band was on break.

"How's Trapp?" he asked.

"Beat up. She's coming in tomorrow."

I decided to bring up Sylvia, as gently as I could.

"Are you any better?" I asked.

"I have my moments but I took your advice and bought a few country CD's,"

"That's a start until you find the perfect woman."

He sipped his beer.

"Have you heard from Sylvia?" I asked.

"Yeah. She emailed me and said that I would always be a very special part of her life but, she knew it would not work between us. She figured out I would never be an East Coast phony who could somehow convince myself that the Harvard-Yale game was right up there with LSU-Alabama."

"She had a lot more insight than you gave her credit for."

"The biggest reason she left was to find someone more compatible than me."

"I thought you two were a matching pair of hyperkinetic acrobats in bed," I said.

"We were. But I could not compete with her mind out of bed."

"She's no brighter than you are."

"Not bright, more insightful. She has vision. I have sight."

"So, I take it you're almost over the heartbreak."

"I'll never get over it, but I'm learning how to use music to help me deal with it. Those songs tell me losing Sylvia is both the best thing and the worst thing that ever happened to me."

* * *

Tim Cagle

Trapp came in on Friday afternoon of Martin Luther King Day weekend. After an early dinner, we fell asleep in each other's arms.

We stayed in bed until after nine o'clock the following morning. After renewing our love, she got up to shower and I headed for the kitchen.

"You seem pretty chipper," I said, as she sat down.

"I have to laugh because I'm really sick of crying. I've been d-d-dealing with one felon after another because Dad spent most of the week with the FBI."

"Tell me how this happened."

"Do you know what stock options are?"

"Not really."

"Options involve stock speculation by the use of puts and calls. A put is a right to sell and a call is a right to buy."

"How did it work?"

"Jack started speculating that stocks would increase or decrease over time by buying options. That meant he could buy low and gamble that the stock would rise, or sell high and bet the stock would fall. If he guessed right, he would make a profit before the options came due. He picked the wrong stocks and shorted them. That meant he had options to sell at a high price, by gambling that the stock would decline. Instead, the stocks rose and Jack was caught flat-footed."

"Couldn't he sell and cut his losses?"

"It was too late. He could have softened the l-l-loss if he made some counterbalancing moves, but he was too pigheaded."

"Didn't your father get monthly statements?"

"Sure, after Jack doctored them."

"How did Jack drain the money from Joe's accounts?"

"Jack would forward a cash transfer order to Dad and leave several spaces between the end of the transfer and where Dad's signatory appeared. After the signed document came back, Jack would add new instructions, pocket the money and send out phony m-monthly statements."

"What about the other clients he stole from?"

"He ran a classic Ponzi scheme. When he made money from one deal, he would use it to replace the money he stole from others."

I was getting infuriated just listening. "Jesus, he needs to be tortured."

"He forged my aunt's signature to some phony real estate transactions and then sold the property out from under her. The dirty bastard even stole from his own father. They had a joint account, and Jack drained it while his father was having s-s-surgery."

"I hope the son-of-a-bitch winds up in the same cell with Jerry Sandusky," I said finally.

"He may never even serve a day. He left a tape describing everything. He begs my father for help and cries out loud about his wife and kids and all I can see is a defense lawyer playing it before p-p-pleading for understanding in front of a jury. And the height of irony is that my father built a very successful career defending creeps like Jack."

The doorbell rang.

"Who could that be?" I asked.

I went to the door and saw Toby's car parked in front.

"Mornin' J. W.," he said after I opened the door. "I hope I'm not out of line for coming by without calling. I need to see you for a minute."

He was carrying his guitar. As Trapp approached, Toby removed his hat and nodded.

"You must be Trapp," he said, smiling.

She shifted her coffee cup and stuck out her right hand.

"And you must be Toby, the gentleman intellectual bass player."

"Want some coffee?" I asked.

"Sure. Black is fine. I've been up all night and I had to show you what I wrote."

"What's the s-song about?" Trapp said softly.

"Love," Toby answered. "And the choices we make for it."

"You've got my attention," she answered.

"What's the name of it?" I asked

"'If I Were There'," he answered.

"Why don't you sing it to us?" Trapp asked.

"OK. I wrote this as a boy slash girl song. So please understand when I sing the girl's part too."

Toby opened his case and removed a battered Guild Dreadnaught acoustic. I thought it was about to fall apart until he strummed a chord. A full, sweet melody filled the air and resonated throughout the room. Externally, it was a cadaver; internally, it was an embryo.

"How old is that Guild?" Trapp asked.

"It's from 1969. My daddy played the circuit for a while before the neon lights, cheap whiskey and unfiltered Camels presented him with a bill his body couldn't pay."

"Shit, that sounds like a lyric," I said.

Toby smiled softly and began to sing while Trapp and I sat back and listened.

* * *

Ribbons from your hair,
Faded now from gold to amber;
Souvenirs so rare,
Photographs that we remember.
Lovers overcoming time,
And dancing through the storm;
Sharing sips of vintage wine,
Reaching out to keep us warm.
Chorus
If I were there,
You'd never have to say to me "I love you";
I'd know it by the way
You filled the empty spaces in my heart;
If you were here,
You'd know I'm always thinking of you;
We'd lie awake together,
While lying to each other;
Making promises that
Never will come true;

* * *

Memories from another time,
Spread across the room;
Old love letters, poems that rhyme,
Scent of your perfume.
Bits and pieces, cracks and lines,
Time to say goodbye;
Proof forever's just a state of mind,
No more tears to cry.

Trapp and I looked at each other before Toby finished. Her eyes were dancing, just like mine.

"OK, stop," she said. "We want to join you."

We sang the song four times. On the final edition, we each let out a cheer at the end.

"We just turned into 'Lady Antebellum'," Toby said, grinning broadly.

CHAPTER SIXTEEN

We went into Nashville on Saturday and spent the day on Broadway, checking in and out of honky-tonks while trying to unwind. Sunday was spent cooking and writing. After dinner, Trapp sat on the sofa plunking out melodies and trying to find lyrics, while I offered suggestions between plays from the Dolphins-slash-Chiefs playoff game.

The contest went into overtime. I stayed up to watch while Trapp wandered off to bed. At midnight, the phone rang. Panic spread over me as I heard Marion's voice. She was hysterical and incoherent. I ran into the bedroom but Trapp was in a deep sleep and it took me three tries to rouse her before she stirred. I handed her the phone as she sat up and took the call.

Her cries began coming out in panic-stricken gasps, like she was wounded. She ended the call, pulled herself together and told me the story.

"My father had a s-s-stroke. He was rushed to the hospital. Mom asked me to come h-h-home right away."

"What do the doctors say?"

She began to sob. I waited until she calmed a little, determined to be the bedrock for both of us.

"His condition is critical. They think he may need s-s-s-surgery."

"I can go online and get you a flight right away," I offered.

She broke down, stepped forward and slipped her arms tightly around me. I held her close until she stopped crying. The first flight with an open seat was not available until the following day. She began to pace, then looked at me.

"Help me p-p-pack. I'm going to drive."

"Are you sure?"

"I am. I'll n-need my car. If we drive, we can be in Houston before my flight even leaves here. I want you to come with me."

"I'll be ready in a flash," I said.

We were on the road by 2:00 a.m. I texted Hooker and outlined our situation, then slid in behind the wheel.

"Can you remember anything your mother said?"

"She told me they were entertaining for the first time since the scandal broke. He was s-s-sitting at the piano with one of his friends and they were having a sing-a-long. Suddenly, he complained that his f-f-face was numb and he had a severe headache so they called an ambulance. The doctor says he's paralyzed on one s-s-side," she said.

"Do you want me to stay in Houston?" I asked.

"No. I'll be overwhelmed for quite a while. You n-need to go back to Nashville."

She squeezed my hand. I tried to sneak my thumbs up to my eyes to neutralize the tears. We rode in silence for the next few hours. Trapp was in the middle of a short catnap when I spied the sign telling us that Houston was only twenty miles away. Gently, I shook her.

"We're looking for St. Mary's Medical Center on the north side," she said.

Forty-five minutes later, we arrived at the hospital complex and were directed to the fourth floor. Trapp left to freshen up, returned and we entered an atrium, took the elevator up to intensive care, then stopped at the reception area.

"Excuse me, I'm Angela Trappani. I'm here to see my f-f-father, Joseph Trappani."

"He has someone with him now," the receptionist said. "Our rules say only two visitors at a time. Here is a copy of our visitation policy. Please take a moment to read it." The receptionist handed Trapp a booklet and looked at me. "Only members of the patient's immediate family are allowed to visit. Is this gentleman your husband?" she asked.

"Of course," Trapp replied, without looking up.

"I'll see if you can go down to his room," the receptionist said.

Trapp finished reading and handed me the booklet. Moments later, the receptionist returned, followed by two extremely attractive women, one middle-aged and one from Trapp's generation.

"Angie, I'm so glad you're here," the older woman said, with a short sob.

"Aunt Lisa. How is he?" Trapp asked as they embraced.

"Not good. He can't speak."

Trapp and the younger woman embraced.

"This is J. W. Steele, my p-p-partner. J. W. this is my m-mother's sister, Lisa, and her daughter, Gina," said Trapp.

I shook hands with each one.

"Where's Mom?" Trapp asked.

"By his side, but she's exhausted. She's been here all night," Gina said.

"Thank you for bringing Angela home," Lisa said, as she shook my hand. "Let me get Marion to step out for a moment so you can see Joe."

"Ma'am, I can wait out here if you all would rather make this a family thing," I answered.

Trapp squeezed my hand. "I w-w-want you with me."

A few moments later, Lisa returned with Marion. We greeted her with a hug and Trapp led everyone over to the waiting area. There were several easy chairs arranged in groups.

"This will give us more privacy, Mom. Lisa said you've been up all night. Why d-d-don't you try to rest for a moment while I go see Dad?" Trapp said.

"I don't think I can rest," Marion said, clutching a linen handkerchief and looking at us through red-tinged, swollen eyes.

"What did the doctor tell you?" Trapp asked.

"That Joe had a stroke and got some kind of drug in the emergency room. I can't remember the name," Marion said.

"He called it tPA, which is short for tissue something," Lisa said.

"They told me he can't talk. He can't even breathe without that damn tube."

"Do you have c-c-confidence in the doctor?" Trapp asked.

"Yes. His name is Dr. Stromberg. I saw him briefly this morning and he said he would come back and talk to all of us."

"All right, J. W. and I are going to see Dad," Trapp said.

I was not prepared for what we saw. Joe was lying in bed with his eyes closed. A plastic tube was inserted into his nose, held in place by adhesive tape. There was also a tube in his throat, which was connected to what I guessed was the ventilator. Without the designer suit and presidential appearance, he looked like just another old man in acute distress.

Trapp gingerly approached the head of the bed. Tears were streaming down her face as she started to stroke Joe's hair. "I'm home, Dad," she whispered softly.

Monitors were situated on each side of the bed. Other pieces of equipment were attached to armatures affixed to the ceiling. I took Trapp's hand and squeezed it as my throat tightened and my body trembled slightly.

"I'm not used to seeing him look h-h-helpless," she said, after several minutes. "My dad was always the one everyone else looked to for solutions. Now, he has to depend on a machine to b-b-breathe for him. I hope the doctors and nurses know what they're doing. The medical field can be such a mystery..." Without warning, she became enraged and hissed, "I'm going to find that b-b-bastard Jack and tear his eyes out!"

I took her in my arms and stroked her hair. "Take it easy," I said. "This won't help Joe or you."

Her grip on my hand intensified. "I'm not saying my father is a saint, but he is a g-good and decent man. He tries to help people the best way he knows how. He doesn't deserve this," she said.

"Things take time. Jack will get what's coming to him," I said, as the door opened.

A man entered, wearing a starched white lab coat over a powder blue shirt and red striped tie. He was about five ten and had a stethoscope hanging out of his left pocket. His dark brown hair was perfectly in place and his facial features seemed to be carved. He appeared to be in his late twenties or early thirties, and looked like he arrived to audition for "The Bachelor."

"Angie, is that you?" he asked.

"Oh, my God," Trapp gasped. "Rick, what are you doing here?"

They walked toward each other and shared a bear hug.

"How long has it been?" Trapp asked.

"Since high school. I finished my residency in neurology last June and joined Dr. Michael Stromberg's practice in July. He asked me to consult on Mr. Trappani's case. When I saw the name, I wondered if you were related." He turned to me and stuck out his hand. "Hi, I'm Dr. Rick Sutherland. You must be Angie's husband," he said, smiling broadly.

"No, J. W. and I are not married. We write s-s-songs and have a s-s-singing act," she replied.

"Can you bring me up to date about my father's condition?"

"Sure. That's what I was about to do with your mother. But it looks like she stepped out."

"She's with my aunt in the waiting area."

"Why don't we go out there, so I can talk to all of you at once?" Rick said.

When we arrived in the waiting area, everyone sat alone at a far table.

"Mom, Aunt Lisa, Gina, do you remember R-R-Rick Sutherland? We went to high school together," Trapp said.

"I remember you talking about him," Lisa said, as Marion tried to smile.

"He's a neurologist now, p-practicing with Dr. Stromberg, and he's taking care of Dad."

"Can you tell us what's going on?" Marion asked.

"Under federal regulations, I am supposed to talk only to Mrs. Trappani," he began, looking at Marion. "But, if you give permission, I can discuss your husband's condition with everyone."

Marion nodded and he continued. "Mr. Trappani is sedated. He had what's called a T-I-A., a transient ischemic attack, before finally suffering the stroke. He was stabilized in the emergency room, given a drug called tPA, which stands for tissue plasminogen activator. The drug has a small window for use and is given to minimize the damage done to the brain. We don't know how much the drug helped. He is still paralyzed on one side and we won't know if it's permanent until we wakes up."

"Will he recover?" Trapp asked.

"We hope so. We have to run some tests to see if he is at risk for another incident."

"What do you mean?" Marion asked.

"We have to check for accumulation of plaque in his carotid arteries. The brain can be very resilient, so there is hope for recovery. The next forty-eight hours are critical."

"What should we do?" Marion asked.

"Go home and get some rest. There's nothing you can do here, and the best way to help your husband is to take care of yourself and save your strength."

Trapp grabbed Marion's hand. They both nodded. "Let's go home, M-M-M-Mom," Trapp said. "We'll get some sleep and come back later."

"I have to continue rounds. Give me your cell number, Angie, and I will keep you updated," Rick said.

After shaking hands with all of us, Dr. Sutherland gave Trapp another hug. Our party went one direction and the doctor went another.

CHAPTER SEVENTEEN

I flew back to Nashville the next day. Trapp and I kept missing each other's calls and did not speak until Monday of the following week.

"Hey, are you OK?" I asked.

"Yes, but r-r-really exhausted," she answered.

"How's your father?"

"Not good. They did another MRI which c-confirmed he needs surgery to prevent another stroke."

"When are they going to do it?"

"He's still r-r-recovering, and they have to make sure he is s-s-stabilized first. They also want to run some tests to make sure his heart is s-strong enough."

"Would it be all right if I came to see you?" I asked.

"It would be f-f-fabulous. I n-n-need to be with you."

"The only reason I've stayed away is because I know how frazzled you are. Why don't I see what flights are available tomorrow?"

"Not tomorrow. I was thinking about t-t-two weeks from tomorrow. I'm still swamped but will have a lot c-cleared up in two weeks."

"OK," I answered, forcing myself to sound upbeat.

"Rick thinks the next t-t-t-two weeks are critical to Dad's recovery and prognosis," she said.

"I'll see what flight I can get and let you know."

"OK, love. I can't wait to s-s-see you."

I felt my spirits surge at the word "love."

* * *

I spent my time writing for the next two weeks, arrived in Houston that Friday and found Trapp waiting. We both broke into a semi-trot and embraced.

"I'm glad you're here," she said.

"How's your father?"

"Making slight progress but it's really slow."

"Is your mother OK?"

"As well as can be expected."

She paused for a moment, then looked into my eyes. "Uh, J. W., I know this is old-fashioned, but I would f-f-f-feel uncomfortable with you staying at my parents' house even with us in separate rooms. Would it be okay if I p-put you up in a hotel?"

"Sure," I said, as she squeezed my hand.

She interlocked her fingers with mine and drove to a Marriott. I changed and we went to dinner at an authentic Texas steak house. We had a few laughs and a couple of beers and it felt like old times. After we arrived at the hotel, I considered how I would ask my next question.

"I hope you'll come in and welcome me to Houston properly," I said lightly.

"I'm s-s-sorry, but something from dinner got me and I'm not feeling well."

I stared into her eyes for a long moment before she turned away.

"OK, call me in the morning," I said.

"You're n-n-not upset, are you?" she asked.

"No. Get a good night's sleep."

Paranoia began to flood my thoughts and I couldn't help but wonder if things between us had changed. Then, I realized she was in the worst crisis of her life and I was acting like a lovesick teenager. After channel-surfing for a while, I gave into the impulse and called Trapp's cell phone at eleven o'clock but got her voice mail. I hung up and called Hooker.

"Hey, man, are you still alive?" I asked.

"Absolutely. I'm really alive," he almost shouted.

"I wasn't sure if I'd find you with a half-gallon of Wild Turkey in one hand and your dialing finger ready for Sylvia."

"I got some incredible news today. Burl got a head coaching job in Division 1 and wants me to go with him to be his Defensive Coordinator."

"That's great. What school?"

"That's the best part!" he yelled. "Texas State in Beaumont. I'm going home!"

I felt my heart begin to pound. "Damn, man, that's the best news I ever heard. Congratulations," I said.

"I have to report in ten days. Burl wants me there before spring practice starts."

After we hung up, I began running through the channels again before falling into a very troubled sleep. I awoke with a thud when my phone rang a little after eight o'clock.

"J. W., are you awake?" asked Trapp.

"Yes. What time is it?"

"Twenty of nine. Sorry I missed your call last night but d-d-dinner got to me so I went to bed. Listen, I have a couple of quick errands and then I thought Mom and I would pick you up and we could visit my father and grab some lunch."

"Outstanding," I said.

"Tonight, I hope you don't mind if we all go to dinner together."

"Great idea," I said, fully awake now.

"I'll c-come by around eleven o'clock," she said.

Trapp and Marion arrived right on schedule and we spent almost an hour with Joe. The good news was he could now breathe on his own. His speech was almost non-existent, and when he tried to talk, it was garbled.

He seemed to grow agitated because he could not form words when he tried to speak. I could see the tears of frustration in his eyes as he seemed to lip-sync phrases.

Trapp and Marion stood on each side of the bed. They both pretended not to notice Joe's trouble with his speech. Trapp told him the practice was all caught up. That made him try to smile.

Afterward, we left for lunch, spent some time with Marion and arrived home shortly after five, with barely enough time to change before dinner. We met Lisa and her husband, Tony, at an upscale Italian restaurant. I felt shock waves when he remembered me from my football days.

"Tony is the uncle I t-told you about who taught me how to play my first guitar," she said.

"You two were magnificent when you opened for Wes McGovern," Tony began. "His music is sure one of a kind."

"Ol' Wes is certainly unique all right," I answered, smiling at Trapp.

"So Angie, are you and J. W. gonna reunite with Wes on his tour?" asked Tony.

"Not for a while. J. W. is w-working up an act on his own."

"Well, you both have an awful lot of talent. I'm sure you'll hit the big time again."

"Right now, I have a lot of drug dealers and c-c-child molesters to try and set free," Trapp said.

Marion grew a look of disapproval, like Trapp had arrived late for church.

"Maybe we should talk about *fettucine* and *marinara* instead of felonies and misdemeanors," Lisa said, winking at Trapp and me.

Dinner was pleasant, and we spent a long time enjoying the surroundings. After dropping Marion at home, Trapp and I drove back to the hotel. I grew preoccupied with how to ask her to come inside with me.

"I hope that invitation to come in is still open," she said, after taking my left hand.

I was overcome by a feeling of euphoria as Deene started growing taller. I took her in my arms. We kissed slowly, deeply. Her kisses grew more passionate and we stumbled toward the bed. We made love sweetly and tenderly but it seemed like something was missing.

"Can you stay tonight?" I asked.

"Sorry, I can't because I have to get ready for a huge trial," she said.

As she headed for the bathroom, I heard the faint ring of a phone and saw her cell had fallen to the floor. I picked it up and read the words RICK CELL. A vision of Joe appeared as I attempted to answer but the call dropped. When she returned, I handed her the phone.

"Rick called while you were gone," I said. "I tried to get it in case it was about your father."

Her eyes seemed to show panic. She confirmed it when she spoke.

"I'll call him back later," she said, sounding like she was caught in a lie. "I'll pick you up in the morning and t-take you to the airport."

My heart sank as I wondered if things between us had changed. I tried to convince myself I was wrong because I had no real evidence.

He's Joe's doctor, you stupid bastard! I thought.

Then, I felt ashamed, because I knew she had to feel abandoned with me still in Nashville and her stuck here. Maybe that's why the lovemaking was not the same.

I thought about having a heart to heart talk with her in the morning, then got pissed at myself because that was really selfish. Suddenly, I grew ashamed for questioning her feelings for me before an image of Erica and Julie scolding me arose and a fresh wave of fear swept over me.

CHAPTER EIGHTEEN

Trapp called me in the morning and said one of the witnesses for her trial was recanting and she had to meet him at ten o'clock. She apologized several times even though I told her I would get a ride to the airport. There were three new voice mails from her when we landed. I called her back and our conversation seemed strained.

Hooker called and asked me to join him for a few beers. He said we were both in the kind of mood that was not conducive to public consumption, so he invited me to come over.

"Son, talk to me about Trapp," he began.

"I feel like we're on the skids. And it means that I'm losing my songwriting partner as well as the love of my life. Rick called her when I was in Texas and she wouldn't call him back in front of me."

"Did you catch them in bed?"

"No. But, he seems to be in her life like a lover."

"Look, pal, I'm here if you need me. If you didn't come along a few weeks ago, God only knows where I would be."

"That's why I have music. I've been told some of the greatest songwriters deliberately break up with their girlfriends so they can get some heart-wrenching thoughts to write about."

He swallowed hard and looked me in the eye.

"Uh, J. W.," he said. "Can I tell you something really heavy?"

I nodded and remembered the only time I ever

saw him this serious was after his brother died.

"Don't think I'm weird but I've been seeing a therapist," he said, dropping his eyes.

I said I was proud of him. His eyes lit up and we high-fived. "I was hoping you'd say that. She gave me insight about my mother and my relationships with women. Also, my commitment issues and fear of abandonment. She helped me see that maybe my Mom did the best she could."

"From what you told me, she was in her own kind of hell," I said.

"She left my dad a few months ago. She's reached out to me but I don't know how to respond."

"Therapy can help you with that, too," I said.

"She's been taking me through the grieving process. Something called Kubler-Ross stages. First is denial, then anger, bargaining, depression and acceptance. It's really opened my eyes about what she called my emotional intelligence."

"Music takes me through those phases," I said, before I got up to leave. Suddenly, I thought about the joy of holding Trapp's body next to mine and the faint touch of her fingertips moving slowly across my skin. Even if I wrote songs that made me immortal, the tradeoff of losing her would always be a complete loss.

* * *

Trapp and I kept calling without connecting. On the morning of Valentine's Day, I texted her and said I'd call that night. Then, I sent her a bouquet of roses. We finally got to speak at nine o'clock.

"How's your father?" I asked.

"They're trying to get him s-strong enough for surgery," she said. She was silent for a long moment. I sensed something was coming down. "We have to t-talk. Things aren't the same anymore," she began.

I felt my entire body shake.

"What do you mean?"

"I don't think we can c-c-continue in our relationship," she said.

"Why?" I stammered.

"I'm s-s-sorry, J. W. but this thing with Rick just happened. I had a t-t-terrific crush on him in high school and when I saw him trying to help Dad, something s-s-s-sparked. I guess I still had some unresolved f-f- feelings for him. I never meant to hurt you. You have to believe that."

I knew there was no way she faked being in love with me. No one is that good an actress, I thought bitterly, as a crushing sensation spread over me. "How could this happen if you loved me like you say you did?"

"You're not here!" she shouted. "I'm alone and my f-f-father almost died, my mother is d-d-destroyed and they're in financial ruin."

"I offered to move down there with you," I said.

"Your place is not here. There is n-n-nothing for you to do except f-f-follow me around."

Another bout of silence. I waited.

"I need someone and R-R-Rick fills a lot of v-v-v-voids. My life in Nashville is over."

I felt hollow inside, like my heart was an empty barrel. She was leaving me, just like Eddie left her. I had an overwhelming urge to punch myself for being so stupid as I heard the old Vince Gill song playing in my mind. It was telling me how there's nobody around who can answer, 'When I Call Your Name.'

"Do you love him?" I asked.

This time the silence was heavy, like waiting for the coroner to declare the cause of death.

"Not l-l-like I love you."

"I'm ready to give up Nashville for you. How can you let what we have go?"

She didn't answer and I grew more frantic.

"What about the music?" I asked.

"That ended when my father had the s-s-stroke."

At once, my chest pounded and my mind panicked. Suddenly, I was transported back in time and could see my mother crying and telling me my dad was just killed.

"I need some t-t-time to figure this out," I said, and we hung up.

Goddamit, that's why I always keep something in reserve. It's every women I've ever been close to all over again, I raged, as my eyes watered. I turned my phone off. I needed some quiet time alone with Kristofferson. In my head, Garth Brooks began singing 'The Dance.' I began to choke up, then felt my anger spike as it sank in. I'd like to punch the shit out of Garth and Tony Arata and every other country songwriter who ever lived!

I began to whisper the lyrics over and over until the anger passed. Tears started flowing like Trapp had just died. Where the hell was George Jones, telling me that I'll find a way to forget in time? Maybe, Patty Loveless can stop by and tell me that tomorrow, Trapp will be just a memory who's 'Over My Shoulder.' Where's Toby Keith explaining why my dreams are too young and fiery to die?

Songs about Houston started playing in my mind. My skin felt like it was being singed as the lyrics started to flow. Suddenly, there was only one Houston song I needed to hear. It was the signature song of a departed superstar, one whose loss could never be overcome. I closed my eyes tightly as I heard Whitney Houston singing, in that magnificently sweet and painfully tormented voice of hers, over and over, 'I Will Always Love You'.

* * *

I did not speak to Trapp for several days. I vowed to find a way to talk to her like someone who loved her, instead of someone whose heart she just shattered, when I felt the time was right.

Toby and I met and he told me the band was officially defunct because Garcia had died the week before after a bar brawl. After the paramedics got him stabilized, he pulled his tubes out in the ambulance so he could attack the other guy, and wound up bleeding to death.

Although we turned out nothing but garbage, the writing sessions became a form of therapy, at times bordering on a ritual of purification. At one point, he asked me if we could write something that didn't remind him of the Bataan Death March. That was when I knew the cathartic effect was beginning to work.

That night, I finally returned Trapp's calls. I had done a lot of thinking to try and sort things out. I refused to be angry with her because I knew she would never lie to me and that her feelings for me were real. It had to be the stress she was under that skewed her judgment. I would smoke out her change of heart and do whatever was needed to fix it.

At first, I was conciliatory. I tried to convince her she was operating out of guilt over her father. That I would be right by her side and she was drawn to Rick because of gratitude, not love. That she would never have with him what she found with me.

Every argument of mine sounded so lucid, I was overcome with enthusiasm. Unfortunately, Trapp rejected everything. At one point, she told me it was time for both of us to move on. Then she broke down and sobbed before hanging up. I redialed her number before breaking the connection and tossing the phone.

I was on my second Coors an hour later when the phone rang. "Hello," I answered.

There was silence on the other end. I tried to speak when she interrupted.

"J. W., Dr. Stromberg just c-c-c-called. My father's d-d-d-dead."

My mind raced and my throat closed as she began to sob.

"Oh, God, Trapp, I'm so sorry."

"They said his heart g-g-g-gave out on him," she said, as her voice quavered before breaking.

I had to swallow several times before my throat would open up.

"He couldn't speak so he wrote me a n-n-note a while back. He said he knew I could be a s-s-star but he never wanted music for me because he was afraid it would break my heart. He said a lot of those big names on his wall told him m-m-m-music was a cruel, nasty business and he didn't want me to get hurt. He also said I was the g-g-greatest singer he'd ever heard."

"What did you do?" I asked, before my throat seemed to slam shut.

"I was so shocked I couldn't s-s-say anything. He finished by writing the happiest day in his life was when he saw me perform. I thought he made me become a lawyer because I wasn't good enough as a singer. But, that n-n-note told me he was watching out for me. All these years I've held a grudge and now I find out he was just p-protecting me."

"At least he got to see you on stage before he died," I said, as we both broke down.

"I need you. Please hurry," she whispered.

I called Hooker and told him what happened. His response bordered on genius. "I have to be in Beaumont in three days. Why don't we drive down together tomorrow? I'll go to the funeral with you so there won't be any awkward moments," he said.

I was thunderstruck. My old pal never ceased to amaze me with his generosity.

"Give me an hour to get my stuff together and I'll come over," I said.

"Do me one favor," he said.

"What?"

"Leave Kristofferson and all the other heartbreakers at home."

* * *

When we arrived at the funeral home, Joe Trappani's burial presentation reminded me of the scene in the *Godfather* when Don Corleone was laid to rest. Hundreds of mourners formed long lines to say their goodbyes.

I was glad Hooker was with me as we paid our respects together. Rick was present at the wake but did not stand next to Trapp in the receiving line. I vowed not to ask Trapp about Rick because I knew that would be the lowest form of insensitivity and selfishness. The time would come when I could get an answer to all my questions, even the ones that broke my heart.

The following day, Joe was laid to rest. It was only the third week in March, but the weather was beautiful and nestled in the high sixties. A row of limousines transported the mourners. The highlight was the eulogy given by Trapp.

The most profound thing she said was that she would picture him next to her when she walked down the aisle someday. At the end, she looked directly at me before quoting Vince Gill, and telling her father to 'Go Rest High On That Mountain', because he had finished his work here on earth. It was a very touching tribute and people were visibly moved.

I realized I would always regret that I never got to know Joe better and felt a stab of pain as I pictured him delivering Trapp to me on our wedding day, if life would have let him live long enough. In my next breath, I pushed that thought aside. Those dreams were gone.

After the service was finished, Trapp walked over and gave Hooker and me a hug. Then she asked me if we could speak alone. We walked until we were out of earshot of the others.

"Thanks for coming. It means the w-w-world to me and my mother."

I stared at the ground and fidgeted. "It was the least I could do. Even though I only met him once, I really liked Joe."

"He told my mom you were the kind of guy he'd always hoped I'd marry."

"He was a great man," I said, trying to smile.

"I have s-s-something to tell you. I got an offer on my condo. I have to come to Nashville in a couple of w-w-weeks to meet my accountant and sign the purchase and sale agreement. I've also got movers lined up so I can get the rest of my stuff," she said.

I told her about Hooker and the job in Beaumont. His lease still had a few months left, so I could move into his place and sublet. I assured her I would be fine. She reached forward, slipped her hand into mine and wore a look like she was dying.

"Things are n-not always as they appear," she said, staring deeply into my eyes.

"What does that mean?"

"I miss you a lot," she said.

"Remember that old Patty Loveless song?" I said.

"What's that?"

I paused and looked at her for a long moment. "'I Miss Who I Was With You'," I said.

She took my hand and squeezed it. It seemed like she had something else she needed to tell me but stopped short. The moment passed as I looked away. "Let's go b-b-back to the others," she said softly.

Two hours later, Trapp and I said goodbye and Hooker drove me to the airport.

"Did you have that soul-searching talk with Trapp?" he asked.

"No. The time wasn't right."

"Maybe she wanted you to make the first move," he said.

"She said things are not always as they appear. I think she was trying to tell me something."

"There's only one way to find out," he said.

After we said good-bye, I went into the airport bar and had a beer. It did not help.

* * *

Trapp called me several days later and confirmed her arrival the following week.

"Do you want me to pick you up at the airport?" I asked.

"I'm driving. I want to take some of my personal stuff back with me in the c-c-car instead of loading it on a truck. I'll be there Tuesday night."

"I be out by then."

"There is one thing you can do for me," she said. "I have to meet my accountant on Wednesday morning at ten o'clock to get my income taxes done. Would you go to my desk and get out the folder in the right-hand drawer that says 'receipts' on it and drop it by his office?"

"Sure," I replied. "What's his name and address?"

"Mark Thomas. His office is located in a building adjacent to the shopping center right before the entrance to my condo complex. He's at the northwest corner by the end of the p-p-parking lot."

"I know where that is."

"April fifteenth is next Friday. So, if you could bring them to him right away, that would save me a lot of time."

I told her about the producer and the audition Dan had just scheduled for next Wednesday.

"I felt you had a right to know and might go with me just to see what they're offering."

"I'm out, J. W. I don't know what you should t-tell Dan."

"To paraphrase Dwight Yoakam, 'I promise to tell the truth except when it's time to lie'."

"That's what s-s-songwriters do," she said.

* * *

I spent the next two days writing. Everywhere I looked reminded me of our time together. Something kept gnawing at me but I couldn't smoke it out. I went into the guest room and got notes from songs we wrote together. Desperate for inspiration, I walked back into the living room and spread them out in a semi-circle.

At midnight, I stopped for a cat nap. I turned on the CD player, lay on the couch and could almost detect our scent when we made love. I kept watching the shadows and waiting for the whispers. They stayed sequestered in a members-only committee meeting, while I was locked out. I kept looking at the songs and thought they reminded me of a flower arrangement.

I guess this is another sterling memory to add to the bouquet, I thought.

Without warning, whispers stirred and I bolted upright. I got up and found one of Trapp's legal writing pads, then began scribbling words and thoughts. After an hour of searching for a word or two and how to phrase them, I picked up the Martin. I stared off into space, then closed my eyes and imagined the room spinning as lights flashed like fireworks displays.

I got up and started to pace, them plopped back on the sofa and crossed my legs with my heels resting on each thigh. My mind raced as I rose and walked to the bathroom, where I splashed my face with cold water. The sensation made me recoil as I closed my eyes again and imagined a laundry list of words that had no meaning, but rhymed with 'mind'. By this time, dawn had broken and the sky was sending signals that the night might be over, but my search for deliverance had just began.

I fumbled with melodies until after seven AM, when my body told me it needed some attention. Two strong cups of coffee later, the whispers picked up and I began to form a crude draft of a verse. An hour later, the start of a chorus appeared. The lyrics were rough, but semi-sparkling. It was a songwriting moment I dreamed of, but never experienced. I was beat up from creating, but still pissy enough to realize I had done some work that made me feel proud.

The melody continued to hide from me. At eight thirty, I called Mark Thomas's office and moved my appointment back from 11:00 a.m. until 2:00 p.m. I was in the zone and nothing could stop me.

At one o'clock, I dressed and made my delivery. The office was located on the first floor and reminded me of a big-time football stadium with Mark's building serving as the end zone area for the home team. I went in and gave the file to the receptionist.

As I left, I watched a delivery truck pull into the first two spaces directly in front of the entrance. When the passenger opened his door, I caught the sounds of Tim McGraw and Faith Hill singing 'Let's Make Love,' emanating from the cab of the truck and filling the whole center.

I exited the parking lot and headed back to the condo, when I was unexpectedly overcome by such an extreme sensation, that I was forced to pull over to the side of the road to get the SUV under control. As I stopped, my entire body started shaking.

I've cracked the code for how to deliver this song to her! I thought frantically.

A tune popped up and I realized the recorder was still at the condo. I was hyperventilating as I searched for something to write on. A Krispy Kreme napkin was all I could find in the glove compartment and my hand began writing like the pen was too hot to hold. After a moment, I turned off the ignition because I would be stopped for a while.

Whispers shattered the silence. Soon, they were shouting so loud I almost needed ear plugs. I was writing like the pen had only two drops of ink left. Ten minutes later, I had the chorus. Then the entire song came together with a thud. Euphoric, I picked up my phone and left myself a voice mail of what I had written.

The perfect plan solidified. This was something that might get Trapp back. Maybe not as a wife, but at least a writing partner. My hands were shaking as I outlined it.

I had to make a series of phone calls. The first was Toby. He said the band was in. Next, I called Galen, the quarterback I helped transform into a star. He told me how much the whole team missed me at the breakup banquet and that he was sorry that he never got to say goodbye. After I gave him the details of my plan, he promised to contact as many of his teammates as he could.

The unpredictable call was to Wendell Dyson, the music director at Tennessee Baptist College. Wendell and I struck up a friendship while I was coaching and I hoped it would carry over into civilian life now that I was exiled from the land of God. We connected on the phone and I outlined my idea. He told me to definitely count him in.

My last call was to Dan. I could almost picture him jumping up and down and doing cartwheels.

"This one is mine exclusively, right?" he asked.

"You're the man on this one, Dan."

"Don't forget, the meeting with the producer is on for three," he said.

"We'll be there," I lied.

I realized this might not work but if things did not go as planned, Dan and I were probably finished anyway. After hanging up, I felt my heart jumping and my pulse racing like a colt on caffeine. This would be my equivalent of a phony deposition. I only had four short days to put everything in place, but the payoff could change my life in ways I always dreamed about.

After returning to the condo, I walked from room to room and stared at the bed where we had moments of joy that would never be equaled. On the night table, I saw our Houston stage picture, and got choked up as I looked at a pair of earrings and the few pieces of clothing she left behind. Everywhere I looked, there was a memory I could either cherish or run away from.

An image arose of Trapp and me, dancing together, like the couple in the *Renoir* painting. When the song was over, she said our time together was through, then kissed me goodbye, like I was a page she had turned. I was overcome by fear that what I had planned would fail, and whether I should call it off before I looked like a fool.

At that moment, the video of 'The Dance' began playing in my subconscious. Tony Arata's lyrics helped me visualize Trapp singing onstage next to me and how that made me feel like royalty. The meaning was clear. If we'd never met, I would not have this heartache; but that price tag was too high, because the memory of her by my side would vanish like daylight in winter.

Looking toward the sky, I remembered the other dances I never had to miss, and saw images of Ann in high school, Melissa Sue in college, and even Carol, before the agony of each parting slowly slipped away, and those memories began to heal. Even if this plan did not work, every time I closed my eyes or pried open my mind, Trapp would be there.

A picture of Garth Brooks, in his black Stetson hat, flashed through my mind as I heard him finish singing. Delicate piano notes began to blend with graceful harmonies just before the video ended, and I could see myself sitting at a poker table, shoving all my chips with both hands into an overflowing, table-stakes pot in the middle.

The last raise is mine and I'm betting my heart, I thought.

Images of the two women who made it possible for me to go all in this time appeared. They whispered that my life really is better off left to chance as I raised an imaginary glass toward them in a toast. For this one moment, my whole world was right.

Thanks, Erica. Love you, Jewels. I owe you both a debt I can never repay.

CHAPTER NINETEEN

Rich shades of blue-grey sky flanked the only cloud that bothered to show up on Wednesday. At 8:00 a.m., I drove by Mark Thomas's office. The parking lot was virtually empty, as only a few shops were open.

I pulled in behind two flatbed trucks and directed them into the area directly in front of Mark's office. They parked with their backends facing the entrance with only a few inches of separation. I outlined instructions to the drivers, then gave them my cell number and left.

I called Toby and Wendell and confirmed that all systems were go. Galen and Dan said they were ready. At nine-fifteen, I drove to the condo. The movers were starting to load the van when I saw Trapp poring over a check list.

"I found out the buyer for this place couldn't get financing, so the deal fell through. But I had to come back anyway, because I need my stuff," she said finally.

"I'm sure it will sell. It has good bones," I told her, taking a deep breath of relief because her arrival meant my plans had not been wasted.

"What did you decide about the audition?" she asked.

"It's on for this afternoon. I'll let you know as soon as I make a decision."

"If you lead them on, this will ruin your c-c-chances with Dan," she said.

"Look, Trapp, this is my version of a fake deposition. I can't let our relationship as writers go without fighting until my last breath to save it."

"I don't think it can be s-saved," she said.

"Well, I can try to stall. Besides, I finally came to terms about you and Rick, knowing that every night you're lying next to him, and I still want to write and perform with you."

She gave me a look of sadness, like she was poring over a scrapbook of memories.

"I'd like to think you don't h-h-hate me so much that you can't at least wish me a little bit of happiness."

"I don't hate you. I hate this moment."

I could see her eyes were moist. Trapp looked at me as if she were waiting for permission to leave. I stayed silent and nervously ran my big toe over the ground in front of me. I looked to my left side so she could not see my eyes.

"I can't say goodbye to you so I'm just going to turn away and go. I do wish you happiness," I began, before walking away.

She stood still for a moment, then turned and drove away. It was time for a miracle; a last-ditch way to keep my dreams alive.

After she rounded the corner, I headed for Mark's office. Trapp had responded exactly the way I figured she would. I followed her to the shopping center, making sure to stay back far enough to avoid detection. As I reached the parking lot, she was opening the door to the office. In what I considered a touch of irony, she had parked in the space next to the flatbed truck on the right.

I texted Toby, then Wendell. On the left, five men carrying musical equipment emerged from behind a building and climbed onto the back of the first empty flatbed. They were followed by the twenty-person choir, resplendent in red and gold ensemble robes, who exited the school bus parked in the middle of the lot, emblazoned with the words "Tennessee Baptist College."

I greeted Wendell and the members of the choir as they climbed aboard the second flat- bed truck.

"We're ready, J. W." he said, while pumping my hand excitedly.

"Outstanding. How did you sneak this field trip past Chantelle and Bartlesville?"

He grinned like a kid skipping school without getting caught. "I told them we had a community event to attend and that the benefactor, who wanted to remain anonymous, would be making a generous contribution to the general scholarship fund," he told me, with a smile.

I reached in my pocket and took out a check in the amount of three thousand dollars, made out to: "Tennessee Baptist College Scholarship Fund." The bank officer's signature made sure I would stay anonymous.

"Excellent. The reverends will give me quite a greeting when I show them this baby," he answered.

The doors to several SUV's and minivans opened and groups of football players dressed in cutoffs and short-sleeved shirts came over to greet me. I shook hands or high-fived each one before leading them over to the back of the SUV.

We unloaded several cardboard boxes filled with tee shirts and began to distribute them. Soon, over forty of Galen's teammates were dressed in white tee shirts. Pictured on the front was a color photograph of Trapp and me opening the show in Houston. The lettering above said, "Nothing Can Change My", and written underneath were the words, "Steele Trapp Mind."

A small crowd formed and the players handed out the remaining shirts. The crowd continued to swell until the size doubled. I realized there were now more people than shirts. Dan walked over with a camera crew. I gave each of them a shirt.

"Damn, boy, you even remembered the advertising," said Dan, holding his shirt up.

Galen walked to the back of the first flatbed and unfurled a four-foot by eight-foot black and gold banner reading "Steele Trapp Mind." After centering it and affixing the banner to the rear of both flatbeds, he unrolled a red carpet. Players cordoned off each side of the area leading from the entrance of the building where Trapp would emerge, and extending all the way up to the back of the trucks. They would provide an unencumbered walkway.

I looked at Toby and Galen, who gave me a thumbs up. I slipped on my black tee shirt and gave the gold one for Trapp, to Galen. Toby extended his hand and helped me to the stage. I picked up my Stratocaster, did a sound check and confirmed the tuning. Nodding to Toby and Wendell, I stepped to the microphone. My heart went from pounding to skyrocketing. The crowd gathered in front of me and my excitement level soared.

"Good morning, ladies and gentlemen. I'm J. W. Steele and my partner is Angela Trappani. We're known as Steele Trapp Mind. We're gonna start off with a song we wrote that you all may have heard Wes McGovern singing on the radio. It's called, 'Reflections of Love.' We expect Trapp to join us in a moment so please help us by singing along. That should get her out here."

Words and music began to flow like champagne on New Year's Eve. As the sound filled the air, Trapp suddenly emerged from the building, wearing a look of astonishment. I pointed to Galen, who handed her the gold tee shirt. My grin was so wide it almost stretched to my ears. He held the front of the tee shirt up for her and said something to her. She nodded and slipped it on. As Galen began to escort her through the gauntlet of football honor guards, she pulled her hands up to her face and seemed to be in shock. The crowd began to clap and cheer wildly in anticipation of the show.

We sang the chorus twice and the crowd joined in. The addition of the choir made it part gospel, part country and part rhythm and blues. They were so good I almost considered passing the collection plate, while applying for membership into their congregation.

Trapp had her hands on her cheeks and was looking from side to side. Galen held her arm to steady her as he walked her toward the trucks. He looked at me and shook his head up and down, as the cheers grew more intense.

"Ladies and gentlemen, it gives me great pleasure to introduce to you my partner, Trapp."

Applause was heavy and sustained. I put down my guitar and extended my hands as Toby ambled up next to me. Galen and two other hefty players stepped forward, swooped Trapp up by her arms and legs and presented her to Toby and me as though she were as light as a fine porcelain statue.

After Trapp was safely aboard, Toby handed her my Martin. She was still in shock as she took her place next to me. "I can't believe you," she said, as she touched her face to mine, then planted a kiss on my cheek. The touch of her tears wet my skin, and drifted to the edge of my lips with their salty taste.

For the next fifty minutes, we went through several of our songs. We ended with the tune Toby had written. By now, the crowd had doubled again and patrons and store keepers were coming out of their businesses to join us. As the crowd sang with us, many locked arms and reminded me of a wave. Dan's camera crew was recording the entire event.

It was time for the finale. Everything was going better than I imagined, but there was one thing left to do. My pulse raced as the show-stopping moment stepped out of the shadows.

"Ladies and gentlemen, before we close, I have one more tune for you. This is a song I wrote a few days ago for my partner, who is the most special person in my life. We hope you enjoy it."

Before we began, I reached into my pocket and handed Trapp a sheet of paper containing the lyrics. Tears flowed again as she silently read the words.

* * *

It's the way you lie beside me
And touch me in the early morning rain
It's the gentle way you kiss me,
That wipes away the traces of the pain
It's a walk on Sunday morning,
Or holding hands at twilight by the bay
But the greatest gift you gave me,
Is wrapped up in your memory bouquet;
Chorus
Steele Trapp mind, never thought I'd find
A way to keep my memories of you.
We'll always stay together,
Wrapped up in a love that won't unwind;
Cause I've stolen every moment,

And trapped them in the pages of my mind.

The crowd became silent. I nodded to Toby and the band began to play. They were followed by the choir, who sang the tag line as an introduction.

Galen and his buddies finished distributing copies of the lyrics. The band and choir sang the first verse again. On the second run-through, the crowd began to join in. Soon, almost everyone in the parking lot was singing about Steele Trapp Mind.

When we finished, there was a cheer that must have registered two hundred and fifty on the Richter Scale. As I looked at Trapp and saw her face filled with the emotion, my body began to relax slightly, when she stared deeply into my eyes.

"My God, I feel l-like Jennifer Grey with Patrick Swayze in 'Dirty Dancing,'" she gasped.

I dropped my voice an octave, like Bill Medley, and sang, 'I've Had The Time of My Life.'

She leaned forward and snuggled up against me. "That's an unbelievable song you wrote for me," she said.

I smiled as she reached up to hug me like I was offering her a life line after a shipwreck. Suddenly, I began to laugh uncontrollably as my mind formed a picture of Jerry Lee Lewis dragging Rick by his lab coat, stethoscope in his ears, onto the back of the truck. After pumping my hand and congratulating me several times, Jerry Lee looked at Rick, picked up the receiving end of the stethoscope and yelled, "Follow that, asshole!"

Trapp and I embraced as the crowd moved toward the trucks. We got down from the truck bed and were besieged with well-wishers.

Dan came over and stuck a microphone in our faces. "We're here with Steele Trapp Mind. It's wonderful to see you both together," he said.

"Thanks, Dan. It's great to be here," I answered.

"Trapp, I think I speak for everyone when I say that I want to extend to you our deepest sympathy on the passing of your father."

Her tears were still flowing but she instantly regained her sense of serenity. "That's very kind of you, Dan."

"I hope your appearance here means that we'll be seeing you on the circuit soon," Dan said.

"Right now, we're taking it one day at a time," Trapp said.

"Do you have any new songs ready for release?" he asked.

"We have a few that are almost ready," I said.

"Well, we all look forward to hearing more music from Steele Trapp Mind real soon," he said, turning to the camera.

When he finished, I called him aside. "Listen, Dan, can we postpone this meeting with the producer today?" I asked.

"I was about to tell you. He called and cancelled. He said he found another act."

We walked back to the trucks, where Trapp hugged Toby and he introduced her to the band. The drummer gave her a rousing drum roll and she embraced the others. Next, I took her to Wendell and they exchanged greetings before Trapp shook everyone's hand and thanked each member individually.

As the crowd dispersed, a man carrying a huge bouquet of white roses approached Trapp and handed them to her. She removed the card from the envelope. The words "For your memory bouquet" were written in bold letters.

"I'll never get over this. You made me feel like a princess," she said.

"I wanted you to see what things could be like. Maybe this is all we can have, but it beats having nothing," I said.

"We have to talk," she answered. "Why don't you meet me at the c-c-condo?"

* * *

Ten minutes later, I pulled in behind her.

"That concert was the most unbelievable t-thing I've ever experienced," she said.

"How could you give up both me and music?" I asked.

"I couldn't destroy your musical dreams like Eddie d-did to me. All I could think of was losing everything at seventeen and leaving N-Nashville. I had to let you go and pray that we'd find each other again," she said. I felt my entire body start to quake. "Do you know that song by Brooks and Dunn, 'The Long Goodbye'?" she asked. I nodded. "The first line says it all. If you're r-r-really in love with someone, sometimes you have to set them free." She stopped, like it was time for a full confession. "Remember when I told you at my Dad's funeral that things are not always as they appear? My life in music was over. Your career was ready to explode. I had to make a clean b-b-break from everything, even loving you." She turned away. "The only one way I could get over you was to f-force myself to move on. Rick was in the picture and someone who I once had a crush on, so I told myself he could t-t-take your place. But, he's not even close."

"I was ready to give up music for you," I said.

"I know. And, you'd always r-r-resent me for that. It's like my father writing me that note telling me he was protecting me from the cruelty of the music business. The same way I wanted to protect you." Her voice had a slight vibrato, like she was ready to weep.

"What about that new life you could have had with Rick?" I asked.

Her eyes became so lively they seemed ready to spew flames. Suddenly, she punched me hard in the arm, then grabbed me and started to pull me back and forth.

"Don't you g-get what I'm saying?" she shouted savagely.

"Ow! What the hell was that for?" I yelled.

She got directly in my face. I didn't know if I should cower, brace myself or call 9-1-1. "Fuck a life with Rick!' she shouted. "And everybody named Rick, and Ricky Ricardo, and Baron von Richthofen, as well as p-p-people who ride in r-rickshaws! Rick could never be you. That concert showed me how much we b-b-belong together," she said.

"Are you telling me the whole story about Rick was bullshit?"

"Not all of it. The part about him wanting to m-m-marry me is semi-true." She put her hand on her hip and looked me right in the eye. "While we're on true confessions here, let's get one other thing straight," she began. "Rick and I never consummated our relationship. We started one night b-but I could not go through with it."

"I thought Rick asked you to marry him. Did he do that even though you two never slept together?" I asked.

"Well, I made him believe I had to wait until the time was right."

"You mean he bought that?"

"I never claimed I was a virgin, but I convinced him I couldn't r-rush into things. Rick is like most doctors. He's married to medicine."

My whole body felt like it was being injected by small gauge hypodermic needles. "Why didn't you tell me this?" I said.

She paused for a long moment, then stared deeply into my eyes. "I didn't want to make you think I was some kind of martyr," she said. "It was t-time for me to put Eddie behind me and for b-both of us to tell that old Catholic guilt to take a hike."

"I did this concert to show you that your place is with me—on stage," I said.

She paused, took my hands, looked me directly in the eyes, then threw her arms around me.

"What about always by your side?" she asked, as she slipped her hands into mine. I tried to respond but was overcome. "I'm sorry, but I'm too short to get down on one knee. Will you m-marry me the next time you come to Houston?" she asked.

At once, I felt euphoric, like I didn't know what to do. I picked her up and we twirled around. I let her go and began to pace back and forth before shoving my right fist skyward and shouting, "Yes!" She started to cry and we clutched each other tightly. "I thought you wanted to be a songwriter more than a wife," I said.

"Not any more. I want to write s-songs together, and be your wife. I knew you were my true love when you told my d-dad about us coming to Houston for our show. He got to see me p-perform before he died. All because you called him," she said. A picture of Richard Gere carrying Debra Winger out of the factory in the movie, *An Officer and A Gentleman* appeared in my mind.

An older man in a tee shirt with a "Southland Movers" logo approached. "We're ready to go, ma'am. Anything else before we pack it in?" he asked.

"Put everything back where you got it," she said, as my chest rose while he looked puzzled and walked back inside.

"What are you going to do about your father's practice?' I asked.

"I'm bringing in someone to help me."

"What about Jack and the SEC?"

"If I can't find a firm to take over, I've got a contact with the local newspaper. If the brokerage house doesn't make an offer of s-settlement soon, I'll blow the lid off this case."

"You'll still be tied up for a long time, right?"

"We can take turns flying back and forth on weekends for a while. I learned you can only d-do so much and I've done everything I can for the sake of guilt."

"Are you sure that won't eat away at you?"

"I've made peace with it. Someone else would have t-take over if I wasn't a lawyer. My father had life insurance, so my m-mother has some cash coming in."

Suddenly, I grew tense. I grabbed her by the upper arms and grew a deeply overwrought look. She seemed worried and confused, like I just caught her robbing my apartment. A vision appeared of Carol's friends flaunting their academic credentials and aristocratic bloodlines. "Before I marry you, I have to know who your family is and where you prepped," I said somberly.

She put her hands on her knees, bent over and belly laughed. I broke up as I watched her pony tail dance up and down with each wave of laughter. Then, she stood up, shook her head, fell into my arms and held me tight again. "We both know I'm the best you can do," she said softly.

"I agree," I said.

"We'll plan everything for June. Is that okay?"

"Can we spend our honeymoon in Vinita?" I asked.

"I'm already there," she told me.

We had both finally gone all in with our feelings. Images of me thanking the women in my past flashed through my mind. I imagined how Trapp was finally able to let go of those bitter memories of leaving Jay and being left by Eddie. I felt my mother and father slipping into a pocket of comfort in my mind, as I gave thanks for the short time we had together.

Our atonement was over; life together had begun. Suddenly, I knew the tee shirts were not only right, they were dead-on prophetic. We were on our way to heaven. And nothing on this earth would ever change my Steele-Trapp Mind.

CHAPTER TWENTY

We stayed up until two o'clock going over wedding plans. From time to time, we would get up and walk around like we were in a tickertape parade, or just fall into each other's arms. We spent most of the night partying, giggling and singing our old songs. After Trapp left for Houston the following morning, Dan called.

"Dan, the man. Talk to me."

"Hey, I'm calling to tell you I'm sorry about the producer backing down. That's why you can't wait on these deals. But, I've got another gig for you."

"Tell me."

"Whoa, pardner, not so fast. I need an agreement with you so that I can act as your agent."

"I would have to talk to Trapp. She does all the negotiating for the act."

"This is not a gig for you and Trapp, J. W. This is for you alone."

Dan said he had a friend who owned a local cable station. Every Friday and Saturday night, they did a country music hour. It was hosted by a country singer who had a string of minor hits ten years ago. The host, Waylon "Buddy" Wilcox, had a certain appeal but the show needed a boost.

"That's where you come in," said Dan.

"If Buddy keeps increasing market share, why does the show need me?"

"Because we never knows when he's gonna be a no-show and he makes gaffes on the air. Plus, he drinks. The owner wants to can his ass, but Buddy has a contract. Also, the boss doesn't want to look like a heavy, so if you come in and the audience starts to like you, they might root for you to take over."

"Can I pick my own guests?"

"Absolutely. You can even team up with Trapp."

"How do you think I'll fit in?"

"You just be your own charming self and some night Buddy will drink a whole barrel full of windshield washer fluid and do an on-air tribute to the Taliban."

"What's your cut as an agent?"

"The standard. Fifteen percent."

"I'll call Trapp tonight. Did I tell you we're getting married?"

"Hot damn, that's the best news I've heard in years. Congratulations to you both."

* * *

I reached Trapp right after ten o'clock. I waited to tell her my news because I knew she was flying high.

"I was on my cell phone for practically the whole trip. My mother is so excited she can't see straight. So is the r-r-rest of my family. After what happened to my dad, this wedding is what we all need," she began. I let her continue because this kind of happiness had been missing for too long.

"I couldn't get the date I wanted, but everything is set for June tenth, six weeks from Saturday. If it's okay with you, we will have the wedding and reception at my mother's house. And Father Giuliano is available to marry us—oh my God—J. W., is it okay if we get married by a p-priest?"

I pretended to protest, even though I knew she was too excited to pay attention.

"I got my best friend, Michelle, for my maid of honor, and Gina as a bridesmaid. My Aunt Lisa g-g-got the caterer I wanted and also the florist. Mom is taking me to Neiman's to look for a w-wedding gown and I have Uncle Tony finding us a band," she almost shouted. "And, we're getting invitations sent out tomorrow and I love you and my f-f-family and my Martin and the concert you gave me more than anything in the world. OK, I can take a b-break. Your turn, cowboy."

I sucked in a deep breath. "Dan Wayland called. He wants to send me for a spot on a television show." I told her about the plans. Me singing our songs. Then, I talked about her joining me on stage and putting our act back together. That sent a spark and she began to warm to the idea. I said Dan wanted to act as my agent.

"Don't sign anything without letting me read it," she said.

After sending Dan a text agreeing to our deal, I called Hooker and asked him to be my best man. He gave a huge shout and we talked for another hour. He said he had been dating a woman he met at TSU for about a month. Nothing serious, but it could be. I told him to bring her to Houston. We hung up and I closed out the happiest day of my life.

* * *

Dan called the following morning.

"What are you doing for lunch?"

"Why?"

"Bull Farnham, the owner of WCAG television, wants to meet you at noon at the Roadhouse."

"Should I bring anything?"

"Yeah, that sparkling wit and charm you carry around."

I arrived on time and saw Dan and another man in a rear booth. We shook hands and I slid in next to

Dan. Bull fit every caricature I knew. Late fifties, about five foot ten and at least thirty pounds overweight. Boots, jeans and a brown suede Western cut sport coat. A full head of dark hair pushed back, a mole on his cheek and at least three chins. His teeth were crooked and reminded me of an assortment of spotted Mentos. Smoking was prohibited, so he chewed an unlit cigar.

"Dan showed me that tape you all made in the parking lot. Really good stuff," Bull said.

"J. W. wrote all those songs, too," Dan said.

"Well, actually I collaborated. My partner, Trapp, and I wrote them together."

"You know this opportunity is only for you? I don't want no misunderstandings," Bull said. I nodded.

"Bull, why don't you tell J. W. what you have in mind."

"It's real simple. I wanna get rid of Buddy. He's got a long-term contract and I can't let him go until I have a replacement."

"Can't you fire him for being drunk and missing shows?" I asked.

"Sure, if I want to be up to mah ass in lawyers and legal fees," Bull said. He told me the show had all its guests booked for the following month. So I would make my debut in six weeks on the Friday night show. "Buddy will introduce you as a guest. You'll get two numbers, then join Buddy and have a conversation," said Bull.

Suddenly, I was struck by thoughts of sheer terror. "There might be a hitch. I'm getting married in Houston the day after the show. I planned on heading down there the Thursday before," I said.

Dan and Bull exchanged glances. Finally, Bull responded. "Ah need to know you got the commitment we need. You cain't let some bullshit over a woman cloud your mind," Bull said as he twirled his cigar.

"You mean I only get one chance?"

"Yeah, and I need your answer this afternoon. Wives come 'n go, but opportunity only shows up once. Ah'm still payin' for two dumbass mistakes I made because of the bullshit of love," Bull said.

"OK, boys, I'm sure you can count me in. I'll fly to Houston on Saturday after the Friday night show." I thought of what Trapp once told me. The word that always follows music is business.

* * *

Trapp and I had a heart to heart talk on Saturday.

"My mother and Lisa are on top of the world. Planning this wedding has turned into a quest for them. I don't have to do anything."

I swallowed hard before I spoke. "I might have a conflict the Friday night before the wedding."

"What do you mean?" she asked.

I told her about my debut with Buddy.

"But J. W., that's the night of the r-r-rehearsal dinner."

"The owner was not moved when I told him. I've tried everything to start appearing on the show after the wedding."

"How am I supposed to go to the rehearsal dinner without you?"

"I have an idea. Can't we have the dinner on Thursday? I can fly back for the show on Friday."

"And then turn around and fly back to Houston on Saturday? That's too much to ask."

"I don't care. I'm willing to do that to make this work."

She became animated. "Sorry if I get a little flustered because I wish it was us performing together. We'll have the d-d-dinner the weekend before."

"I knew we could figure this out. I'll see you in two weeks."

* * *

I agreed to meet with Dan, Bull and Buddy the following Thursday. Everyone was waiting when I entered. To the left of Bull was a clone of Charlie Sheen.

"J. W., this here is Buddy," Bull said.

I stuck out my hand but it was ignored. I could see Buddy was agitated. I would also bet my last dollar he had a hangover that required major medication.

"Let's get something straight. I'm the star and I don't need no other wannabes," Buddy said, jerking his thumb at me.

Bull started chomping on his cigar like it was a steak bone. "Let's get one other thing straight," he said, biting the cigar in half, so that the nearest end fell on the table. "I'm the goddamned owner and I will say what you need."

Dan took over like a federal mediator called in to settle a six-month-old miners' strike.

"Now, boys, take it easy. Bull, we know it's your baby and you call the shots. Buddy, you're the star and J. W. is being brought in just to take some of the load off," said Dan.

"As long as he understands his place," Buddy said, sneering at me.

"Why don't we have us a little jam session," Bull said.

Dan walked with me out to the SUV to retrieve the Martin. "Buddy's in kind of a foul mood today," he said.

"No, Buddy's a smalltime prick. Bull had better hope he pulls some heavy duty shit or they're never gonna get rid of him."

"With you on board, he'll be so pissed he's bound to do something to mess things up. So keep your cool and wait your turn."

I followed Dan back into the studio. Bull was chewing a new cigar and tapping lightly on the table. Buddy wore a disinterested look. I led with some of my new tunes while Buddy's look changed to boredom, followed by a speck of interest. After my third song, he got up and grudgingly retrieved his guitar. "Ah think I can improve that sumbitch," he said caustically. We stopped after two more songs. Buddy had mellowed a bit but was still hostile.

"Boys, that was a real winner," said Bull as Dan nodded.

* * *

The rehearsal dinner went off without a flaw. Trapp and I both spoke about Joe and how we wished he could have been with us.

After the dinner, Trapp showed me the presents she bought for our bridal party. Cody got a set of sterling silver cufflinks, Hooker a Swiss watch. Gina got platinum earrings and Michelle a gold and topaz bracelet. Each was inscribed with our wedding date and love from both of us.

Hooker was in Oklahoma recruiting and Michelle was stuck in surgery. Trapp told me Michelle was looking forward to meeting me, but threatened to boycott the ceremony unless we wrote a song for her. She told me she invited Julie and the twins to the wedding and they had an emotional conversation. Julie told Trapp she was bringing me a special surprise.

Trapp said the leader of the band called her a few days ago and asked if we would do a couple of numbers with them at the reception. He said we were like royalty and it would be their honor to back us up. I told her to count me in.

Suddenly, inspiration tapped me on the shoulder. I told Trapp we needed to supplement our gifts to our best friends with a musical tribute. After I told her my plan, she got so excited she did a short gospel-like two-step.

* * *

I was back in Nashville on Tuesday. An idea for a new song popped up when I was leaving Houston, when Trapp said marrying me would help her deal with us being separated. She said it was like the songs where you have to die to stop loving someone. That line about dying stuck with me. By the time we landed, half a verse was finished. It took me several days until the song finally came together.

On Friday, I got to the station a little after five o'clock. At a quarter to eight, Bull asked me to do a few songs in order to warm up the crowd. After I did three tunes and got a nice ovation, Buddy appeared in the wings and kept looking from me back to the audience.

The curtain lifted, Buddy took the stage and opened the show with a medley of his old songs. They flowed easily on the mind but his lyrics were basic, not memorable. At a quarter to nine, I took my place in the wings.

"And now, ladies and gentlemen, we have a real special guest who's dying to meet you. I want to introduce a singer and songwriter who used to be a pro football player. Give it up for John Steele."

I walked on stage and tipped my hat to the crowd. "Howdy folks. I'd like to thank Waylon for that great introduction." I looked to my right and grinned at how annoyed he looked when I called him Waylon. I turned to the band and we slid easily into my first song. When I finished, the applause was sustained. Buoyed, I continued as several people in the audience stood and whistled. When we finished, the entire audience broke into a sustained cheer as Buddy closed the show.

"Jesus Christ, J. W., that switchboard is lightin' up like a Tahitian volcano," Bull said.

"You're a big hit, J. W. I knew this would work," Dan said.

We heard a loud crash.

"What the hell was that?" Bull asked.

We started to head toward the sound when an assistant ran up to us.

"Bull, Buddy threw his guitar against the wall so hard it broke through the sheetrock. Then he stormed out of here."

"Good. Maybe he will be a no-show tomorrow. J. W., you get ready to take over in case that sumbitch drinks a whole silo full of hand sanitizer."

"Boys, as much as I'd like to take you up on the offer, I'm marrying the woman of my dreams tomorrow," I said.

Bull began chewing furiously on his cigar. "Yeah, I forgot. Guess it's too late for you to postpone that, right?"

"If I can't take some time for my own wedding, then the hell with being a star," I said.

"Yeah, okay. You're right. Still, I never knowed me a bride, at any stage of mah life, that I'd trade for bein' a star. No offense to your betrothed, J. W.," Bull said.

"Bull is just bein' a good businessman," Dan said.

"Gentlemen, I am taking care of business by leaving," I said.

"I'd admire it if you could explain that one," said Bull.

"If I was a hit, the audience will want me back and they'll let you know. If I stay away for a while, maybe we can milk it."

"Damn, I think you found a way to bail us out," Dan said.

CHAPTER TWENTY-ONE

On Saturday morning, I arrived in Houston just before eleven o'clock. When I got off the plane, Hooker was waiting for me, accompanied by a stunning brunette.

"This is Linda Palmer," he said.

"J. W., I feel like I've known you for years," she said, extending her hand.

"Linda, it's a pleasure. I'm happy you're here."

Hooker told me they arrived last night and met everyone for dinner. Trapp invited Linda to come over early today to congregate with the family and wedding party, so we offered to let her get ready first as we headed for the bar.

"Looks like you hit the jackpot with Linda. Do you two split the same underwear drawer?" I asked.

He gave me a grin like he was talking to his parole officer.

"Naw, I've been on the lingerie wagon since we met. I don't know what I did to deserve her."

"How'd you meet?"

"She's a professor in the engineering department. Refuses to be an ornament, but happy to be a partner."

"You seem like a new man. I'm happy for you," I told him.

"Son, speaking of hitting the jackpot, you are in for a real treat when you meet Trapp's maid of honor, Michelle. Between her, Trapp, Julie, the twins, Gina,

Linda and Cody's wife, Amy, I felt like you and I are two dumbass jocks at a Mensa meeting."

"Aren't Julie and the twins everything I said they were?" I asked.

"Are you sure you two are just friends?"

"Trust me, I'm sure."

"The twins sang for us last night. Said you were their teacher and they owe it all to you."

"They have so much talent I didn't have to do much," I said.

"Tell me about your television gig," he said.

I said it looked like a pathway to success but there were impediments along the way.

"What do you mean?" he asked.

"Bull is the man with the kingdom, the power and the glory. Plus, he's got a ruthless streak in him. He asked if there was some way I could postpone the wedding and be on tonight's show."

"I'm not surprised. You know nothing in life comes without a price tag. You have to give up something to get what you want. I think this will come down to you choosing Trapp and a life together, or giving that up for the spotlight."

"Why can't I have both?" I asked.

"It's impossible because nothing's free. I'm pretty content now, but look what I gave up to get here."

"But Sylvia left you. That choice was made for you."

"Not exactly. In the beginning, she hinted about a life together, but I couldn't commit." He picked up his beer and sipped. "I hope this decision isn't made for you," he said.

"How?"

"You need to prepare yourself to pick what you want most out of life, a wife, Trapp, or a mistress, music."

His cell phone buzzed.

"Linda's ready. Why don't I get a cab and run her over to Trapp's? I picked up your tux and left it in the closet," he said, after handing me the keys to the rental car.

I stumbled over my next words. "Listen, Hooker, I love Trapp more than life itself. She'll always be my number one choice."

"Son, it's not me you have to convince. You found the perfect woman. Music is beating on your door. Remember that Sinatra song you're always quoting. You're 'riding high as a rocket in April and you get shot in the ass in May.'"

I handed him the gift for Trapp, a string of pearls, and asked if Linda would give it to her before the ceremony. He left with Linda to help Cody escort guests to their seats, and I texted Trapp that all systems were go, before I went to get ready.

* * *

I arrived thirty minutes before the wedding was scheduled to begin. People were raving about the style of our tuxedos, black tailcoats and trousers, contrasted with white on white dress shirts, waistcoats and white bow ties. The florist also presented my attendants with periwinkle boutonnieres which matched the color of the gowns worn by Michelle and Gina. As a tribute to our heritage, Hooker and I wore black ostrich boots.

The grounds were decorated with light blue delphiniums and pink peonies. A group of dogwood trees were in full bloom, bursting with pink and white flowers.

A canopy was placed to the left of the lake at the rear of the property. It was surrounded by over one hundred ivory chairs. A white carpet led from the rear of the house and served as an aisle.

A huge tent was erected on the other side of the pool in case Mother Nature was in a surly mood. Bars were strategically located near the rear, as servers in black vests, white shirts and orchid bowties scurried around making last minute adjustments. Three chefs manned different food stations. Organ music flowed softly in the background.

I watched Cody and Hooker finish seating our guests. The florist came over and fitted me with a white boutonniere. I spotted Julie and the twins, went over and we all embraced. I was puzzled that the twins wore gowns that matched the bridesmaids. I was ready to ask about the dresses when Julie whispered they had a surprise for me. I felt someone take my arm and looked up to see Cody and Amy. We all exchanged hugs. I was also introduced to Trapp's cousin, Mario.

I said hello to everyone else. Tony and I shook hands as he told me everything I emailed him about was ready, before he introduced me to the priest.

As we waited for the ceremony to begin, I thought of my mom, dad and grandmother. This was a day they would have treasured.

Linda came over and told me Trapp was the most magnificent bride she had ever seen. She described her gown in glowing terms—a silk and satin strapless sheath, covered with Alencon lace adorned with appliqués of white pearls, and finished with a handmade lace bolero. She got a little choked up when she told me my gift to Trapp was perfect.

Right before the ceremony began, the twins rose and walked over to the two microphones beside the altar. Tony followed them and handed Trapp's Martin to Lexi. I felt a ripple in my chest and a hush come over the congregation as they began to sing. The song was Clint Black's mega-hit, claiming that love is 'Something That We Do.' The harmony was precise, the girls' performance was flawless and the mystery of the matching dresses was solved.

I felt overcome with emotion when they finished. Then, Lexi handed the Martin to Emily, before they slipped into John Barry's old hit, 'Your Love Amazes Me.' Their guitar performance was simple, but polished. It was their voices that excelled, a result of maturity and blossoming into womanhood, a huge step from when we first started almost two years ago. Emily had turned into a superb *mezzo* soprano while Lexi had emerged as a solid alto. The blend of their voices was smooth and rich, just like a laser-cut diamond.

When they finished, faint murmurs swept through the crowd. I caught Julie's eye and we exchanged looks like proud parents. Tony retrieved the Martin and the twins took their seats next to Julie, beaming like two starbursts.

At that moment, the organist began to play 'Ave Maria' by Bach and Gounod. Gina stepped forward first and walked down the aisle to where Cody was standing. When she reached his side, the contrast was startling. Gina, at five foot three, standing next to Cody in his tux, reminded me of a periwinkle smart car parked beside a black Mack truck. I walked over, gave Gina a kiss, then Cody escorted her to her place before returning to his side.

Michelle appeared and walked slowly down the white carpet. At once, I knew Hooker's over-the-top description was an understatement. She was stunning, and her face was lit up like a Roman candle. Her smile shouted that she was up for some old-time fun with some new-found friends. I remembered the stories Trapp told me and felt an instant connection.

She stood about five foot six, with auburn hair and sparkling blue eyes, wore an exquisite strapless periwinkle gown and carried a bouquet of lilac and white orchids. Hooker met her and took her arm. I walked over and gave her a peck on the cheek.

"Trapp said you're Henley and she's Frey," she whispered, with a smile as wide as a canyon.

"That's because I'm a 'Victim of Love' and she's still looking for 'Life In The Fast Lane'," I said. She giggled before they walked toward the makeshift altar.

I turned to face the rear of the house as the organist broke into Beethoven's 'Ode to Joy.'

Trapp and Marion emerged from the sunroom with smiles as broad as Texas as they slowly approached. On the way, Trapp touched the pearls around her neck and blew me a kiss. The priest asked who was presenting Trapp and Marion replied, "Her father, who is looking down and smiling, and me, her mother." If there was a dry eye to be found, I'm sure we would have discovered their tear ducts were welded shut.

The ceremony was short and moving. After taking traditional vows, Trapp and I added one more promise in a short whisper heard only by the wedding party. "What God and a few diminished chords have joined together, let no lyric or harmonic put asunder."

The priest looked puzzled as we both laughed softly. Out of the corner of my eye, I saw Tony rise and approach us carrying Trapp's Martin.

"It's time, Father," I whispered, and he gave a short nod.

Trapp looked at me quizzically as I retrieved the guitar and slid the strap around my neck. I turned toward the congregation and said, "I'm taking a huge risk by following Emily and Lexi."

Sprinkles of laughter followed as I faced Trapp and said, "This is my gift to you. It's called, 'Until We Are No More'." Silence swept over us as I began to sing.

* * *

I'll hold your hand and take my vows;
Love has touched us, here and now;
I'll take your arm, we'll beat the storm;
And when it's cold, I'll keep you warm;
If I get weak, you'll make me strong;
For that, I'll give to you this song;
To steal a kiss between our souls;
This life we'll share, as we grow old
Chorus
Our love is like a song we sing
A book of poems, our wedding ring
A walk beside a peaceful shore
In love until we are no more

* * *

If you get lost, I'll make you found;
And always help you stand your ground;
As we stand here all aglow;
Hand in hand, to face tomorrow;
Love is music; so sublime;
Love forever; yours and mine;

When we tap on heaven's door;
In love until we are no more

I handed Tony the guitar, rejoined Trapp and looked toward the priest, who nodded his approval.

"Do you have the ring?" the priest asked, as Hooker extended an envelope to me.

I repeated my vows and slipped the wedding ring on Trapp's finger. Hooker then produced another envelope to Trapp, whose hands were shaking as she faced me. She repeated her vows and slipped my wedding band on. Then, she made another withdrawal from the envelope and said, "Julie and I send this to you with love."

She opened her hand and showed me my Super Bowl ring. My eyes grew misty as I thought about how I planned to make sure Trapp and I were stable financially before I redeemed the ring. I became overwhelmed at her gesture of love and did everything in my power to keep from breaking down, but could not stop one very persistent tear that insisted on falling.

"By the power vested in me, by God and the great state of Texas, I now pronounce you husband and wife," the priest said.

Rousing applause broke out as we shared a kiss, then made our first walk as a married couple. Handshakes were everywhere as the organist cranked up the volume. Photographs finished in record time, as the picture-perfect weather planted a kiss on every pose.

Michelle was like an old friend. I told her how much she meant to Trapp and thanked her for everything she did so long ago. After we got to the head table, Hooker gave the best man toast.

"Ladies and gentlemen, there are few events in life that can equal a wedding. In honor of my two best friends and greatest songwriters, I propose this toast, in their own words:

* * *

'We'll always stay together,
Wrapped up in a love that won't unwind
Cause I've stolen every moment,
And trapped them in the pages of my mind'."

The feast was on. Everything was served buffet style and presented with the usual Texas understatement. A waiter brought us barbeque, chicken fried steaks, and kick-ass Texas chili with jalapeño biscuits. Trapp told me the menu was her gift to me.

"What's for dessert?" Hooker asked the waiter.

"You have a choice of hazelnut chocolate truffles and bing cherry tart *petit fours.*"

"Like a bridge over truffled water," I said.

Trapp's eyes lit up.

"Swing low, s-sweet cherry tart," she added.

Those within hearing distance rolled their eyes.

"I'm starting to regret I gave up two nose jobs and a butt tuck for this," said Michelle.

"I could be at a slide-rule symposium," added Linda, as Michelle raised her glass and clinked it with hers.

"I should be giving a lecture on benzodiazepines," Julie said, as everyone chuckled.

Hooker shrugged and gave me a look of hopelessness that suggested we were being held back together to repeat the third grade.

The band warmed up and a makeshift dance floor was put in place. Trapp and I danced our first dance to 'Stars Over Texas,' by Tracy Lawrence. The highlight of the evening was a medley of the band's rendition of top ten songs by Alabama, until the front man spoke to the crowd, while additional microphones were put in place.

"Ladies and gentlemen, I have been asked to give you a rare treat. We all know the bride and groom are professional singers and songwriters. Let's see if they will favor us with one of their songs. Trapp, J. W., will you join me?"

I looked at Trapp and saw the glint in her eyes. She nodded. We rose and headed for the bandstand, hand in hand. All the band members were applauding as we approached the stage and headed to our microphones. Cody and Hooker were standing at the bar laughing like old friends. Julie and Mario were having a glass of wine and the twins stopped their conversation with Linda, moved closer and looked at Trapp and me like we were about to be deified.

"Ladies and gentlemen, we're thrilled to be here with you," I began, and made a sweeping gesture to Trapp. "We'd like to start with a vocal tribute to our oldest friends, Michelle and Billy, our maid of honor and best man. We wanted to write a song for them but someone else beat us to it."

The band broke into the opening strains of the Beatles hit, 'Michelle.' Trapp and I accentuated the French phrasing and Michelle and Hooker started to dance a Texas two-step as the crowd whistled and cheered.

Afterward, the drummer and lead guitarist ramped up the intro to an old Robert Palmer hit in Hooker's honor. Trapp and I held our mikes in our left hands and waved our right index fingers at him. Linda, Julie and Mario moved next to Michelle as they all began pointing at Hooker as they were joined by Gina, Cody, Amy and the twins. Everyone started to yell that it was it time for him to just stand up and face it because he was 'Addicted To Love!'

When we finished, a standing ovation broke out. Even the servers, chefs and bartenders stopped and joined in. We joined hands and took several bows. Two songs turned into six and the congratulations and best wishes did not stop for almost half an hour after we finished.

* * *

The party did not end until after midnight. Trapp and I said our goodbyes and headed for our suite at the downtown Westin. We made love, giggled, reviewed the day and held each other.

"That song you wrote was beautiful," she whispered.

"My Super Bowl ring was unbelievable. How did you pull that off?"

"Julie told me about the ring but didn't know the n-name of the pawn shop. I asked Hooker and he told me about Morrie. I sent Julie a check and had her pick it up." She took a deep breath before continuing. "We need to talk about s-s-something else," she said, growing solemn. I considered making a joke but could see she was serious. "You once told me you didn't have kids with Carol because you weren't sure about her, right?"

"That's right."

"But you like kids, don't you?"

"The twins can be my references."

"What would you do if we had a child?"

"It would be unbelievable," I said.

She lifted her head and looked me directly in the eyes. "We're going to have a b-b-baby, J. W. It must have happened the night after we did that concert outside Mark Thomas's office."

Her words hit me like a jug of ice water flung directly into my face. "I thought you were on the pill."

"I am, but I got a sinus infection and had to take antibiotics. I had no idea they would interfere with my birth control p-pills, but they did." I was dumbfounded, and then elated as I let out a shout. She threw her arms around my neck like I was saving her from drowning. I could feel droplets from her eyes moisten my neck.

"I didn't t-think I could ever be this happy," she said.

"When are you due?" I asked.

"The second week in January. Seven months from now."

"Are we having a boy or a girl?"

"Does it matter?"

"Not really. I want to know if I should go out and buy a pink or blue Martin."

She brushed away a tear and smiled. "I'm having an ultrasound in a f-few weeks. We'll know then."

"Have you thought about names?"

"If it's a b-boy, I'd like to call him Joseph."

"Me too. What about a girl?"

"I'll let you p-p-pick. That way you can spoil her rotten."

I was suddenly struck with a semi-terrifying thought. "Jesus, Trapp, the world is really in deep shit now. Our child will be half German and half Italian."

"So?"

I struck a serious pose, like I was about to deliver a speech advocating a unilateral nuclear arms freeze.

"The kid's German side will fight with the Italian side over whether to leave the gun and take the *canolis*, or vice versa."

CHAPTER TWENTY-TWO

I called Dan on Wednesday and he told me the next show was not set until the end of July. Since I was free for a while, Trapp rented us a place on the water in Galveston. A week in the sun and surf turned into a cleansing of the soul.

June melted into July. Trapp flew in with Hooker and Linda the night before the show. I got word shortly before nine that Buddy had a family emergency and I would be hosting. I told Bull I wanted Trapp to perform with me and he agreed. She was overjoyed when I told her that we would be appearing together for the first time on live television. We spent two hours polishing our top three songs and arrived at the station shortly after five. I opened the show and Trapp joined me. When we finished, the audience was on their feet cheering.

After a few moments, the band broke into the introduction for 'Steele Trapp Mind.' As I started to sing, I heard a commotion and saw Buddy entering the studio. He waved his hat at the crowd and began to speak.

"Thank you, ladies and gentlemen. I want to thank the Lord, Jesus Christ, for helping cure mah daddy and letting me get back in time to be here with you all."

The crowd responded as Buddy shot us a triumphant look.

"I'd like to thank John, here, for standin' in for me, but I'm back and the show is again in my strong hands."

Good strong hands, my ass. Let's put it to a vote.

"Isn't that the best news ever, folks?" I said, waving my arms to encourage a cheer. We're thrilled for Waylon Senior and wouldn't want to impose on Junior to perform under such stress. So, why don't we pick up where we were before we got the good news?'

Trapp and I did two more songs. When the show ended, Buddy was in my face before the curtain hit the floor. The odor of alcohol was strong enough to press my pants.

"Who the fuck do you think you are?" he screamed.

I started to reply when he swung. I managed to get my forearm up in time to deflect the blow. Buddy staggered slightly as he moved forward, then lost his balance as I tossed the Martin to a stage hand. A security guard came over as Buddy started screaming at the top of his voice.

"Bull, you'd better tell this sonofabitch it's mah show. We have a contract, so tell him to git outta here," Buddy said.

"It was yer show. But now, it ain't. Check out Section eighteen of your contract. You violated the conduct detrimental clause when you swung at J. W. You're fired."

Buddy was dragged to the exit by two stagehands. Bull stepped in front of me and put his hands on my shoulders as his grin intensified.

"J. W., I want you to take over the show when we come back next month. We'll work on a new guest list soon," Bull said.

I felt my chest swell and my heart surge. Trapp stepped up and brought me back to reality.

"What about a contract?' she asked.

"Not yet," Bull said. "I gotta make sure the folks are on board. Then we'll talk contract. For now, it's strictly on a per diem basis."

* * *

For the next month, I continued to work on arrangements. On Tuesday before the next show, Dan told me to come in for a meeting at noon. He sounded excited and said he did not want to spoil the surprise. Bull was twirling his cigar like it was a maestro's baton, when I walked in.

"Two major developments. First, Friday night's show is being moved to Saturday. Guess who your special guest will be on Saturday? None other than Wes McGovern," Dan said.

I sat there in silence as my mind ran a sprint. Dan and Bull grew engorged with excitement.

Bull started shifting his cigar like a mini-drumstick. My mind became flooded with conflicting thoughts, especially Wes telling Trapp that I was second rate. I thought for a long moment and decided it was time to act happy.

"Hot damn, let's start making calls to our advertisers. This sumbitch is gonna be bigger than the Super Bowl," Bull said.

Bull told me Wes was going to be my only guest. Dan told me to talk as much as I could about Wes, our show together in Houston and Wes's latest cuts for his new album.

There was a little tension between me and Wes at rehearsal. I decided not to tell him I thought he was an asshole for that stunt he pulled trying to split me and Trapp up. I also got a scent of alcohol coming from his direction and knew it would be pointless to say anything.

The crowd was standing room only. After my opening number, Wes came out to thunderous applause, did two of his old hits and then joined me for a chat. A coffee cup sat on the table next to him. I could not tell what beverage it contained, but ruled out no-foam latte.

"So Wes, you're sounding better than a fine-tuned symphony. Tell us what you've been doing," I began.

Wes brought us up to date. Then, he picked up his guitar and asked me to do a number together. I panicked because we had not rehearsed. Relief came when he said, "How about 'Reflections of Love'?"

We did the song and the crowd gave us a massive ovation. I heard a huge noise off to the right of the set. Buddy Wilcox staggered onto the stage, whiskey bottle in one hand and waving a baseball bat with the other.

"This is my fuckin' show!" he screamed, as Wes ducked behind the couch. I stayed in place, as people dove for cover or tried to run for the exits.

Lowering my shoulder, I drove it right into Buddy's side, like he forgot to call for a fair catch. He went down in a heap as the bat went flying. Buddy jumped up and swung at me, but I ducked as two deputy sheriffs entered the stage and put him in handcuffs. Turning, I saw Wes scampering off the stage. Bull came out and addressed the crowd.

"Folks, we're right sorry about this interruption. We're gonna call off the rest of the show, but you all come back next week."

"I wonder how ol' Wes is," Dan said when Bull finished.

"He ran out of here faster than an Olympic sprinter. Wes is definitely not the guy I'd want beside me if we had to go into combat," I said.

"I'm bettin' the ratings will be through the roof on this, Bull," Dan said.

"Well, boys, as much fun as this was, I'm going to Houston tomorrow," I said.

"When are you coming back?" Dan asked.

"The end of the week. In time for the show next Friday," I said.

* * *

I arrived in Houston on Sunday morning of the Labor Day weekend and found Trapp waiting. She gave me a hug and we headed toward home. "I have a present for you," she said, as she handed me an envelope with a return address of St. Luke's Medical Center.

I began to read.

"Are you disappointed it's not a b-b-b-boy?" she asked.

"Are you crazy? I'm going to spoil her so rotten you'll have to hire an ex-CIA body guard to accompany her to pre-school. I get to name her. You promised."

"What's her n-name?"

"It's Charlotte, after Charlotte Bronte, my favorite writer. It will remind me of that line from *Jane Eyre*, about 'asking you to pass through life by my side, and to be my second self.'"

We walked inside where Marion met us. "Quick, come see the news," she said.

We entered the family room and found Lisa and Tony.

"There was a wild scene in Nashville last night. A near brawl broke out on a cable station when the man who was ousted as host of a weekly music show, came back with a baseball bat and tried to crash the party. Here's a portion of one of the videos now," the announcer said.

The screen lit up with me and Wes talking as Buddy came onstage. It then changed to all Buddy as he went into his rant. Suddenly, a figure in a black Stetson hat tackled Buddy, before the cops arrived and took him out in handcuffs.

"Now, we'll go to our colleague in Nashville, Heather Tyler," the anchor said.

The screen flashed to the front of the station where Bull was standing next to a news reporter.

"Phil, I'm here with station owner Bull Farnham. Bull, can you tell us what happened?"

"Well, we was airin' our weekend extravaganza. Our host was J. W. Steele and our special guest was ol' Wes McGovern. Toward the end of the program, the ex-host, Buddy Wilcox, tried to take over, but ol' Wes was successful in disarmin' him."

"Wait a minute!" I yelled. "Wes ain't unique enough to do that."

"What about J. W. Steele, the host? Was he injured?" Heather asked.

"Naw, J. W. is a tough ol' bird. He's fine, especially after Wes did all the heavy liftin'."

Heather turned toward the camera. "Check out our website for the whole video. Back to you, Phil."

"Who subdued Buddy?" Lisa asked.

"Had to be J. W.," Tony said. "I recognize a hit from special teams when I see one."

"Why did Bull say Wes c-c-cleaned house?" Trapp asked.

"I don't know. We were both wearing black hats. Maybe he got confused."

"J. W., you're six foot three. Wes might be five foot nine if they put him on a shoe stretcher for six m-m-months. No way Bull could have made that mistake," Trapp said.

"Maybe not. But, we both know Bull is not exactly the go-to guy at a Phi Beta Kappa retreat," I said.

"I think you should straighten him out when you get back," Marion said.

"That will be my first order of business."

CHAPTER TWENTY-THREE

I flew back to Nashville on Thursday after Labor Day. Neither Bull nor Dan would take my calls while I was away. I finally reached Dan after I landed.

"I've been calling for a week and have left you a dozen messages since Sunday," I said.

"Sorry, I've been tied up."

"What is this bullshit that Bull has been telling everyone Wes was the one who put Buddy out of commission?"

"You know Bull. He gets confused sometimes."

"Confused is one thing. That's retrograde amnesia. You know Bull lied."

"I know. We've even gotten a couple of videos from people with their phones," Dan said.

"I've got some ideas for the next show. When can we sit down?" I asked.

"Uh, J. W., we need to talk," Dan said, as I grew anxious. "Bull signed a deal with Wes McGovern to host the show."

I felt waves of betrayal and sabotage, then outrage as I pictured Dan and Bull.

"Why?"

"Lots of reasons. Wes is a big name. Now that the show got plastered all over the news, the ratings will be sky high and Bull will make a fortune from ad revenues and syndication rights."

"That sleazy son-of-a-bitch. What was all that shit about me taking over?"

"At one time, that was the plan. But when Wes became available, all that changed."

"So Bull made up that crap about Wes stopping Buddy so he could sweeten the deal," I said.

"That's partly true. Bull was also afraid your heart wasn't in this, J. W. You were just like Buddy, except you have a wife instead of a love affair with whiskey."

I tried to mount a defense even though I realized there was truth to what Dan was saying.

"This would have all worked out. Trapp is getting ready to join me any day now," I said.

"Too late. Bull has his mind made up. Plus, Wes has already signed the contract. You've got a lot of talent, don't give up," Dan said.

* * *

It took me about ten seconds to realize that Dan was right. I texted Toby, but he was on tour with his band. Next, I called Jake Skylar. He promised to get back to me if and when he had something.

I reached Trapp and she said Bull played this one beautifully. By refusing to give me a contract, he could dump me and I could not sue.

I drove into the city and headed for the Outlaw Lounge, a legendary home for songwriters and artists trying to make a name. I briefly considered trying the Bluebird Café, but decided it was too much in demand and I would have a better shot catching on at a place less popular.

A crimson awning with the name "Outlaw's" scrolled on it, welcomed me. Photos and posters covered the glass doors at the entrance. I walked inside and approached the bar. The bartender, a huge man with a full beard and shoulder-length dark hair, was loading beer bottles into coolers.

"What can I git ya, pardner?" he asked.

"A Coors Light and some info," I said.

"Info is free. Beer's four-fifty," he said, shoving the bottle in front of me.

"Deal. How can I get to play here?" I asked.

"Simple. Write a killer song, play and sing like a legend, and make sure your music sizzles. Monday's open mic night and we try to fit everyone in. Be in line by 4:30 p.m."

"Will I get on stage?"

"Unlikely. We always have more people than time. If your name gets drawn, it's yer night in the box. If not, you might get a raincheck. No drums, and no backin' tracks. Yer on yer own and mah advice is to do yer best not to suck."

"I'll be back Monday."

"Don't bother. We're booked for two months solid. Try us in a few weeks."

He told me about a new place down by the river that had just been revamped. He said the name escaped him, but it was some term used by football teams.

A few minutes later, I reached the river bank and turned up First Avenue. Immediately, I saw a huge sign reading, "The Huddle." The place was located almost directly across from the stadium. A sign in the window read, "Artists welcome. Open mic night Friday and Saturday. Come in and become a fightin' Titan."

I went in and spoke to the bartender who reminded me of a geriatric Matthew McConaughey. He was chewing on a toothpick and wore old faded levis, a blue cowboy shirt with pearl buttons, a beat-up pair of leather boots and a look that said he had traveled down a lot of roads, all of them unpaved.

He said I needed to audition and went to get the manager. Although the place was clean, there was a faint odor of beer and fried food that must have avoided the housekeeping crew.

The bandstand was situated directly in front of me. It was about twelve foot square and had just enough room for guitars and drums. There was a small dance floor covered in dull gray and white tiles. A limited menu was available, consisting mostly of sandwiches and appetizers. A row of black stools faced the bar, with swiveling capability so people could turn and face the band, or watch the crowd.

A minute later, the bartender returned. "The boss wants to see you. Follow me," he said, jerking his thumb toward the rear.

We walked to the back to an office in the last room on the left where a woman was on the telephone. Her conversation ended and she stood up to greet me. She was middle-aged, classically professional and very attractive. Her scent was rich and provocative without overloading the senses. I found myself staring into her eyes as she stepped forward and extended her hand. She was sexual, but sultry is the term I would pick to describe her. I looked into her face and thought she resembled an aging Dina Meyer, the actress from *NCIS* and *Castle*.

"Hi, I'm Sunny Sterling," she said.
"I'm J. W. Steele," I said.
"Can you play and sing?"
"I can."
"Show me."

"I don't have my guitar with me. It's in my car."

"How far away?"

"Fifteen minutes."

"Too far, I can't wait half an hour."

She walked to the closet, opened the door, removed a Golden Ovation and handed it to me.

"You can use this. One of the musicians left it behind," she said.

The Ovation was a bitch to tune, but I did two songs and they stared at me intently.

"Yer good, son, don't let nobody tell you otherwise," Garland said.

"Not just good, but damn good," Sunny said.

Suddenly, I got inspired and broke out into the old Bobby Hebb song, 'Sunny,' and sang the opening line about how my life was filled with sorrow until she smiled at me and really erased the pain. She tossed her head back and laughed as Garland left for the bar.

"Do I get to take the stage on open mic night?" I asked finally.

"No, I have something else in mind," she said. "I have to know what I'm getting. Tell me about yourself."

I gave her the short version of my life. Her eyes lit up when I told her about my football career.

"OK, here's the deal. I got this place as part of a divorce settlement. My ex-husband is an idiot who ran it into the ground by wasting money on young babes and stupid bets with his bookie. I want to do something to appeal to the football crowd," she said.

She looked at the ring on my left hand.

"Tell me about your wife."

"We live in Franklin. She's in Houston now."

"Are you separated?"

"No. She has some business to wrap up before she can return."

"I want you to come to work for me," she said. "I'm offering you a job playing cocktail hour, six to eight o'clock. I can pay you four-fifty a week. If business starts to increase, your money will go up. There's just a couple of conditions you have to agree to or this won't work."

"Like what?" I asked.

"You have to show up regularly. Don't drink while onstage or hook up with any women."

I shook my head before I answered. "I don't intend to hook up. I told you, I'm married."

"Everybody is married unless they're alone or with someone. Don't let it interfere with your gig here, that's all I'm asking. We're selling sex to the crowd here, but it's only a side dish. The entrée is music and you're gonna be my head chef," she said.

"You can count on me, Sunny." I smiled.

* * *

I spent the rest of the night polishing my act. I called Trapp and told her I was now employed, and was planning to have her join me onstage.

The following day, I arrived at the Huddle at five thirty. Sunny came out, wished me good luck and found a seat at the end of the bar.

At two minutes to six o'clock, I took the stage. There were only half a dozen people in the bar. I did a sound check and spoke to the crowd, but there was no response.

Sunny gave me a brief smile while Garland watched with his arms folded. I did three songs and no one noticed, so I started to play to the people at the only three tables that were occupied.

"Ladies and gentlemen, I'm told we have a verdict. Mister Foreperson, would you please tell the court what the jury has decided about convicting me for this act," I said, looking at the hairy guy with three empty beer bottles in front of him.

"If ah'm votin', you get life at hard labor," he said.

"Folks, we have life. Does anyone want to go for the death penalty?" I asked, as even Garland grinned.

A few patrons trickled in. When a group of twelve entered, I broke into the old Beatles song 'A Little Help From My Friends.' They high-fived and clapped and the party was on for the next hour. After a short break, I went back on until eight o'clock. When finished, I got word that Sunny wanted to see me. She was seated behind the desk and motioned for me to sit.

"That was outstanding," she began.

"I just hope the word gets out about cocktail hour," I said.

"I want you to understand the dynamics here. This place is saving me. I have a daughter who hasn't spoken to me for years. My ex-husband is giving me fits. You may have heard of him. His name is Richmond Silver. He's a former big-time car dealer who pissed everything away."

"His name's not familiar," I said.

"In his commercials he calls himself 'High Dollar Ritchie' whose slogan is he'll bend over backwards to do business with you. His most obnoxious spot showed him bending over about to show his bare butt and saying he would make a deal with you even in the moonlight. The station was forced to pull it."

"What's his problem?" I asked.

"He's a cancer. Garland worked for him here for over twenty years and even lent Ritchie eighteen grand. My lawyer told me the debt was discharged when Ritchie filed for bankruptcy. I was forced to sell my real estate agency to pay our debts. I got about fifty cents on the dollar."

"I'm not sure why you're telling me this, Sunny."

"The divorce is not final and we're trying to finish the negotiations. He comes by here from time to time just to upset me. My lawyer says I can't keep him out because he's still part owner. So, if I happen to be in a funk or downright nasty, I'm asking you to overlook it," she said.

I reflected for a moment and decided it was time for me to let down a bit. "Let me say it again. I won't let you down," I told her.

* * *

As I settled into the gig, the crowds started to grow. In no time, the word about me, my music and the party-like scene began spreading all over town. Sunny said business had doubled in the two weeks since I made my debut.

I got to the club early the following afternoon and sat at the bar. Garland slid a beer toward me, then came over to talk.

"What's the story with Sunny? Is that her real name or a nickname?" I asked.

"Sunshine Dylan Sterling. She told me her parents were in their hippie phase in college when she was conceived. It was after they smuggled in some killer weed from North Carolina called 'Outer Banks Sunshine,' before they went to a Bob Dylan concert. She says it was before they discovered that antiseptic sprays and hefty bank accounts could peacefully co-exist with peace, love and dope."

"Did she come from the nightclub business?"

"No, but Sunny said hard work is the key to success in any business. She got this place by agreeing not to dig too deep into the assets Ritchie is hiding," he said.

"Sounds like she's having a tough time with him."

"She is. That asshole had ten automobile dealerships but only has one left."

"What's his story?" I asked.

Garland grew a look of anger, then disgust. "He's a compulsive gambler who ran his business into the ground and spent all his money on loan sharks."

"Why would he turn this place over to Sunny?"

"So he didn't have to pay alimony."

"What did she see in him?" I asked.

"I think he dazzled her at first. He even flew her to Vegas on their first date. Stuff like that clouded her judgment."

"He ran this place for a while?"

"Almost twenty years. I was his head bartender."

"How long were they together?" I asked

"Almost twelve years. He's a real scumbag. He even had Sunny's mother mortgage her house for him. Sunny's mom died a year later so he just refused to pay her back."

"Why'd she put up with him for so long?" I

asked.

"She's a good woman who tried hard to make it work."

Ten minutes later, I took the stage and formed a kinship with the crowd. Sunny was sitting at the end of the bar when I finished and asked me to meet her in the office.

"Business is really up, so I'm not the only one who thinks you're a star," she said. She gave me a short hug and I told her about Trapp joining me onstage. She smiled and said that would transform the music scene into an all-out party that would draw an ever bigger crowd.

She gave me another hug and I felt like I had found a home.

CHAPTER TWENTY-FOUR

Tuesday's mail brought a letter from Jake Skylar. He told me he represented Doc Grayson, a big name country singer who wanted to discuss cutting one of my songs. I cradled the letter like it was an inheritance check and called Trapp.

"Don't sign anything without letting me see it," she warned.

My hands shook as I waited for Jake to come on the line.

"J. W., how are you? Doc Grayson wants to see if we can put a deal together."

He gave me several options. I explained Trapp's situation with Joe's fraud case and the practice in Houston, as well as the baby and told him she would be in town next week.

"Why don't we set it up for Friday, around noon, in my office?"

I called Trapp and could barely contain my excitement. She was much more pragmatic, and brought me down to reality, telling me that she would pack a business suit for our lunch with Jake and Doc.

On Thursday of the following week, Trapp arrived at noon, looking amazing despite the fact she was seven months pregnant. I took her to the condo before we left for the Huddle.

I was flying high as I introduced her to Sunny. After my first set, Trapp told me she was not feeling well, then left for home. When I arrived an hour later, she was better and started going over her notes. She told me that we must have something Doc wanted and we had to figure out what they were willing to pay. I kept saying they liked the music and she said there was more to it than that. She told me we would find a way to smoke it out into the open.

* * *

On Friday, we arrived at Skylar's office and were escorted into the conference room where Jake and a tall man in a silver Stetson hat were waiting.

"Trapp, J. W., this is Doc Grayson," Jake said.

Doc tipped his hat and stuck out his hand. He shook hers first, then mine. He put his hat on the table and we saw he was blessed with a head full of salt and pepper hair flowing like a mane.

"Where's Ace?" I asked.

Jake seemed to grow somber.

"He had another meeting but sends you his best," he said.

"Tell him we missed him," I said.

Jake nodded briefly and we got down to business.

"I love your music, Doc," Trapp said. "Although 'That's What She Told Me' has caused a lot of red faces in the c-c-circles I travel in."

That was Doc's signature song and it involved some highly suggestive, if not downright pornographic, lyrics. It consisted of a series of sayings, followed by the words: "that's what she told me." My favorite line was, "this thing between us is 'bout to get bigger," followed by everybody singing that magical line and then chugging their beer.

"That one was really huge, that's for sure," said Jake.

"That's what she told me," said Doc, as we all roared.

We took our seats and got acquainted.

"Is Doc your real name?" Trapp began.

"It's a nickname. First name is Ken. I spent a year in medical school before deciding I wanted music more than medicine. I gave up paroxysmal ventricular tachycardia during the week and replaced it with the boot scootin' boogie on the weekends."

"Any regrets?" I asked.

"Only that I couldn't find tunes for some of the lyrics I wrote back then. Somehow, I don't think there's a memorable melody for:

* * *

'You broke my heart
Like you gave it ischemia
When I saw your fat ass,
It gave me bulimia.

I decided to play.

* * *

You shattered my life
Down in Grove, Oklahoma,
Made my love blind
Like closed angle glaucoma.

It was Trapp's turn. She sang her entry, a move I recognized as one designed to keep her stuttering in check.

* * *

My love for you
Was like credit card debts;
That I'll never pay off

'Cause I've got Tourette's

By now we were all laughing uproariously. Finally, Jake spoke.

"Why don't we rename the band, 'Musical Malpractice'?" he asked, and we all broke up.

In no time, we were swapping stories like old friends. Finally, Jake brought us back to the business of music.

"Trapp, J. W., Doc wants to record some of your material and write together. Is that something you'd be interested in?"

"Of course we're interested. We respect Doc, both as an artist and a s-s-songwriter. We just need to know exactly what you are proposing," Trapp said.

"Doc is offering to buy the rights for the song 'The Promise of a Lie.' You all would get a flat fee and Doc would retain all publishing and royalty rights."

"You mean give up all rights to the music and not be listed as a writer?" Trapp asked.

"That's the way we always do it. We could also talk about you two opening for the band."

"First of all, I won't be able to tour for a while because there's so m-m-much to finish up in Houston, Also. I'm due in January. Why can't Doc cut whatever s-song he wants and we share the royalties?" Trapp asked.

"That won't work," Doc said.

"It worked well for Glen Campbell and Jimmy Webb," I countered.

No one spoke for a moment. Finally, Doc responded. "I've been down this road before. I don't mean to be a hardass, but that point's non-negotiable."

"Sorry, but as we say in Texas, that hound dog won't hunt. Thank you for m-m-meeting with us. We wish you all the best," Trapp said.

"I'm sorry, too," Doc said finally. "Good luck to you both."

"Maybe we all need a little time to see if there is a way to compromise," Jake said.

Trapp and I walked in silence to the elevator.

"Trust me on this one, J. W. It would not have worked."

"You have all my confidence. I'll do whatever you say."

"We have to keep the p-publishing rights. If we give that up, Doc could claim he wrote our stuff and no one would ever know they're our songs."

"Don't second guess yourself."

"Then why does it feel like I couldn't c-c-come across for us?"

I shot her a naughty grin. "As Doc might say, 'That's What She Told Me'."

* * *

Trapp wanted to skip my performance at the Huddle, but I convinced her to come and offered to have her join me on stage. She declined, saying she was not up to performing.

Sunny came over to greet us as I took the stage. I was ready to begin my first set as I saw them head off toward the office. It was almost an hour later when they reappeared. Trapp threw her head back and belly-laughed. After finishing my final set and packing up my guitars, Trapp and Sunny shared a brief hug.

"What was with you and Sunny and the love fest?" I asked when we reached the outside.

"She is one helluva woman. I can see why you think she's so attractive," said Trapp.

"What do you mean?" I asked, as my voice broke despite myself.

"C'mon, J. W. She a beauty and incredibly lonely. She's also v-v-vulnerable even without the 'let's have a two-day hump session' pumps. Don't tell me you never noticed."

"I swear to you nothing happened. I wouldn't let it," I said.

"I know it d-didn't," she said finally. "One, I trust you. Two, I believe her. There's a helluva lot more to her than physical attributes. She's been f-f-flogged by life and survived some real turmoil. Plus, if you two would have gotten together, she would have t-told me. I am a pretty good judge of character credibility and she has both."

"I would not cheat."

"I know that. You know what convinced me? She admitted she thought you were h-h-hot but would not interfere in our marriage because she couldn't do that to another woman. But, that took second place to her biggest bona-fide truth disclosure."

"What?"

"She said you made her feel like a grandmother waiting for you outside a n-nursery school."

I chuckled and pictured Sunny saying that.

"Being around a beauty like Sunny makes me feel pretty inhibited. I don't feel like my old feminine self with the b-b-baby due and I'm dealing with the hormones and mood swings."

"What were you two laughing about when you came into the bar?"

"Sunny also told me she knew right away that you were not the answer for her. She said the only reason women need men is because vibrators can't take out the trash." I laughed as she continued. She also said something that's not funny. She told me she's not l-looking for love again. She said commitment is tough enough even with the right man at the right time."

"She has a helluva lot of insight."

"She constantly gets hit on by fools and married men. I'll also bet she d-d-discovered she liked you too much to take you to bed."

* * *

On the second Friday in December, I had just started my first set, when Sunny motioned to me to leave the stage. She told me Trapp was rushed to the hospital and they couldn't get me on my cell phone because I had turned it off.

Panic-stricken, I called Marion who told me Trapp went into premature labor and to get to Houston as soon as possible. The airline said no flights were available until the one I was on tomorrow afternoon which would not arrive until almost four o'clock. I could be there by 11:00 a.m. if I drove.

I made it to Houston, located the hospital and headed for the maternity wing. Lisa and Marion met me outside Trapp's room. Charlotte had decided to make her entrance. She had some slight respiratory distress and would be hospitalized for a couple of days.

I went to see Trapp first. She was sitting up and trying to rest while her arms were hanging listlessly at her sides. I kissed her cheek and she smiled at me. "Go meet your daughter," she said. "You're in for the b-b-biggest treat in your life."

"After finding you," I said, as Trapp rolled her eyes and made a 'yeah, right' motion with her left hand.

Marion led me to the nursery where a small, white-blanketed bundle was resting. A tube was feeding oxygen to her and she seemed to have her left fist formed in such a manner that it resembled the finger positions for a C chord.

I thought of at least two dozen things to say but none seemed appropriate. My own tear ducts ramped up production as I looked at that tiny helpless face. Charlotte's head seemed a little big for her body. Her legs seemed scrunched up, her skin was bright pink and she had lots of wrinkles. They told me all these things would disappear with time.

After a quick lunch, I called Sunny to give her the update. She was thrilled about Charlotte and sent Trapp her best. Since it was December tenth, I told her I wanted to spend the next few days in Houston and would return after Christmas.

She said business would likely slack off so I could take whatever time I needed. She said she would see me on New Year's Eve.

* * *

Charlotte came home two days later and began to explore a brand new world. Her skin had turned from bright pink to creamy white. The wrinkles were gone and her full head of coal-black hair was wispy and wild.

As I wiggled my index finger into her hand, she cooed and shook her arms. A lyric began to whisper. I was unable to concentrate and could only remember the line '*laugh and start to dance*." The chorus stayed hidden so the song went on hold.

Our first Christmas Day as a family arrived. Lisa and Tony and several friends arrived shortly after 1:00 p.m.. Hooker and Linda called later that afternoon. He sounded serious as he asked me to get Trapp on the phone.

"I've got a gig for you two. Are you free on June twelfth?"

I looked at Trapp and shrugged.

"I think so. That's quite a long time out. Why?" I asked.

"We want you two to sing at our wedding," he said, his voice rising.

We all stopped and shrieked with joy.

"I'll bet I know where you two are going for your honeymoon," Trapp said, looking over at me and winking.

A silence ensued before Hooker and I answered in tandem with a rising shout, "Vinita!"

* * *

New Year's Eve was a rocking success. After my sets, I sat in with the band for several numbers. The crowd was swaying and singing like they had just discovered partying and the celebration did not end until almost 4:00 a.m.

The following Tuesday, Trapp called and said the attorney for the brokerage firm had made some overtures for settling Joe's case. It all came about because Jake Skylar gave her the name of an expert witness who wrote a scathing report that linked Joe Trappani's death to the stress he underwent because of the embezzlement and conversion of his personal accounts. She opined that Jack's taped confession confirmed he acted intentionally.

When the brokerage company lawyers realized this testimony would be offered in a Texas courtroom under oath, where every potential investor would hear and see it, the price tag on silence soared.

She told me she had entered into talks to merge her father's law firm with another practice. She would soon be chasing the music with me again.

Two weeks later, a settlement was reached. The firm also agreed to pay an additional sum for Joe's wrongful death and their unfair and deceptive business practices. Trapp said the deal included a confidentiality agreement so she could not give me details. That seemed strange since we were married, but she said the law required her to stay silent, even to me. She also said confidentiality was the cornerstone and vital to ensure no one except the parties knew the terms. She also said if word leaked out, they could sue her and Marion to recover the entire amount.

"I can tell you that my mother is set for life," Trapp said. "I also worked a deal where they will pay my legal fees and expenses," she said.

"Can you tell me how much that is?" I asked

"Over two hundred thousand. Add that to what I've earned since I took over the practice and the only work we'll have to do when I move back is writing songs."

"I don't know if you've considered the irony," I told her. "You ran from the law to find music. Now, it's the law that is letting you finally become the singer and songwriter you always wanted."

She told me there was only one thing she wanted from all the money. "We have enough cash to look for a house. I want Charlotte to grow up like I did, with plenty of land and trees and birds and everything that goes with it." I started to reply when she added her last wish. "Most of all, I want the three of us to someday turn into the f-f-four of us," she said as her voice broke.

"We will definitely need a drummer in about ten years," I said as she broke into a half-giggle.

* * *

Trapp arrived on the following Friday morning for her debut with me at the Huddle. She had lost all the baby weight and diet and an exercise regimen had her looking and feeling like a personal trainer. We had a lively conversation as we drove to the condo. She told me she was heading back to Houston next week to execute the settlement documents. Then, she, Marion and Charlotte would drive back to Nashville. Marion agreed to stay for a few weeks while we looked for a house.

We rehearsed half a dozen numbers and got to the Huddle shortly before six o'clock. Trapp and I walked to the bandstand as Sunny came over and exchanged hugs with us. After a sound check, I warmed up the crowd until Trapp joined me onstage.

It was standing room only again. Sunny and Garland wore grins that stretched across their faces. After our last set finished, Trapp and I posed for pictures.

On Monday morning, we met with Doc and Jake. Doc told us he wanted to write with us without an outright purchase of our songs. It was a major concession on his part. An hour later, we all signed an agreement for two songs now and two more to be written.

Trapp gave Jake a twenty-four carat gold Montblanc pen for referring her to his expert witness friend. Ace was not in, so Trapp gave Jake a second pen for him because he represented us against Bryson.

"Where is Ace?" I asked.

"In the hospital having some tests," he said softly.

"I hope it's not serious," Trapp said,

"Well, the findings so far are not encouraging. He's afraid those damn cigarettes finally caught up with him," he said.

"Can we do anything?" Doc asked

"Pray, if you think that will help. Keep the faith and hope if you don't," Jake said. Each of us shifted uncomfortably until Jake continued. "Look folks, Ace appreciates your concern but he doesn't want your tears. We both know you only live once. Besides, when you live like he and I have, once is more than enough."

* * *

After Trapp left for Houston on Wednesday morning, Doc called me. We agreed to meet on a daily basis to write. Our first meetings were tedious, as we took the time to get used to each other's creative process.

The following day, I got inspired right after he left, picked out a tune and soon had a tag line. Suddenly, I felt like the day I wrote 'Steele Trapp Mind', as I had a vision of Charlotte and remembered the line that appeared when I was watching her in her bassinet.

The words appeared. Whispers began to scream. I was up until four o'clock in the morning.

Doc came over around ten o'clock and I showed him what I had written. He sipped his coffee as I began.

* * *

May you never hear the thunder
In the canyons of your soul;
Or watch jagged streaks of lightning
As you fight to gain control;

It's the love that can't be faithful
That's bound to leave you bitter;
Or memories from a broken heart
That tell you you're a quitter;
Remember time is but a debt
That never can be squandered;
And destiny is not by chance
So keep your sense of wonder
Chorus:
There's another storm forming,
On the road that lies ahead;
It's time to make a choice,
To lead or to be led;
You can try to find the shelter,
And never take a chance;
Or look the storm right in the eye,
Laugh and start to dance

*   * * *

May you always have the courage
To think and do for others;
And show the grace and wisdom
Of blessings from your mother;
May you always live the life
That lies buried in your mind;
And die just like a hero,
Instead of pleading for more time;
And I will live just for the day
I get to see your smile;
When we are arm in arm
As I walk you down the aisle

When I finished, he put his cup down.
"That's absolutely beautiful. What do you call

it?" he asked.

"'Charlotte's Song'."

"You and Trapp should record it together."

"You're right. But I want the line about walking her down the aisle all to myself."

"You're coming to the show on Friday night, right?" Doc asked.

"I'll be there."

"You and I will do a couple of tunes right at the end. We'll go out afterward for a few pops with the band."

"Good idea. Let's hope they inspire us to keep writing."

CHAPTER TWENTY-FIVE

On Friday, Trapp left to take over my gig at the Huddle as I drove to the Country Palace Theater. Doc gave me a backstage pass and security led me to the assembly area where I was introduced to everyone.

For the next fifteen minutes, I mingled with the guys. We had a quick rehearsal and I left to watch the show until it was my turn to perform. The arena was packed as the warm-up band took the stage at exactly nine o'clock.

At nine-thirty, Doc and the band appeared. For the next ninety minutes, several thousand people were clapping, swaying and having the time of their lives.

I headed backstage with half an hour left in the show. After my introduction, Doc and I did the two new songs and the crowd gave a hearty response. Two women held up signs with marriage proposals for anyone in the band.

After the show, I went out for a few beers with Doc, lead guitarist Trace Allen and the drummer, Carl Nash. I texted Trapp and told her I would be late. She told me to take my time because she and Sunny were sharing a table and having fun with all the patrons.

We went to a dive on the outskirts of town called "Nashville Flash." Unfortunately, the only flash we found was reflected in the chrome door handles of the pickups parked outside. Doc said he liked the place because he rarely was recognized.

"I thought the new stuff went great. The crowd really got into it," Doc said.

"I could see people swaying back and forth in the aisles," I said.

"There was this blonde honey in the front row who couldn't take her eyes off me. I looked for her after the show, but she was gone," Carl said.

"She probably had to leave because she's got a curfew," Doc said, grinning.

We all laughed as a man in a dirty, off-white cowboy hat approached and stopped at our table. He had tattoos on both arms and his belt was about six inches too long as it flapped back and forth against his oversized buckle. His face had not collided with a razor for some time.

"Ain't you Doc Grayson?" he asked.

Doc looked the man up and down before he replied.

"No, I'm Leroy Jethro Gibbs, a micro-paleontologist from Clemson," he said.

"Bullshit," said the cowboy. "You sang that song, 'I Won't Lie If You Won't Ask'."

"Look, pal, we're trying to have a private conversation. So why don't you move along?" I said.

"My girl left me because of that song, asshole," the cowboy said.

He flashed a knife and swung it at Doc as I grabbed for his arm. At the same time, Trace moved in front of Doc to shield him and took the force of the knife thrust in his left hand. He went down screaming.

Carl grabbed the cowboy in a headlock and started to pummel him. By this time, the bouncers came over and held the man until the cops came. An ambulance arrived to take Trace to the hospital. Doc inspected his wound and applied first-aid, before riding to the hospital with him. Carl and I went back to the Country Palace to get our cars. I arrived home shortly after 1:00 a.m. when my cell phone rang.

"Hey, Doc. How's Trace?"

"It's too early to tell. They think the knife cut a tendon in his hand so he'll be out for quite a while."

"Maybe we should have gone somewhere else."

"Can't, J. W. It was only a dipshit cowboy, that's all."

"What are you going to do for a guitarist?"

Doc hesitated for a moment. "I want you to join the band. You can start tomorrow night for our show here at the Palace."

I could almost hear Bull asking me if I wanted to be a husband or a star.

"I need you, J. W. We've been working together so you can jump right in. This is your chance to hit the big time," Doc pleaded.

I felt flushed and my mind raced. "Let me talk to Trapp. We agreed any gig had to include both of us."

"I know, but the act doesn't include a female singer."

"Doc, I don't want to move on without her," I said.

He raised the stakes. "If you join me, J. W., I'll produce you and Trapp recording 'Charlotte's Song'."

Jesus Christ, he was offering me a record deal with Trapp. All I had to do was take the gig with the band. My thoughts moved like lightning bolts ricocheting off metal platforms. I stared at the phone before I replied. "Plan on me being there tomorrow night."

Trapp was still awake when I walked in. I told her what had happened and said Doc asked me to join the band.

"I think you should do it. This isn't like b-before where we never knew what was coming next," she said. I took her in my arms. "Besides," she continued. "You just got us a record deal. I'll work out the details with Jake. If it takes you playing with Doc and the b-b-band for a while, that's a small price to pay."

"There's one other thing. Can you take over again at the Huddle tomorrow night?"

"I've got you c-c-covered, kid," she replied.

* * *

The next night, I took the stage with the band. After the show, I was feeling ecstatic because the big time and I were becoming really comfortable. My heart sank when I turned on my phone and saw several text messages as well as multiple calls.

The first message said call Garland because Trapp and Sunny were both taken to the hospital. I panicked and tried to call, but my hands were shaking too hard. Finally, I connected.

"Garland, is Trapp okay?" I shouted.

"We think so. Sunny's in bad shape. That asshole Ritchie's dead."

"What the hell happened?"

"From what we can figure, Ritchie broke in and stole the night's receipts. Sunny and Trapp were sitting together when Sunny got up to clean out the registers. When she got to the office, Ritchie had the cash box and

Sunny chased him. That's when Ritchie's partner, who was driving the getaway car, shot her."

"How did Trapp get shot?" I almost screamed.

"She saw Sunny lying on the floor and Ritchie leaving. She yelled and the guy fired and hit her in her right side."

"Where is she?" I asked, as I ran to the parking lot.

"Parkway Hospital on State Street and Pine. They left about twenty minutes ago," Garland said, and I started sprinting.

At the hospital, I found the emergency room and approached a nurse who gave me an update.

"Mr. Steele, your wife is in surgery. She just went up and is expected to make a full recovery."

My throat parched as I asked the next question. "Ms. Sterling was also brought in. What's her condition?"

"Are you a relative?" asked the nurse.

"No, just a friend."

"I'm afraid I can't discuss her condition with you. I can say she is also in surgery."

"Are her wounds life-threatening?" I asked.

"I'm afraid I have to let the doctor discuss that with you," said the nurse. "The operating room is on the third floor."

It was almost two hours later before I got an update. I was paged and found a doctor dressed in surgical scrubs who was writing in a chart.

"Mr. Steele, I'm Doctor Delaney. Your wife is a very lucky woman. The bullet hit her on the right side of the abdomen. No vital organs were hit and blood loss was minimal. She will be sore for a while and we need to keep her here for now."

"Thank God. Can I see her?"

"She's still out. Why don't you go get some sleep and come back later? We'll call you if anything changes."

"Ms. Sterling was brought in also. Can you tell me anything about her condition?"

"You're not related, are you?"

"No."

"All I can say is she was not so lucky. She's still in surgery and will go to ICU when she gets out of recovery."

"Will she be okay?"

The doctor hesitated as she looked into my eyes. "Let's hope for the best," she said, touching my arm.

* * *

The next day, I was not allowed to see Trapp until almost noon. When I entered the room, she was lying in bed, staring at me. I walked over and she raised her left hand toward me. After kissing her fingers, I fought back tears.

"Too bad Sunny was not as l-lucky as me," she said, as her voice broke.

"What do you mean?"

"We came together in the ambulance. They had to shock her twice. The doc said she doesn't have much of a chance."

I felt my entire body stiffen with fear.

"Do you feel well enough to tell me what happened?"

"Sunny and I were having a drink when she went to c-c-clean the cash out of the registers. She does that around midnight so she can make the night deposit at the bank."

"Did she tell you how much cash?" I asked.

"She figured it was over six thousand. They were six or seven deep at the bar and Sunny kept t-t-taking the cash so it wouldn't build up. She went to the office and I heard what sounded like a gunshot. I ran back and saw her lying on the floor. She said, 'Ritchie just robbed me and r-r-ran out the back."

"What happened next?"

"I went to the door and saw Ritchie hand the strongbox to another m-m-man. Ritchie said, 'There's over four grand in there. I'll get you the rest next week.' The guy said, 'How do you know what's in there? Ritchie said there was a deposit slip. The guy opened the box and said, 'There's no deposit slip here. You asshole, you skimmed off the top.' Then he s-s-shot Ritchie. I yelled and he turned and fired at me."

"Can you tell the cops anything about the van?"

"I took a photo of the license number with my c-cell phone before I passed out."

"Garland told me there was a surveillance camera in the back alley," I said. "Maybe that caught some of the action."

* * *

Jake and Doc were at the hospital when I arrived the next day.

"You're one lucky gal," Jake said. "I heard if the bullet was an inch or so higher or lower, you would have had kidney or hip damage."

"I'll still have a scar my b-bikini can't hide," Trapp said, trying to smile.

"It's too bad about Ms. Sterling," Doc said.

"What do you mean?" I asked.

"I heard on the news she died this morning," Doc said.

I slipped my hand into Trapp's as we both teared up.

Doc told us the report on Trace said the tendon was not severed but merely nicked. He needed some physical therapy but should be ready to go when the tour started. Then, he told me the best news. "J. W., my label wants to record you and Trapp doing 'Charlotte's Song.' I will produce and I want my band to cover instead of session musicians."

Trapp said she would contact Jake about representing us on the recording contracts. She said she had an idea about the Huddle. "What would you think about us b-buying the club?" she asked. "When I sell the condo, that will get us enough money."

"That's genius," I answered. "It means we would have our own stage and we could limit how much we tour."

"Do you know who Sunny's lawyer was?"

"I'll ask Garland."

* * *

It took me a day to finally reach Garland. He said he was leaving Nashville because there was nothing left for him here. I asked him if he would run the club if we bought it and he shouted, "Yes!"

Sunny's lawyer was a guy named Roger Castle. I told Garland to sit tight until he heard from us. Trapp was on the telephone with Castle for almost half an hour, carrying on a spirited conversation.

"You're not going to b-believe this," she said.

"As Prince Charles once said, 'I'm all ears'," I told her.

"Did you know Sunny executed a new will a couple of weeks ago?"

"No. What difference does it make?"

"We don't have to buy the club. S-Sunny left it to us."

I was dumbfounded as I reached for her hand. "You're kidding me."

"We now own it outright."

"I thought Ritchie had forty-nine percent."

"He did. But he died first, so Sunny survived him. The d-divorce was not final so she inherited his share and the club was all hers."

"What about everything that Ritchie owed?"

"The lawyer said all his debts were unsecured. They died with him."

"What about her daughter or anybody else who could inherit?"

"She had what's called an *in terrorum* clause in the will. That says if anyone who could inherit c-c-contests the will, they will automatically get nothing if the challenge fails. Castle said they can't find the daughter. By law, he has to p-publish a notice in the newspaper. If she doesn't respond, she's out. If she contacts him, the court will decide what happens."

"What if someone sues us?"

"They would have to show undue influence. We both tried to help her make the club a success. They don't stand a chance if they sue."

"I can't believe this," I said.

"Sunny and I got pretty close in a short time. She had few friends because most women thought she was trying to take their man away. Her daughter was from her first marriage before Ritchie, and she ran off with a drug dealer."

"Why do you think she took to us so fast?" I asked.

"She said she looked at us as the k-k-kids she never had. Ritchie was a dipshit but he still managed to get a long-term lease. It still has eighteen years to run. Castle told me the rent would be double now if we had to negotiate a new agreement."

"I've got some ideas about changes at the club," I said.

"Tell me."

"I'd like to change the name to Vinita Dreams."

"Please, J. W., I'm b-begging you not to do that. It's bad enough Charlotte's middle name is Vinita. I've got a name for you. I want to call the club 'Whispers.'"

CHAPTER TWENTY-SIX

Spring slipped into summer. Trapp and I kept writing and working on our act. Charlotte got her first teeth. Marion stayed with us and took care of the baby as we worked toward recording our first CD.

Sunny's estate cleared probate. No one responded to the newspaper notice. The club became ours with music as our roommate.

We paid Garland back his eighteen thousand dollars and gave him another seven thousand as interest. Our first order of business was to talk about expanding and redecorating. Garland showed us his ideas like streamlining the menu, adding a private function room and expanding the bandstand.

We got financing approved, did a complete renovation of the club's interior and added a banquet room for parties while expanding the lounge capacity. The reopening was set for July first.

A month before the club was scheduled to open, Trapp reached a deal on winding down the practice. Her firm was merged with another in Houston and she went on their letterhead as 'Of Counsel.' That allowed her to draw an income for several years without having to have a caseload. It was ideal for tax purposes, because the money was spread out instead of given as a lump sum payment.

It wasn't long before we found a house on a lot bordered by woods and a small lake. It had five acres and was big enough for a pony or two. The lake had perch and bass and reflected sunsets like a prism.

Two days later, we got an offer on the condo from a struggling husband and wife songwriting team who had just published their first song. As a wedding present, Trapp dropped the selling price by a thousand dollars.

We listened to some of their tunes but felt no spark. We decided they were a little too country, and not enough rock and roll.

* * *

On the first Saturday in June, Trapp and I attended Hooker and Linda's wedding. I was his best man and Trapp was one of the bridesmaids.

Hooker's mother came to the wedding and kept clinging to Linda like Krazy Glue. She told him Linda was the daughter she'd always wanted and how her life changed when she left his father. Now, she was always asking what she could do for her last son.

He asked me if I would do the song I wrote for Trapp during the ceremony at the church. I told him we had worked it into a duet. His eyes lit up as he said it would be his gift to Linda.

"You're a tough act to follow, J. W. I'm not a poet or a singer so I need you to help me out. The only talent I have is knocking ball carriers down.

"I've got your back, man," I said.

Trapp and I performed and it became the highlight of the ceremony. We were mobbed at the reception and asked to do several numbers with the band. Afterward, Hooker asked me to meet him at the bar for a drink.

"I don't know how to thank you," he said. "If it wasn't for you, I wouldn't be here."

"Neither would I," I said. "There's an old song by Ian and Sylvia called 'These Friends Of Mine.' The last line talks about being a better man because I know you."

"One final gift from a woman named Sylvia," he said, as his eyes briefly took on a look of reflection.

I asked how he liked being back in Beaumont. He said it was a vindication of sorts. "It's where I learned to stand up for myself in places besides the football field. Now, I can show other kids how to do that."

"That's what life is all about," I told him.

"Son, maybe that's why this wedding could be considered an allegory," he said.

"Not really," I told him. "That's the name of some dipshit author who wrote a book about impacted third molars called *An Inconvenient Tooth*."

* * *

Jake helped us form a publishing company and we met with Doc to record 'Charlotte's Song.' The record label said we needed at least four more songs before they would give us a deal for our first solo CD. They also agreed that 'Clouded Soul' would be the second cut. I called Julie and told her to expect a royalty check when it was released.

We moved into our new home a few days before the club opened. As we stood arm in arm and looked out over the water, I thought of what I would say to Bob Seger about not needing it all.

"I may not need it all or deserve it, but I certainly found it."

* * *

On the day of Whispers' grand opening, we put the finishing touches on the interior. I got a ladder and moved it inside the entrance. After taking out a small, richly-finished wooden sign, I nailed it above the doorway, so that it would be visible to every person who left. The sign read, 'Leaving Vinita', with a smaller inscription below, "When Dreams Have Faded, and Destiny's Sealed, the Power of Friendship, Stays Strong as Steele."

After the sign was hung, I walked behind the bar and placed a gilt-framed photograph of Trapp, Sunny and me right in the center of bar, above the mirror covering the wall. It was the one taken on the night when Trapp and I first performed together at the Huddle. The three of us were smiling like the world was ours for the taking, and nothing could stand in our way. At the bottom of the frame, we had these words inscribed: "'Ain't No Sunshine' now that she's gone." It was the best tribute we could compose. We figured even Bill Withers would approve.

At one o'clock, Jake met us at the club with proposed revisions to our recording contract. The label was thrilled about 'Charlotte's Song', our other new tunes and said we were only one song away from a deal. Jake said they wanted the final song in two weeks.

"We'll have to bribe the s-shadows so they'll talk to us," Trapp said.

"I'll remind them we named the club in their honor," I added.

* * *

Just before four o'clock that afternoon, we received a delivery of roses from Julie and the twins. I had invited them to our first night but they could not get away until August. I told the twins that we had a spot for them to sing when they finally came to Nashville and they promised to keep working on their act.

Jake and Doc came by several minutes later. Doc told us he was ready to take the stage with us at six o'clock. He was honored to help us christen our new ownership.

"I wish I could join you all on stage," Jake said. "But, at my age, the audience would probably expect a medley of Civil War campfire songs."

"I hope you'll be here tonight," Trapp said

"I wouldn't miss it," he said.

"Any way you can bring Ace?" Doc asked.

"Let me see if he feels up to it and could use a night out."

"Is he any better?" I asked.

"He's working on it," Jake said.

"Tell him we're thinking of him," Trapp said.

"I will. He told me to send you all his best wishes."

"I'm really happy for you two. You deserve all of this," Doc said, looking around at the freshly painted walls and expanded stage. He focused on the photographs of us with him and the band, located over the center of the bar, on each side of the picture of us and Sunny.

"There's only one thing left to do," Jake said, as he put one arm around me and the other around Trapp.

"What's that?" Trapp asked.

"Go home and hug the stuffing out of Charlotte. She's what really counts in life when you get right down to it."

"Her grandmother is already starting to p-prepare her to join us," Trapp said.

"What do you mean?" Jake asked.

"She keeps telling people Charlotte is destined to become a country singer like her parents," I said.

"Why?" Doc asked.

"Because she is the only one in h-history who had an authentic Steele Trapp Mind installed at the factory," Trapp said.

"God help us all," I added

About the Author

TIMOTHY R. CAGLE

Tim Cagle is a practicing trial attorney in the fields of Medical Malpractice, Products Liability, and Personal Injury law. He has also served as co-counsel to other trial lawyers by conducting the cross examination of adverse expert witnesses during trials.

In addition, he was a law professor and taught courses in Torts, Evidence, Medical Malpractice and Negotiations. He is admitted to practice law in the Commonwealth of Massachusetts, State of Missouri, before the Federal District Court in Boston, and has been admitted *pro hac vice* for the trial of cases in the State of New Hampshire, the State of Rhode Island, and before the Federal District Court in the State of New Jersey.

He received a Bachelor of Arts Degree from Kansas State College and a Doctor of Jurisprudence Degree from Suffolk University, Boston, Massachusetts.

His memberships have included the American Bar Association, Massachusetts Bar Association, Academy of Trial Attorneys, Massachusetts Academy of Trial Attorneys, Nashville Songwriters Association, American Legion, Boston Pacemaker Club and Sigma Chi Alumni Association. He served as a First Lieutenant in the United States Army, was assigned to Military Intelligence and was honorably discharged.

After playing college football, he served as an assistant high school football coach. He has written over three hundred and fifty songs, played professionally in groups and as a single performer and spent time in Nashville as a songwriter. He is also the author of *Whispers From The Silence*, a novel based on his experiences writing songs and his career as a singer/songwriter. It was released in June, 2017.

His biggest regret in life is that he did not spend more time concentrating on guitar riffs, lyrical hooks and finger-popping melodies, and less time learning about when to blitz if the guards pull on third and long, blistering cross-examination techniques and expert witness fee schedules.

You can find more stories such as this at www.bookstogonow.com

If you enjoy this Books to Go Now story please leave a review for the author on Amazon, Goodreads or the site which you purchased the ebook. Thanks!

We pride ourselves with representing great stories at low prices. We want to take you into the digital age offering a market that will allow you to grow along with us in our journey through the new frontier of digital publishing.
Some of our favorite award-winning authors have now joined us. We welcome readers and writers into our community.

We want to make sure that as a reader you are supplied with never-ending great stories. As a company, Books to Go Now, wants its readers and writers supplied with positive experience and encouragement so they will return again and again.

We want to hear from you. Our readers and writers are the cornerstone of our company. If there is something you would like to say or a genre that you would like to see, please email us at inquiry@bookstogonow.com

Made in the USA
Middletown, DE
07 June 2019